DEATH *of a* MODERN KING

A STORMY DAY NOVEL

BOOK #4

ANGELA PEPPER

CHAPTER 1

INSIDE THE SPACIOUS KITCHEN of the mansion, Erica Garcia dropped a handful of roasted nuts on a cutting board and pulverized them with a sharp knife, releasing her frustration.

Erica had worked as a maid for the Koenig family for twelve years, three months, and five days. She'd witnessed a number of changes, but nothing had rattled her quite so much until now.

A disaster of these proportions was bound to happen, given how much Mr. Dieter Koenig loved his entertainment.

The family's last name, Koenig, was German for king, and Dieter embraced his role as the unofficial king of Misty Falls. After the death of his wife, he'd taken to throwing grand dinner parties, inviting guests he found *interesting*.

Eight months ago, he'd brought in a fortune teller. She'd been murdered not long after her visit to the mansion. After that, a dark pall settled over the estate. Erica was the most superstitious of the staff, but even the non-believers couldn't deny the fog of danger that filled the mansion's rooms and rolled through long, darkened hallways. The once-boisterous staff now spoke in hushed tones and startled like mice over the clatter of a dropped knife.

Spring came, along with the public tours for the town's Cherry Blossom Festival, but still the dark pall wouldn't lift.

In June, Mr. Koenig threw a lavish, weekend-long party. He invited several guests, including a notorious local woman, an aspiring singer. Mr. Koenig, a man of seventy-five, fell for the singer's charms and became as smitten as a schoolboy. Despite the protests of his children, Dieter began dating the woman, who was nearly fifty years his junior.

Now she'd moved herself into a guest room, wanting to spend more time with the man she'd revoltingly nicknamed *Deets*.

Erica tried to stay positive in the face of it all. She took pride in her work. She cared for the Koenig family as if they were her own. Every day for the last twelve years, three months, and five days, Erica Garcia had counted her blessings.

Today, though, it was difficult to see her blessings, much less count them. The new girlfriend was a magnet for drama. If she wasn't at dinner, starting fights, the family was fighting over her. Dieter's sons hated their father dating the woman, but only because they loved him so much. Or so they claimed.

Something dark moved at the edge of Erica's vision. She whipped her head around guiltily. The darkness moved like wisps of smoke, taking the form of a pack mule. An omen of bad luck.

Erica's heart raced. She clutched the medal of Saint Benedict on her necklace. The smoky dark apparition dissipated as quickly as it had appeared. She whispered a prayer to Saint Benedict, shook her head, and got back to work.

When Verity, the all-seeing head of the household staff, came in to check on the kitchen, she could tell something was bothering Erica.

"I'll take over the breakfast service," Verity told her sternly.

"I can handle this," Erica insisted, clutching her Saint Benedict.

"You superstitious ninny," Verity said with a sigh. "Your forehead is waxy, and you're sweating. Are you coming down with something, or have you been seeing ghosts in the kitchen again?" She looked around as though expecting to catch a glimpse of a spirit. "What was it this time? Another demon chicken coming to peck out our eyes?"

Erica looked down at her hands and answered, "I saw a dark mule, over by the door. It means somebody could fall and hurt themselves."

Verity sighed. "It must have been the spirit of Juan Valdez reminding you to grind fresh coffee beans." She clapped her hands three times. "Let's go, Erica. If you're going to serve breakfast, get to it."

Erica gathered the nuts into a serving bowl and added it to the tray with the other bowls. She checked her appearance in the room's small mirror—her dark curls were frizzing their way out of her bun—before taking the tray through the hallway toward the conservatory.

The morning's routine was not the usual one for a weekday. Mr. Dieter Koenig had sprung it on the staff that morning that he would be entertaining two mystery guests in the glass-walled room overlooking the pool.

Erica reached the door to the conservatory and found it locked. This door was never locked, so she didn't have the key with her.

Switching the tray to one arm, Erica knocked on the door while pressing her ear against the wood. She heard movement. She knocked again. "Hello? It's me, Erica. I'm just here to set up for breakfast, Mr. Koenig. Would you prefer that I come back in ten minutes?"

Something clicked.

She tried the door handle again, but it was still locked. Furiously, she blamed the new girlfriend, who'd been giving Erica nasty looks last night at dinner.

Under her breath, Erica muttered, "Evil Brat. Trying to make me look bad again? I'll show you."

The other entrance to the room was from the exterior, from the courtyard, and she did have that key.

Nine serving dishes chattered on the tray as Erica marched down the hall and exited through an exterior door. She walked across the grass, along the paver stones, then through the opening in the hedge. As she passed the pool, she caught a glimpse of something dark in the water but refused to look. The smoky dark omens were just her mind playing tricks on her.

The exterior door for the conservatory was unlocked. She entered, leaving the door open for pent-up heat to escape while she arranged the tables and chairs to seat a party of four. The room wasn't as hot as she'd expected. She turned on the air conditioning, unlocked the interior door leading to the hallway, and started closing the double doors leading to the pool.

Again, something dark in the pool caught her eye. As Erica moved closer, she could see the darkness was red at the center. It seemed to be blood, coming from a body that floated, unmoving, near the bottom of the deep end.

Erica screamed. She kicked off her shoes and ran to the pool's edge.

She screamed again, and then she dove in after the body.

CHAPTER 2

STORMY DAY

"Drop everything, Stormy. We're going to the Koenig Mansion for breakfast."

Logan Sanderson was standing on my front step, grinning.

Was this really my life now?

Logan and I had officially become boyfriend and girlfriend at the Misty Falls Annual Cherry Blossom Festival, in the spring.

According to my best friend, Jessica, my kissing sessions with Logan under the falling petals put us in the running for Most Mushy Couple. Luckily for us, there was no such award given, or the entire town would have been treated to an acceptance speech by Logan.

If Logan hadn't become a lawyer, he could have been an actor. He loved having everyone's attention, whether he was telling a dirty joke for a group of friends or dramatically asking questions in a deposition. The support staff at his office jokingly called him *Mr. Standerson,* adding a T to his last name to make it a pun. Logan would never *sit* and ask questions when he could *stand* and ask those questions with more flair.

I didn't hold his wit and charm against him. In return, he didn't roll his eyes at my detective work. He loved that I was as busy as he was. Secretly, I wanted a little more playtime, but I didn't dare slow him down.

In early August, Logan proudly announced that he was on retainer for the richest man in Misty Falls, Dieter Koenig. I was elated, because I would *also* be on retainer for the richest man in town.

In my former career in venture capital, I'd met plenty of wealthy people, including billionaires, but I'd never met Dieter Koenig, and I wanted to. He was the unofficial king of the town, and who wouldn't want to meet someone like that?

It seemed I'd gotten my wish one Sunday in the middle of August, when Logan knocked on my door and told me to drop everything because we were going to the Koenig Mansion for breakfast. But then again, Logan was also a big tease and loved tricking me.

"Nice try," I said, clutching my fragrant cinnamon bun, still warm from the oven. "If you want a cinnamon bun, help yourself. You don't need to steal mine."

He followed me into the kitchen and playfully yanked the pastry from my hand. "Don't spoil your appetite," he said. "Mr. Koenig might be uncomfortable if you don't eat."

I stole back my breakfast. "You're going to be uncomfortable if you keep taking my food away." I took a huge bite and started chewing.

He leaned against the kitchen counter and watched me, his blue eyes twinkling with amusement under his thick, black eyelashes. His dark beard had been trimmed to its summer length, just a bit longer than stubble.

After a minute, he said, "If you eat any slower, we're going to be late."

I set down the remainder of the bun. "You're not joking. We really are invited to the Koenig Mansion for breakfast?"

He grinned. "Is that what you're wearing?"

I looked down and laughed at the thought of entertaining anyone, let alone members of the Koenig family, in my tacky, multi-colored bathrobe.

Logan said, "You have two minutes to change," and started a countdown.

I ran. I was spruced up and spiffy with ten seconds to spare, thanks to a little pink dress borrowed from Jessica's wardrobe plus my no-fuss short hairstyle.

We got into Logan's truck, and I actually clapped my hands with excitement. My new private investigation career was a blast, I was falling in love with a handsome lawyer, and we were going to share a meal with the unofficial king of Misty Falls. Could life get any better?

* * *

We pulled up to the iron gates for the Koenig Mansion. They opened for us automatically.

Logan reached over and squeezed my hand. We drove up the road, passing gracious trees gently waving in greeting.

"Not bad," Logan said as the stately home came into view at the top of the hill.

The Koenig Mansion resembled a castle, with Romanesque arches, recessed entryways, and at least four cylindrical towers with conical caps.

I agreed. "Not bad for a little cabin near the woods."

"A cozy summer shack," he said. "It's a shame they don't have a mudhole for skinny dipping. I hear they have to make do with one of those heated, in-ground swimming pools."

"Those poor souls," I said.

Logan chuckled as he steered to the right, following the signs directing us to the Visitor Parking lot, which was empty.

"Turn around," I said. "We're too early. I don't want to be the first to arrive."

Logan parked and turned off the engine. "We are a bit early, but as far as I know, we're the only guests."

"How early are we? You can't show up to someone's house early. It's worse than being late."

He leaned over and kissed my cheek. "You're adorable when you're flustered. Don't be nervous. Mr. Koenig is going to love you." He pulled back and looked over my curve-hugging dress. "On second thought, do you have a jacket or a big scarf you could wear over that skimpy dress? You look cold."

I smiled and unbuckled my seat belt. "Very funny. I hear he's in excellent shape for his age." I winked. "Not that I'm looking to trade up."

Logan gasped with mock indignation. "Trade up? Hilarious. Even if he did steal you away from me, it would be more of a lateral trade." He got out of the truck and circled around to meet me on the passenger side. "Not that Mr. Koenig is in the market for a new wife, anyway."

"Oh?" I linked my arm with his, and we started toward the entrance. "Does he have a girlfriend? His wife passed away about three years ago, as I recall, so it's not out of the question."

Logan mimed locking his lips and throwing away the key. "I've said too much already. Do your best to act surprised if he mentions anything of a romantic nature at breakfast."

"What's this meeting officially about?"

"I don't know," Logan said. It was a phrase I didn't hear from him that often. His usual style was to be so prepared nothing surprised him.

As we neared the door, he seemed to be lost in thought. He didn't knock or ring the doorbell. I pressed the button for the bell and heard what seemed to be a woman screaming.

Logan turned to me, his eyebrows colliding like two dark trains on the wrong tracks. Doorbells didn't usually sound like screams. We stared at each other in confusion, and then he reached up and rang the bell.

Again, there was the sound of a woman screaming.

"That's not coming from inside," I said.

I pressed the button a third time. There was only silence. If a doorbell was ringing inside the home, the door was too thick for us to hear it. Nobody opened the door.

"That's ominous," I said. "And those screams didn't sound like kids playing."

"Let's check around the back." He led the way, moving left along the large, castle-shaped building.

Jogging, we followed a path of paving stones that wove through lush gardens. The mansion was so large, it took ages before we turned the first corner, marked by a round tower.

Logan was breathing hard when I overtook him.

I called back over my shoulder, "You should come running with me and Jessica!"

He laughed between puffs.

I slowed for him to catch up. We cleared the side of the building and turned right. We hadn't seen another soul, but I could hear people shouting nearby. The panic in their voices sent a chill up my back.

"The pool," Logan puffed. "It's on the other side of that hedge." He pointed to the large wall of green that began at the path's edge and stretched out of sight.

As we were looking, a figure in workman's clothing and a hat emerged from the greenery about forty feet from us.

"Hey, you!" Logan yelled.

The figure jerked to attention and began running away.

Logan was off and running, before I could even warn him to be careful.

A woman wailed on the other side of the hedge, pleading for help.

I left Logan to his chase and ran along the path, emerging into a courtyard containing an enormous pool and a group of people dressed in staff uniforms.

I ran toward the cluster of staff, where I saw a familiar face.

Erica Garcia, a maid at the mansion, was sobbing and soaking wet, down on her knees.

Before her lay a trim man in swimming trunks. He wasn't moving, or even breathing. Pale-blue eyes stared up at the cloudless sky, unseeing. A dark pool spread on the ruddy stones beneath his head.

"He's dead," Erica sobbed. She locked eyes with me. "Miss Day! Is your father with you?"

The three other staff members whipped their heads to face me.

"I'm here with Logan Sanderson," I said, though he wasn't technically with me at the moment. "He's chasing after someone," I added.

"Who?" Erica asked, but she didn't wait for me to answer before she cried, "He's dead, Miss Day! Mr. Koenig is dead!"

CHAPTER 3

Mr. Dieter Koenig, the wealthiest man in Misty Falls as well as Logan's newest client, was dead.

I did my best to comfort the maid, who was kneeling and visibly trembling next to the body. Erica Garcia was a thirty-seven-year-old woman who'd worked at the Koenig Estate for over a decade. I'd met her before, and she was familiar with my father from his days working as a policeman, which was why she'd asked for him when she recognized me.

I asked gently, "Erica, what happened? You're soaking wet. Did you dive in and pull him out?"

"I think so," she said shakily. "I mean, yes. I'm not a good swimmer, Miss Day. I don't know what I was thinking, but there he was, and there was so much blood, and he wasn't moving."

"Did you scream? I heard two screams a few minutes ago."

She nodded. "And there was a sign. An omen." She clutched a coin medallion on her necklace and began to pray, too fast for me to catch the words.

Another member of the staff, a young man in kitchen whites, was trying to resuscitate Mr. Koenig. By the look on his face, he'd given up hope, but continued doing chest compressions.

A sharp-faced woman of about fifty kept watch as she spoke into her phone. After a moment, she dropped the phone from her ear and announced, "The paramedics are on their way."

The fourth staff member, a soft-bellied man in his fifties, dressed in dark slacks and a half-buttoned white shirt, shuffled from one foot to the other with a stunned look on his face. With a flat voice, the man said, "I'll go wait by the front door and bring the paramedics through the house to save time."

The sharp-faced woman sniffed. "To save time?" She gave him a withering look. "He's dead, Randy. Half his blood is currently staining the sides of the pool."

Randy turned to the pool, where a dark stain lurked, spreading in one quadrant.

"I'll drain the pool," Randy said. "What else should I do, Verity?"

I had been kneeling next to Erica, but now I stood up. "Don't drain the pool," I said. "It's evidence."

Verity, the sharp-faced woman who seemed to be the head of staff, turned her withering gaze on me.

"*You* need to leave," Verity said.

"But I had a breakfast meeting with—"

She cut me off. "I know exactly who you are, Miss Day. I think we can assume, given Mr. Koenig's lack of proper attire, not to mention half his blood being in the pool, that your breakfast meeting is cancelled until further notice."

I replied, "I'll see myself out."

Erica jumped up and grabbed my forearm, her wet hand as cold as an icy claw. "Don't go, Miss Day," she pleaded.

"I won't go far." I patted her hand.

I joined Randy, who stood dumbfounded near a wide-open pair of glass doors leading into the home. The instant Verity turned her hawk-like scrutiny back to the body, I switched into detective mode.

I pulled my phone from my purse and took several photos of the scene. With my elbows braced against my lower ribs, I used my body as a rotating tripod and snapped a series of photos for a complete 360-degree panorama.

The courtyard was the type featured on the covers of architectural magazines or in TV shows about the lifestyles of the wealthy. A lush green hedge formed a fence-like boundary, probably as much for safety as for looks, for it looked difficult to penetrate. The hedge would keep out deer and other large local wildlife.

The ground was paved in slate stones, a dark contrast to the white statues of cherubs, marble urns of bright flowers, and lounging furniture. Apparently, the decorator had opted for a classic symmetrical theme. Every item had a twin on the opposite side. The courtyard was the picture of perfect symmetry, except for the dead body and staff members.

Randy didn't notice me taking pictures. He stared stupidly at the buttons of his shirt and the smear of watery blood along the hem.

The sound of sirens approaching shook him out of his reverie. He blinked at me and asked, "Should I drain the pool?"

"Let's get the front door first," I suggested.

"Of course." Randy led me through the house. The direct route was much faster than my previous journey around the exterior.

We stopped at the front door, where Randy faced himself in a full-length mirror. He snapped into focus at his reflection, re-buttoning his shirt and tucking the stained hem into his waistband.

"My jacket," he said, as much to himself as to me. "I don't have my jacket."

I looked into his watery eyes and caught a glimpse of the abyss. I patted him on the shoulder and spoke soothingly.

"Randy, you're in shock right now, but you're going to be okay. The Koenig family needs you as much today as any other day. How long have you worked here?"

"Twenty-two years," he said.

I gave his shoulder a squeeze. "Then you know your job. Trust me, it's okay if you don't have your jacket. Just do what you can."

"Jacket, jacket, jacket," he muttered as he opened a nearby closet. He took out a black suit jacket and pulled it on with an expert flourish. He straightened up, smoothed his hair, and buttoned the jacket, transforming before my eyes from a schlubby, soft-bellied lost soul into a straight-backed butler.

He turned to me and asked archly, "Who are you?"

"Stormy Day. I'm here with Logan Sanderson. He's... around."

Randy said stiffly, "Mr. Sanderson cannot be wandering around the estate unaccompanied."

"Mr. Sanderson is currently chasing down the suspicious man we saw emerging from the hedges right after the screaming."

Randy stared blankly. "Suspicious man?"

"Someone in workman's clothes and a hat. Could it have been someone on staff? Say, a gardener?"

"No," he said. "The only people on the schedule this morning are the ones you saw. Why do you ask?"

I patted him on the back again. "Just get the door."

He opened the door to sirens. The ambulance had arrived. The sirens went quiet as the vehicle slowed to enter the circular driveway that curled around a fountain. A male and a female EMT jumped out and approached the house, gloves on and kits in hand.

"Right this way," Randy said graciously.

He was calm and composed, every bit the dignified butler, escorting them through the stately home toward the courtyard.

I lagged behind to call Logan on my phone.

Logan answered, breathing heavily. "What happened?"

I countered, "Did you catch the guy?"

"No." He sounded disgusted at himself. "Is Mr. Koenig okay?"

"Not by a mile," I said. "Barring some resurrection miracle at the hands of the EMTs, he's dead."

Logan swore.

I explained everything I'd seen so far while he made concerned noises.

When I'd caught him up, he said, "This is beyond messed up."

"Where are you?" I asked. "Are you heading back to the house?"

He swore again. "This is exactly what I was worried about. I told him to be more careful, to stay away from the mansion for a little while, but he wouldn't listen to me."

Ahead of me, Randy and the EMTs were attending the scene. I ducked back into the house and into a quiet alcove.

I spoke softly into my phone. "Logan, what are you hinting at? Was Mr. Koenig worried about someone killing him?"

"Stormy, the less you know, the better. Do you hear something?"

I listened. The interior of the home was as quiet as a library after closing time.

"All I hear is the air conditioning," I said.

"There's a plane approaching. It's coming in low, and the only airstrip within a hundred miles is right here in the backyard." He let out a single dark laugh. "As much as you could call it a *backyard*."

"Hurry back," I said. "I guess I'll go meet you by your truck?"

"The truck!" he exclaimed. "You've still got the spare key, right? Go jump in and drive. I'll meet you on the access road. I'm already about a third of the way to the airstrip. I'll run along the side of the road so you can see me to pick me up."

"We're going to the airstrip?"

"You bet we are," he said. "With Dieter Koenig dead, thirty million dollars are about to change hands. Maybe the death was an accident, maybe it wasn't. But I need to see which of his heirs are on that plane."

CHAPTER 4

THE BEAUTIFUL TOWN of Misty Falls, Oregon, isn't big enough to have a McDonalds, let alone its own commercial airport. We do, however, have a private airstrip on the Koenig Estate.

I stepped outside, where I could hear the jet coming in for its landing. Some or all of Dieter's heirs were on that plane. The thirty-million-dollar question was *who?*

I jumped into Logan's truck and started it with my spare key. I started driving down the access road. The jet came in alongside me, aiming for a paved runway strip that ran parallel to the gravel access road. The aircraft slowed for landing but was still much faster than Logan's truck, even with the gas pedal touching the floor. The plane landed smoothly and taxied out of sight, turning past the hangar.

I kept lookout for Logan, but he wasn't on the side of the road where he said he'd be, and he wasn't answering his phone. I reached the hangar, parked, and jumped out, calling his name. Nobody answered.

The hangar resembled a topped-off mountain made of corrugated metal. I approached a door that was covered in signs warning against trespassing. The handle turned, but the door wouldn't open. I knocked and tried the handle again. This time, the handle didn't even turn. Had someone on the other side intentionally locked me out? I banged on the door in frustration. For good measure, I also kicked it.

"There you are," Logan said, running up to join me. He'd loosened his tie and looked sweaty.

"Someone's in there." I gave the door another kick.

"Easy, tiger. That's not how you kick down a door."

"It's steel-framed," I said. "We'd need a battering ram. It's a shame you don't have a winch on your truck."

He wiped his forehead with the back of his hand. "Are you always this intrepid?"

"Yes. That's a good word for what I am."

He gently pulled me away from the door and knocked on it. "This is an emergency," he said, his voice booming and forceful yet controlled. "Open up, *please*."

"The magic P-word," I said, nodding. "An interesting alternative to kicking things."

"I'm not as intrepid as you, so I need my other tricks." He banged on the door again, repeating his request and identifying himself as Mr. Koenig's attorney.

This time, a muffled voice answered with what sounded like, "Hold your horses."

While we waited, Logan slipped an arm behind my back and pulled me against him in a half-hug. "How are you holding up, Ladybug?"

His use of the pet name added a layer of surreality to the moment. I rested my head against his chest, inhaling deeply. His jog around the mansion and to the hangar had made him sweat, and the musky scent was as comforting as his solid body against mine.

I answered with a croaky voice, "I'm doing better than poor Mr. Koenig."

"We're okay," he said. "This is some serious business, but as long as we keep our heads, we'll be fine." He squeezed me and kissed the top of my head. "When we get inside, I'll do the talking. Would you mind recording everything on your phone?"

I got my phone ready and gave him a grin. "My usual rates apply."

He looked up at the sky and frowned. "Where did those rain clouds come from?"

I thought he was teasing me, referring to my family's running joke that my moods affected the weather, but then I felt a cool spot on my cheek. It was a raindrop from the gathering clouds.

The metal door suddenly opened with enough velocity to damage a person who wasn't standing a few feet back, as we were.

Two men, Dieter Koenig's sons, stood before us. Both resembled young European princes, with golden hair, high cheekbones, and piercing blue eyes.

On the left was the family playboy, Drake Koenig—tall and handsome, forty-something and never married. On the right was Brandon Koenig, the glasses-wearing, conservative, older son who was poised to take over the Koenig empire. I'd never formally met either one, but I'd seen Drake around town, and I'd read about Brandon in the *Misty Falls Mirror* whenever one of the family businesses was in the news. Drake looked calm and cool, while his brother Brandon's face was red, especially his cheeks.

Both of the men had phones at their ears and signaled for us to wait. They didn't invite us inside the hangar but came out and joined us on the exterior walkway. The rain was little more than mist—nothing to flee from if you were used to life in the Pacific Northwest.

Logan and I exchanged a look. His expression conveyed the same suspicion I felt. Neither Koenig brother seemed surprised to see us or terribly upset over the news they were getting over their phones.

Drake finished his phone call first. He nodded briefly at Logan before turning to me.

"You're Stormy Day," Drake said. "I've read about you in the *Mirror*."

"I'm so sorry for your loss," I said. "It must be such a shock."

"He was old," Drake said. He looked up at the sky and blinked repeatedly. "What I mean is, I knew it was bound to happen someday, but I never expected it so soon. If I'd known, I wouldn't have left right after an argument."

"You were arguing?"

Drake sniffed and returned his gaze to me. "Nobody was a fan of Dad's new girlfriend."

"Well, I'm very sorry," I said. I stopped myself out of politeness, though I was dying to ask who the girlfriend was.

Logan peered around Drake, trying to catch a glimpse inside the hangar. "Did you see someone running in here to hide?" he asked. "Someone in workman clothes? With overalls and a big hat?"

"Do you mean Ol' Tim?" Drake asked. "I was looking out the windows when we came in for landing, and now that you mention it, I did see Tim near one of the supply sheds."

"I checked the shed," Logan said. "He wasn't in there. He just disappeared into thin air."

Drake tilted his head to the side. "What does Ol' Tim have to do with anything? He's a kooky-spooky sort of guy. If there was some sort of shouting going on, he might have climbed a tree. I've seen him do that to get away from Verity sometimes."

Logan glanced at me. "I didn't check the trees," he said apologetically.

Drake continued to stare into my eyes. "Stormy, I enjoyed reading about you in the *Mirror*. They really ought to run more photos with those stories. It would increase readership."

Drake Koenig was shaking my hand firmly, though I didn't remember offering it to him.

He continued, oozing charm, "Such a pleasure to meet a local celebrity."

"Sorry it had to be under these circumstances," I said.

Drake released my hand and shrugged one shoulder. "And I'm sorry you had to witness everything," he said. "You'll be compensated for your time, naturally. Please send us a bill for your hours this morning, and I'll bug my big brother to make sure you get paid." He nodded at his glasses-wearing brother, who was still giving monosyllabic responses over the phone.

Logan said, "We won't be charging for today. The visit we had scheduled with your father was purely social."

Ignoring Logan completely, Drake kept his piercing blue eyes on me. "Purely social?" He quirked one gold-brown eyebrow. "You weren't at the house this morning for business?"

"Just to eat," I said with a smile. "If you happen to hear my stomach rumbling, it's because we didn't quite make it to breakfast."

Drake looked over my head, in the direction of the mansion. "That means Dad died on an empty stomach. What a shame. All that food, and he died as hungry as the day he immigrated to this country with barely more than the clothes on his back."

Logan said, "I'm sorry for your loss. He was a great man, and he will be sorely missed by the entire community."

Drake turned and looked him in the eyes. Dispassionately, he said, "Don't be too sorry, now. You'll be handling the estate, and that'll keep you in billable hours for six months, at least."

Despite the daggers in Drake's words, Logan didn't even flinch.

"I'll start shopping for my own private jet," Logan said. "Speaking of which, where did you come from this morning?"

"New York," Drake answered while yawning and stretching. "Long flight across the country. Not that it's any of your business, but we were visiting a dear family friend."

"And your friend will attest to your whereabouts?"

"Our friend came to the airport and saw us onto the plane. Again, not that it's any of your business." Drake adjusted his tie and glanced over at his red-faced brother. "I suppose we'll be in touch about the estate and all that transfer and trust fund nonsense soon enough. Don't worry about rushing us a copy of the will. I've got the last revision in my files somewhere."

"Good," Logan said, handing Drake a business card. "Please call me if I can be of any service to the family in this time of crisis. Our office will be in contact, of course."

Drake tucked the card into his suit pocket. He held his hand out, palm up, before me. "And what about the lady?" he asked me, maintaining eye contact.

"Can *she* be of any service to the family in our time of terrible, heartbreaking crisis?"

"Any time," I said, and I handed him my own card.

Drake took the card, touching my hand and stroking my forearm with the dexterity of a stage magician. I'd only realized the extent of his contact after it was done, when the sweat from his fingers on my skin dried in the misty breeze. His face wasn't as red as his brother's, but he was sweating despite his cool appearance.

"We'll be in touch," Drake said dismissively.

He nudged Brandon, and the two brothers started walking away. Brandon was still talking on his phone, head bent forward as they approached a vehicle that was bigger than a golf cart and smaller than a Jeep—the sort of thing you'd call a dune buggy.

Drake put one arm around his brother's back and called to us over his shoulder, "See you around!"

They climbed into the dune buggy, with Drake at the wheel. The tires kicked up dirt and grass as they tore off toward the access road and the mansion.

I turned to Logan as I brought the speaker of my phone up to my mouth. For the benefit of the recorded memo, I said, "Ladies and gentlemen, that was Drake Koenig, taking the news of his father's demise with remarkable resilience."

Logan reached for the device and touched the red button to stop the recording. He nodded for me to follow him into the hangar, through the door he'd kept open with his foot.

I followed him in, blinking rapidly in the relative darkness and hoping kooky-spooky Ol' Tim wasn't up in the rafters, waiting to drop down on us.

CHAPTER 5

THE HANGAR WAS BIG enough to hold two private jets but was currently empty. The barn-style sliding gates at the far end were wide open, and the family's private jet was visible in the distance. They must have gotten the news as soon as they touched down and decided to park it later. I saw nobody else attending to the plane.

I said to Logan, "There's no pilot or crew. Do you think the brothers were flying the plane?"

"Probably," he said. "They both have licenses to fly, and I don't see anyone else around." He sniffed the air. "Is that gasoline, or booze?"

We were near the only furnished area within the hangar, a cozy seating arrangement with comfortable leather couches plus a wet bar.

I inhaled deeply. "Some fumes are blowing inside from the plane, but I do smell hard liquor." I leaned over the wet bar's sink and smelled the two tumblers sitting in the basin. "Whiskey," I said. "And not the cheap stuff, so it wasn't staff or crewmen." I pointed to the nearby whiskey bottle, which was a premium top-shelf brand.

"There's a story here." Logan leaned over the sink, examining the tumblers without touching them. "So, the boys are coming in for a landing when they get the news about dear old Dad. Then they lock themselves in the hangar and toss back a toast. Does that seem suspicious to you, or just distasteful?"

"People don't just drink to celebrate," I said. "They might have been steadying their nerves."

Logan pulled out his phone and snapped some pictures of the wet bar and the still-wet tumblers.

We were still mulling over the scene when someone yelled, "FREEZE!"

The voice was male and coming from behind us.

He shouted, "Put your hands up!"

We did. Logan glanced over at me as he muttered, "Please, tell me that's not your friend Tony behind us. As much fun as it is to wrestle with the guy, I'm not in the mood for his style of male bonding."

I turned to look and immediately dropped my hands.

"Dimples, you scared the dickens out of us," I said.

Officer Kyle Dempsey, also known as Dimples, on account of his cute-as-a-baby good looks, moved his hand away from his holster, shook out his arm, and let out a sigh as he visibly relaxed.

He said, "Stormy, is that your black truck I clocked speeding over here?"

I countered, "Is it really speeding if you're on private property?"

"Yes," Kyle said.

"That's my truck," Logan said gruffly, extending his hand to shake. "Officer Dempsey, I'm sure Stormy wouldn't knowingly break the law by speeding."

They shook hands, and Kyle said, "Mr. Sanderson, it's good to see a little stabbing hasn't slowed you down."

Logan responded by looking pointedly at Kyle's sidearm. "And I'm glad to see your piece is still in that holster and not in the hands of a ninety-pound lady."

Kyle grinned, putting his boyish dimples on display. "We all have our blind spots," he said.

"Some of us more than others," Logan said.

Kyle kept up his grin. "As much as I'd like to socialize, I am going to have to escort you off the premises. Let's step outside, where you folks can get into that truck and drive off at a reasonable speed so I don't have to issue you a ticket."

I pointed to the sink. "We'll go, but get out your little notepad and write this down. Have the CSI techs pull prints and DNA from these tumblers and the bottle. Oh, and Logan saw someone, possibly a gardener, leaving the pool area when we arrived on the scene. He called out to the person, but they ran away like they had something to hide. They came out of the hedge." I snapped my fingers. "You guys need to do a sweep of the hedge. The person might have been taking a shortcut, or they might have been hiding something. At the very least, they might be a witness."

Kyle's dimples grew even larger. "Last I checked, Miss Day, you weren't the captain." He waved for us to proceed toward the door.

"Dimples, I'm not joking around," I said. "You don't have to tell anyone it was my idea. Act like you thought of it all yourself."

Kyle nodded. "Prints and DNA on some suspicious tumblers, and then beat the bushes for clues. Got it."

Logan said, "Officer Dempsey, with all due respect, may I speak with you in private for a moment?"

"If it's outside, sure," Kyle said.

We followed him to the door and exited the hangar. During the few minutes we'd been inside, the mist had turned into actual rain.

I didn't know what Logan wanted to talk to Kyle about privately, but I trusted his judgment. I got into the truck and waited.

As the two men talked, Kyle's expression became more somber. Logan pointed to the sky a few times. Kyle used his police radio to communicate with someone else and then shook Logan's hand. He jumped into his police cruiser and drove away, back toward the mansion.

Logan returned, slid into the driver's side, and started the engine.

I said, "Do you think he understands what's going on here? I hope you mentioned the thirty million dollars."

"That boy's just a smidge smarter than he looks."

"But not smart enough to take me seriously," I said. "You, however, had him eating out of the palm of your hand, like a horse to sugar cubes."

Logan put the vehicle in gear and started driving. "I have a few tricks." We drove toward the mansion, as it was the only way to exit the property.

"What did you tell Dimples?"

"The exact same thing you did, but in a man's voice." He pulled on his seat belt at the request of the female voice coming from the vehicle's navigation system.

"That's not much of a trick," I said.

"Don't hold it against me," he said. "You know I take you very seriously. Young Officer Dempsey probably wasn't able to think straight, since he's so in love with you."

I laughed. "Oh, please."

"At least I made you laugh," Logan said. "Enjoy it while it lasts."

We reached the front of the mansion, where an ambulance was pulling away just as several more police vehicles arrived.

"This is bad," Logan said. "And things are only going to get worse."

I got the terrible feeling he wasn't just being pessimistic.

CHAPTER 6

IF YOU'RE EVER in Misty Falls around lunchtime, and you've got a hankering for pasta, stop by the Olive Grove. This quaint Italian restaurant pre-dates the large Olive Garden chain, so any similarities are coincidental. In fact, if you mention to your waiter or waitress that the Olive Grove is *much nicer* than the similarly named chain, you may be the recipient of a complimentary take-home box of freshly-baked almond biscotti. The biscotti are famously crunchy and absolutely *must* be dipped in coffee.

"How about the Olive Grove?" I suggested to Logan.

He was driving, a good ten miles below the speed limit, and silently lost in his thoughts. He hadn't said a word since we'd exited the iron gates of the Koenig Estate.

"Why?" he asked.

"Food. Coffee. And if you need a third reason, almond biscotti."

"Okay," he said, putting on the turn signal as we approached Broad Avenue.

I didn't voice my concerns, but I could tell my boyfriend was off balance. Technically, almond biscotti fit within the general category of food, which was the first reason I'd cited, so it wasn't a legitimate third reason. It wasn't at all like detail-oriented, always-ready-for-battle Logan Sanderson to let my error go without a challenge.

We parked in the restaurant's parking lot and went in. The air smelled of lemon and herbs. The lunch rush hadn't started yet, so we would have our choice of seats in the near-empty restaurant.

A blonde with dark lipstick greeted us. She held up her hands and joked, "Don't hit me, Stormy. I'm unarmed!"

I shook my head and smiled. "How are you, Harper?"

She rolled her eyes. "Eager for the school year to start so I can get Hayley off to school. She's driving me nuts."

I asked, "What grade?"

"Eleventh grade. She's sixteen now, and she wants to drive my Torino." Harper steered us to a corner booth and set the menus on the table while we slid into the seats. "They grow up so fast." She cleared away the extra place settings. "Coffee? Vanilla latte for you, Stormy?"

I agreed, and Logan said he'd have the same, even though he often switched to tea by mid-day.

"How about breakfast?" I asked. "Are we too late?"

She answered, "We can rustle up some eggs if that's what you're craving." She glanced over at Logan and then gave me a knowing look. "Sleeping in late with your boyfriend can really fire up the appetite."

"That's not... we were... oh, never mind." I waved her away.

After Harper left, Logan said to me, "How does that girl have a sixteen-year-old daughter?"

"Hayley is her little sister," I explained, and then I reminded him of how I'd met the girls. He knew about the whole incident, including how I'd assaulted poor Harper with an economy-sized jug of laundry detergent, but hadn't connected her face with the story. That was also very unlike him.

Harper brought our two cups of coffee. We both ordered the day's brunch special, a one-egg omelet and a half waffle—the perfect mix of savory and sweet.

We sat in silence until Logan said, "Sorry I'm not better company."

"Do you want to talk about what's bothering you?" I glanced around to make sure no one was within hearing range. "Or is this location not private enough?"

He frowned at his coffee. "Like I said earlier, the less you know, the better. Paranoia is a bit like yawning or the common cold. It's contagious."

"Are you saying Dieter Koenig was paranoid? Did he think someone was planning to kill him? His son Drake certainly had an interesting reaction to his father's death. He's lucky he was on that jet, or he'd be getting grilled by Tony and the gang right about now."

Logan winced. "Lucky, indeed. Drake and Brandon Koenig are his only children. Their grief is probably mitigated by the belief they'll be inheriting fifteen million dollars each." He pressed his lips together and made a sound that suggested there was more to the story but he wasn't telling.

I gave him a sidelong look. "The *belief* they'll be inheriting that dough? Is there some reason they won't get everything? What is it? Are there other children they don't know about splitting the family jewels? Business deals gone wrong and more debt than cash?"

I had a thousand more questions but stopped talking when Harper arrived with our breakfast. We started eating, and I waited patiently for Logan to divulge more details.

Finally, he said, "How well does your father know the maid, Erica Garcia?"

I leaned in and focused on my omelet. "How well? You'll have to ask my father yourself." I took two bites and chewed. "Why?"

"She'd be a good resource for finding out the general mood of things at the mansion. I have some questions, but I don't want to tip anyone off that I'm snooping around."

"Because it could be dangerous?" I asked.

"Maybe. But I've also got to think about my long-term business plans in this town. I've made enemies in the past, and I'm not eager to make those mistakes again."

I worked my way through the remainder of my small omelet. Logan could be very open about some things, such as his emotions, but he didn't discuss his past. I respected his request for privacy, and hadn't done so much as an internet search on his name. My father wasn't nearly as respectful of Logan's wishes, but then again, he was my father. He'd assured me there were no red flags, so I'd left the matter alone for the time being.

"I could talk to Erica," I said. "As a friend, unofficially."

"You'd get paid," Logan said.

"I'm not worried about that." I studied his face, which gave away little. "But I am worried about you. This whole thing has really rattled you."

He scoffed as he poured maple syrup over his waffle. "Rattled? No way. Let's not forget, I ran that mile to the hangar in under four minutes, and on an empty stomach."

"There's *no way* you ran a four-minute mile," I said.

"And I did it in dress shoes," he said with a smile.

I pried the maple syrup container from his hand before he used it all up. "Whether it was four minutes or not, you were very heroic to run after that guy, whoever he was."

The smile dropped off his face. "But I let him get away."

"You're assuming something sinister happened. It might have been a simple accident. It would appear that Dieter slipped and hit his head, probably on the diving board, and either that killed him or he drowned." I shivered and rubbed my arms. "Poor guy. I hope he didn't suffer."

"He really was a great man," Logan said. "I was just getting to know him, and I genuinely liked him. He had big ideas for the town, and he wasn't ready to shuffle off into retirement."

"Like what? More factories?"

"He wanted to boost tourism. He wanted to buy more land and invest in infrastructure, in things that might take twenty years to start seeing a profit."

I took a slow sip of my latte. "Have you ever seen one of those bumper stickers on a motorhome? The ones that say *We're spending the kids' inheritance*?"

He let out a dark laugh. "I see your point. His sons might not have approved of his plans." He shook his head. "I just wish I could have caught the guy in the hat. He was so fast."

"We'll get him again," I said. "You're a great lawyer, and I know you'll stop at nothing for your clients. If someone killed Dieter Koenig, they're in big trouble."

"Big trouble," he agreed.

"Now, are you going to tell me who he was dating, or do I need to drag it out of you?"

He looked down at his plate and frowned.

"Do I know her?" I asked.

"Unfortunately, yes."

"And? Mr. Sanderson, I will resort to drastic measures if you don't tell me. I'll eat your waffle."

He looked around, took a deep breath, and said, "Della."

"Very funny. Who was he really dating?"

"I'm not joking," he said.

"Della." My stomach clenched.

CHAPTER 7

"THE SINGER?" asked my father. "*That* Della? The woman who ran the karaoke night at the Fox and Hound?"

"Among other things," I said. "May I have another dinner roll?"

He handed me the basket across the table.

It was Sunday night, and I was at his house for a quiet dinner with just the two of us.

After my late breakfast at the Olive Grove, Logan dropped me off at the house and left for his office, warning me not to wait up. I puttered around in the garden for a few hours, wreaking havoc on some weeds, before heading over to my father's for dinner.

"I hear she's a good singer," he said.

"Dad, haven't you seen Della sing a bunch of times when you go to karaoke nights with your friends?"

"I've seen her," he said, grinning. "But with the way she dresses, it's hard to tell what she sounds like, unless you look away, and why would you do that?"

I palmed my forehead. "You wouldn't be such a fan if she'd thrown *you* down in the mud and wrestled her way on top of you."

With perfect timing, he said, "Maybe I'd like her even more."

I pretended to throw a dinner roll at his head.

He helped himself to a second serving of the roast, as well as more of the tomato salad.

"Have yourself plenty of salad," he said. "Tomatoes are supposed to be good for reducing inflammation."

"Are you saying my face looks puffy? It feels puffy."

"You look fine for your age. Not a day over forty."

I shook my head. I'd be turning thirty-four in October, and he'd been giving me a hard time about catching up to him.

I took some salad, including extra tomatoes.

"Tell me more about this favor Logan wants," he said.

I added a splash of dressing to the salad and finished catching him up on the events of the day, including Logan's request.

My father, Finnegan Day, made many friends during his years working as a police officer in the town of Misty Falls. Even the people he'd arrested or issued tickets to showed him begrudging respect on account of his professional, fair treatment.

Women in particular appreciated his *even fairer* treatment. With a few charming words and a quirk of his eyebrow, Finnegan Day could turn the most reluctant witness into an eager criminal informant, especially if she was his type—and my father's type was any woman who found him charming.

He'd helped the Koenig family's maid, Erica Garcia, during a domestic dispute years ago. I didn't need to hear the details to understand the impact. I could tell by the reverence in Erica's voice that my father had been a hero in her time of need.

I explained how Logan wanted to put out some unofficial feelers to get a sense of the mood at the Koenig Estate.

My father called Erica's home and got her on the phone.

"How are you holding up, my dear?" he asked.

He nodded for a moment then said, "That's all to be expected, after discovering your employer doing the full float in the pool. I hear you were a real hero and you dove right in there after him. You should be commended for your bravery."

More nodding.

"Don't blame yourself," he told her. "You couldn't have known there was suntan lotion on the diving board."

My ears perked up. Suntan lotion would support the theory of an accident, unless it had been put on the diving board on purpose.

"I suppose we'll never know for certain," he said.

I frowned. He was just offering comfort, but I refused to believe we'd never know what happened to Dieter that morning.

I cleaned up the dinner dishes while my father spoke to Erica. They talked for nearly thirty minutes. The conversation moved upstairs to his den, where I couldn't overhear his side.

When the call was finished, my father came downstairs and reported that Erica was shaken up but taking the events with her usual sweetness and grace.

"She's got the day off work tomorrow," he told me. "We shall be stopping by her house at eleven in the morning for a social call."

"In person? I thought you were going to get the information over the phone. Don't tell me we're going over there just so you can flirt with her in person."

He pretended to be offended. "Me? Flirt? You're confusing flirtation with being nice."

"Why haven't you dated Erica, anyway? She likes you a lot."

"Since when do you offer your old man dating advice? You've gotten cheeky since you turned fifty."

It was my turn to act offended.

"We'll have fun tomorrow," he said. "You can drive us in the Batmobile."

He cracked open a can of his favorite cheap beer, and we settled in to watch some of our favorite true-crime shows. Around ten, I returned home to my cat and roommate.

Jessica had heard the news through various sources, so I caught her up on everything I could divulge before retiring for the night.

My dreams were relentless and confusing. Each one featured Drake Koenig. He played my friend and my foe, charming and evil, my enemy and my lover. I awoke in a guilty sweat around two o'clock and took a sleeping pill to keep him at bay.

* * *

The next morning, yawning from the lingering effects of the bad dreams and sleeping pill, I drove to my father's house.

I turned onto Warbler Drive at 10:44 a.m., a minute early. He was already waiting, standing on the sidewalk in front of his house. He wore a suit, dark sunglasses, and a summer-weight fedora. The sun glinted off his cane's handle—the handle that also served as the hilt for the sword hidden within. He'd recovered robustly from a total hip replacement on one side nine months earlier and didn't need the cane, but as he put it, "Once you've had a cane sword, you can't live without a cane sword."

I turned off the stereo as he slid into the passenger side.

"Dad, what's with the hat?" I asked. "You look like you're auditioning for the Blues Brothers."

He set the fedora on his lap and shot me a grin. With an exaggerated thickness to his usual Irish brogue, he replied, "The world's a stage, and we're all unrehearsed, but at the very least, we can make our entrance with some style."

He gave me the address for the Garcia residence.

As we drove there, he expounded on his philosophy of style versus fashion.

"Stormy, the thing is, fashions come and go, but style is eternal, because it's an expression of your true self."

I took another sip of the coffee I'd brought from home in a thermal mug. I tried to pay attention to what he was saying, but my mind kept wandering back to the scene by the pool and Erica, trembling and wet next to her employer.

The day had been warm, and the pool was heated. Had she been shaking from the shock alone, or did she know something she hadn't disclosed to the police? As soon as she'd seen me, she'd asked for my father. Was it possible he was the only one she trusted?

CHAPTER 8

ERICA GARCIA LIVED in the Parkhill neighborhood, which was full of modest bungalows that compensated for their size with elaborate, eccentric front yards. Her street alone featured one property fenced by polka-dotted tires, one home built from a retired paddleboat, and one lawn decorated with the rear quarter of a 1958 Ford Fairlane Skyliner angled so it appeared to be driving toward some subterranean freeway.

Erica's home was the most low-key one on the block, even though, with its flat roof and green-and-brown paint, it resembled a chocolate-peppermint wafer.

A dark-haired teenage boy with sleepy brown eyes opened the door. He wore a too-big T-shirt advertising a soft drink with a too-short pair of jeans that ended an inch above the tops of his socks.

"No soliciting," the boy said, pointing to the handwritten note on the mailbox and then slamming shut the door.

Through the door came the muffled sounds of Erica scolding her son for being rude.

The door opened again.

"What are you selling?" the boy asked.

I pointed my thumb at my father. "Tickets to see the Blues Brothers," I replied.

At this, the boy rubbed his chin. The sleepiness disappeared from his eyes, replaced by a mischievous twinkle.

"Are the tickets free?" he asked.

My father answered, "Only if you come up on stage and help me sing."

The boy's eyes flicked up and down shyly. He hugged the doorframe and asked, "Do I have to wear a suit like yours?"

"Have to? I think you mean *get to*. You can wear one of my old ones, Bobby. You're darn-near tall enough now."

The boy straightened up, his brown eyes wide. "How do you know my name?" He called over his shoulder, "Mom!"

Erica Garcia came to the door, apologizing for keeping us waiting on the front step. She wasn't wearing her maid uniform and looked completely different in a pair of curve-hugging jeans and tunic-style top with a purple-and-gold batik pattern. Her curly dark hair was loose around her shoulders, varying from gentle waves at the front to tight ringlets at the back.

"Mr. Day and Miss Day, please come in. I tried to clean, but this little hurricane makes a mess three steps behind me."

We went inside her tidy home, assuring her there was no need for apologies. We sat at the vintage arborite table inside her simple kitchen, which had dark-wood cabinets and a green-tile backsplash, matching the exterior's chocolate-peppermint-wafer theme. She served us fresh coffee and cold cookies, homemade but still defrosting from the freezer.

My father set his hat on top of Bobby's head and completed the look with his sunglasses. "I'll just leave my things on this handsome hat stand," he joked.

Bobby held out his hands in the manner of a butler. "Your jacket, sir?"

My father handed him the jacket, and Bobby ran off grinning, probably in search of a mirror. From elsewhere in the house, he called out asking his mother if he could record some videos on the computer while wearing the cool clothes. My father and Erica gave permission in unison.

"You look well, considering," my father said to Erica once we were all seated.

She gave us a tired smile. "Better than poor Mr. Koenig, God rest his soul. How are you, Mr. Day? Or should I call you Officer Day?"

He said, "Like I told you on the phone, I'm not here as a policeman. I'm retired now, and that life is behind me."

"But you still have friends on the force," Erica said.

"I have friends everywhere." He smiled and helped himself to a cookie. "Anyway, I'm sure the police already have all the information they need. It looks like the whole thing was just an unfortunate accident."

She asked, "What do the police say?"

"I did speak to one of my contacts," he said.

"Was it Kyle?" I asked. My father had been mentoring the young rookie, or at least letting him bring beer over to the house, since January.

"My sources are secret," he said cryptically.

Erica shifted impatiently on her chair. "It was an accident, yes?"

"Here's what the police think so far," he said. "Mr. Koenig went out to take his morning swim, and either he tried something new or he slipped on the diving board. The suntan lotion on the diving board may have been a factor. He struck the back of his head with the end of the diving board. The impact knocked him unconscious and caused the bleeding wound. He might have died on impact before he hit the water. They'll know once the coroner's checked his lungs for water."

"When?" asked Erica.

He checked the time on a clock hanging on the wall below a framed Sacred Heart image. "If the wheels are turning as they should, that report might be in already."

"Now what?"

My father explained what would happen over the next few days. Even though the death appeared to be an accident, the police would likely visit the estate a few more times and interview each member of staff thoroughly.

"That won't take long," Erica said. "Only four of us were working. The butler, Randy, and Verity, the head of staff, plus myself, and Carlos, the cook."

"No gardener or handyman?" I asked.

"We had someone in to trim the hedges around the pool, but that was Saturday."

My father leaned in. "Do you think he came in to finish the job on Sunday? What did he look like?"

"It was a woman," Erica said. "She was short, barely taller than my Bobby."

My father gave me an eyebrow raise. Could it have been a short woman fleeing the scene? I didn't think so. I shook my head, no.

We were on our second cup of coffee when he got down to brass tacks with Erica.

"Strictly off the record, has anything unusual been happening around the Koenig mansion lately?" He gave her a friendly smile. "Items going missing? Staff getting into quarrels with each other or with the family?"

Erica played with one of her dark ringlets. "Unusual?" Her voice was high and squeaky. "No, nothing that isn't normal... for that family."

My father raised his eyebrows and sipped his coffee.

Erica continued, "I suppose the family has been fighting more lately, but that always happens when both of the sons are single and at home a lot. Those boys should have gotten married and had kids already. It would have settled them down. But Brandon is always too busy working, and Drake is... well, he's always busy with other things."

"Drake Koenig is very friendly," I commented. "I only met him briefly yesterday, but I noticed he has a certain way with women."

My father caught my eye. "How friendly?"

"Quite friendly," I said.

"Good for you." He chuckled. "Don't get me wrong, Stormy. I'm a great fan of Mr. Sanderson, but you could do worse than date someone worth half of thirty million dollars."

Erica gasped. "Thirty million? Is it really that much?"

I kicked my father under the table. "That's just a rumor," I said. "We couldn't possibly know how much the Koenig Estate is worth, could we, Dad?"

"Just a guess," he said. "You work at the mansion, though. You'd probably know more than most people."

She muttered, almost sub-audibly, "I know more than I care to know."

My father nodded and gave me a subtle hand gesture to wait.

Erica took a deep breath, her curves filling out her batik-patterned tunic. She exhaled the words, "Mr. Koenig had a new girlfriend."

"Interesting," my father said, playing dumb.

She took another breath, and the words came loose from wherever she had them locked down. "A young, stupid idiot of a girlfriend." She held one hand to her chest and said directly to me, "I'm not trying to be mean, but you know. Stormy, you met her. You know what she's like."

"I do?" The confusion in my voice was also an act. I wouldn't normally lie, but I was following my father's lead.

He prompted her, "Who is it?"

Erica spat out, "Della. The singer. The one whose brother was..." She trailed off as she looked up at the cross on the wall. "It's bad luck to speak of such darkness. Please forgive me for mentioning anything." She touched the medallion on her necklace and whispered a prayer.

I shot my father a look. I did know Della had a thing for older men who wanted to take care of her. She also had a thing for drama. And violence. We hadn't spoken since the night she'd aimed a gun at me and my friends.

Bobby came into the kitchen with the hat and sunglasses on, snapping his fingers and strutting. "Yo. Check me out." He'd put on a pair of black shoes, and performed a rehearsed dance move for us. "That's my new signature move," he said.

"Very slick," I said.

His mother got to her feet and squeezed him in a loving embrace. The louder he complained about her embarrassing him, the tighter she hugged him.

To us, she said, "Thank you both for coming to check on me. I am very grateful for your friendship. If you'll excuse me, I have to make sure this one does his chores, so he can get paid his allowance. You have to keep up your regular routines, even when life gets crazy."

My father stood and began collecting his hat, sunglasses, and jacket from the boy.

As we walked toward the front door, he asked, "Erica, did all of the estate staff take today off?"

"All except for the cook," she answered. "He stayed to make sure the boys were eating. The rest of us were dismissed for the day, to give the family privacy. We will be back tomorrow, and we'll be very busy. Many relatives will be coming to town for the funeral, and they will be staying at the house."

Someone knocked on the other side of the door. Erica pulled aside some net curtains covering a vertical window next to the front door.

"Look at that," she exclaimed with surprise. "Here is the estate's handyman. He must be here to check up on me, too."

She opened the door to reveal a tall, fit man with gray whisker stubble, wearing a loose-fitting, long-sleeved shirt, old jeans, and a big hat.

My nervous system jolted with adrenaline. If this was the estate handyman, Tim Barber, he had to be the same man Logan and I spotted emerging from the hedge when Erica was screaming for help.

The handyman said, "Sorry, Erica. I didn't realize you had guests. I'll come back in a few hours." He backed away from the step. "I left the sprinkler going on the lawn, anyway, and I should shut it off."

"Tim, don't go," she said, but he was already at the front sidewalk, heading up the street.

I leaned over to my father and whispered, "He's the one I saw running away from the pool yesterday."

My father murmured, "He's on foot, too." He turned and said to Erica, "The handyman lives in this neighborhood?"

"Just up the street," she said. "Tim is so nice. It's a shame he didn't stay and meet you. He gives me a ride to the estate some days, when my sister needs to borrow my car." She waved at Tim as he peered back over his shoulder.

I turned to Erica and bluffed, "Why did Tim run away from the pool yesterday instead of helping you with Mr. Koenig?"

Erica frowned. "Who said that? If Tim heard me calling for help, he would have dropped everything. And he wasn't on the schedule to work, anyway."

"I saw him there," I said. "Logan called for him to stop, but he just ran."

Erica shook her head. "No. It wasn't him."

I shrugged and offered her an apologetic smile. "I must be mistaken, then. Everything happened so fast."

My father said, "Eyewitnesses get confused all the time. Your friend Tim isn't in any trouble. You said he lives on this street?"

She smiled, relaxing again. "Tim lives in the house with the funny car fender sticking out of the lawn. He tells me the whole car is buried in there, and he's going to pull it out one day and we'll ride around in style."

"I love those old Ford Fairlanes," my father said. "I might have to walk over there and take a look."

"Be careful," Erica warned.

We both asked, "Why?"

She smiled. "Because Tim's a real talker, and he'll chew your ear off."

CHAPTER 9

"Luck of the Irish," my father commented as we walked up the street toward Tim Barber's house. "And it's a good sign for an investigation when the witnesses start coming to you."

"We have to be careful," I said. "If this guy's lying about being at the estate yesterday, he might feel threatened by us questioning him."

"I've got my cane sword. What have you got?"

"My sweet disposition," I said.

"Then we're well armed." He pointed to the assortment of colorful garden gnomes in the yard next to Erica's house. "But you could borrow one of those guys if you'd feel better holding something terrifying."

I chuckled. "Dad, you're the only one who finds garden gnomes terrifying."

"They multiply," he said. "They're pure evil. A gnome infestation starts off innocently enough. You see a cute ceramic gnome with a wheelbarrow that's the same color as your house, and it's on sale, so you think, what's the harm in just getting one? Then, a week later, you see another gnome who catches your eye with his impish grin, and you feel terrible about leaving it in the store when you have a lonely single gnome in your garden who could use a friend. What fun is life without friends, after all?"

"Oh, Dad."

The next home had a similar infestation, but with pink flamingos.

We continued up the street until we reached the home of Tim, the handyman.

I stopped to admire the peaches-and-cream-colored Ford Fairlane tailfins emerging from the ground amidst late-blooming summer perennials.

My father stepped over a decorative picket lawn border and leaned over the jaunty car structure.

He asked loudly, "Do these tail lights still light up?"

Tim was hunched over a brass spigot near the base of his house, turning off the water for a nearby lawn sprinkler. He moved into an upright position slowly, one hand on his back. I'd guessed him to be about fifty when we first saw each other at Erica's house, but now that I saw how he moved, I was inclined to put him in his sixties.

Tim stared blankly at us. "What do you want with me? Who sent you?"

My father nodded to the tailfins and repeated, "Do these tail lights still light up?"

"No," Tim said then, "Yes. But they've been modified."

"How's that?"

Tim eyed us with suspicion as he answered, "I've got some low-power LED lights inside, so it lets out a nice glow at night but not so bright that people call in reports to the police."

My father chuckled. "That's good. You wouldn't want those clumsy police officers stomping around in your flowers."

"No, sir," Tim said. "I don't have a problem with them doing their job, but sometimes they get in a fighting sort of mood, and they go around harassing regular citizens who are minding their own business."

My father said casually, "Is that so?"

Tim walked toward us and removed his floppy hat to ruffle his light-gray hair with one hand. "People who get into that line of work are just the sort who want a badge so they can push people around and nobody can say nothin' about it."

My father continued to admire the car, commenting evenly, "That's the sort of thing I've heard before."

"I coulda been a cop, but I ain't no bully," Tim said, picking up steam. "That's what I figure, anyway. They wouldn't say. Just that I didn't pass their test. They've got all sorts of mumbo jumbo they use, but the truth is it's like a clubhouse, and if they don't want you in their clubhouse gang, then you're not invited. They label you with all sorts of things, but they won't come out and say you're stupid." Tim tapped the side of his forehead. "You know who's really stupid, though? Anyone who lets on that they know exactly what's happening. That's right. If you really are a genius, you better not let anyone know, or they'll haul you off and do experiments on your brain."

My father murmured an agreeable sound.

"Especially the cops," Tim said. "They'll hook you up to one of those lie-detectin' machines and shoot electricity into you until you do what they tell you to. Yes, sir! No, sir! Right this way, sir! And you'd better do whatever they say or they'll beat you with a telephone book."

My father leaned over the car and tapped the peach-hued stretch of paint. "Is that the original color?"

"I sure as heck don't know," Tim spat out angrily, apparently frustrated at my father's continued interest in the car. "It was there when I moved in. I didn't have anything to do with it, and I sure don't know where the rest of it is, so don't even bother asking." He crouched down and yanked some weeds from the flower bed, muttering about police conspiracies.

My father stepped back over the decorative picket lawn border and joined me on the sidewalk.

"You have a good day," he said.

Tim barely looked up from the flower bed. He kept talking to himself about electricity and voltage.

My father and I walked back to my car in silence.

Once we were driving, leaving the neighborhood, I said, "Tim the handyman seems to be a few numbers short of a bingo card."

My father drew in a long, audible breath. "His full name's Timothy Andrew Richard Barber, and he's perfectly harmless. I've had a few...*interactions* with Mr. Barber over the years."

"You're lucky he didn't recognize you as a cop. It's a good thing you had your sunglasses on."

He leaned in and adjusted the air conditioning controls. "Don't be so sure he didn't know who I was. Maybe not consciously, but he did leap right into talking about the police at the first opportunity."

"Almost like someone with a guilty conscience?"

"Perhaps," he said. "Then again, maybe he had the local police on his zapped-out brain because they questioned him yesterday."

I glanced over, eyebrows raised. "His *zapped-out brain*? What are you saying?"

"Timothy Barber has had ECT, electroconvulsive therapy, a few times, but not the newer, gentler kind. I'm afraid ol' Tim Barber rode the full-power Lightning Express back in the old days. He's doing well these days, considering."

"Barber," I said. "That name sounds familiar."

"He's the nephew of Ray Barber, from the Credit Union."

"That explains it," I said. I'd been just a kid when the bank was robbed in a bizarre case that grabbed national headlines. The names of those involved had continued to reverberate for years.

We drove for a while before I asked, "Do you think Tim could have hurt Dieter Koenig? Erica kept saying how sweet he is, but I know a short fuse when I see one."

"You would," he said. "And even the sweetest person can commit unspeakable acts when cornered or frightened."

"Or maybe he loosened something on the diving board and caused the accident. Like some bolts, maybe. Then he fixed it before Erica discovered the body. That might have been why he was hiding in those bushes."

"Possibly," he said. "However, that shows a level of planning and forethought I'm not sure the man's capable of." He adjusted the air conditioning again before adding, "Not to mention there's a real lack of motive. Why would Tim kill his employer?"

I scoffed. "I'm thinking someone paid him off. Specifically, two someones. There are thirty million reasons the man's heirs might pay someone to do their dirty work."

He made a thoughtful noise and stared out of the window for a minute before saying, "That would be awfully foolish of Tim Barber to get involved with those two. He'd be outmatched in every way."

"Plus you know what they say about secrets," I said. "The only way two people can keep a secret is if one of them is dead. And with two Koenig sons plus Tim, that makes three people in on the secret, which is a real crowd."

"You're assuming both brothers were in on it," he said. "If you were planning to pull off a big crime, such as the heist of the century, would you tell your sister, Sunny?"

I laughed. "Only if I wanted to give her future blackmail material."

He chuckled in agreement.

After a few minutes, he said, "Is it possible you're fixating on the handyman for personal reasons?"

"I don't think I've ever met the man before today."

He took off his sunglasses and shot me a look. "I meant, might you be fixating on him because you don't want to deal with a certain person? A certain young woman by the name of Della?"

I groaned. He was right.

"She's evil, Dad."

"Worse than a garden gnome?"

"Way worse, because she doesn't even know she's evil. She's the type of person who acts like she's the victim in everything, even when she lies and hides things to get what she wants. The type who thinks anything she does is justified because it's for the greater good—the greater good being her getting whatever she wants."

"I thought you didn't know her that well?"

The car was hot. I rolled down my window.

"I know her type," I said. "I'm not saying everyone who craves the spotlight is the same way. Some entertainers are really nice people. But narcissism infects a person's soul. I've felt the darkness myself, when people are talking about me around town but they're not saying the things I want them to say. I feel this urge to control the narrative, you know?"

"I do know," he said. "Why do you think police wear uniforms? It's not just so the public can identify us. It's also to remind us that the job is not about us. We're part of something bigger than ourselves. When you're secure in that, you can let go of the idea of your image and just do the work."

I focused on driving for a few minutes, thinking over what he'd said.

"Dad, you're kinda deep and philosophical sometimes."

"Better to be deep than wide," he said.

I laughed, even though I didn't quite get it.

After a moment, he said, "Are you going to look into Della as a suspect?"

"Only if Logan asks me to, but so far she doesn't have much motivation. Unless he recently changed his will to provide for a woman he'd barely started dating, I can't see why she'd benefit from him being dead."

"There are other motivations besides money," he said. "Revenge, anger, jealousy, self-protection, and so forth."

"You think the old man was going to break up with her and she was angry about it?"

"Hell hath no fury like a woman scorned."

"Well, nobody likes being scorned."

"Try to have an open mind," he said. "Let your personal experience inform you without prejudicing you."

"That sounds hard."

"If it were easy, we'd live in a perfect world."

"Good point," I said, and I tried to think about Della without imagining her falling into canyons or being eaten by a pack of wolves.

He wanted me to have an open mind, but how could I? The woman had nearly shot off one of my most favorite body parts—my head.

CHAPTER 10

"Logan, Dad and I met with Erica Garcia this morning, and guess what? We have our Running Man. His name is Tim Barber, and he's the handyman. He wasn't on the schedule Sunday morning, but seeing is believing. I'll tell you when I see you, which will be in ten minutes."

I pressed the button to confirm my voicemail, ended the call, and steered the car back onto the road.

"Turn left up here," my father said.

"I'm not taking you home?"

"Not unless someone put in a wood-burning bagel oven while we were out. I'm meeting some friends at the bagel place. Drop me off there, and I'll find my way home."

"How's your hip for driving these days? You don't seem to use your car much."

"That car's boring," he said. "It's an old-man car."

"No comment," I said. He'd thought the car was the bee's knees a year ago when he bought it, but he wasn't wrong about it being boring. If he dropped by the seniors' center to play cards, it took two or three tries to figure out which car in the parking lot was his.

I went into the bagel place with him and ordered some lunch to go. Logan might be disappointed I hadn't cracked the case entirely yet, but he'd be happy to get a ham-and-cheese bagel with three kinds of spicy mustard.

With my bag of warm takeout food, I drove toward Logan's office.

If you're ever visiting the Pacific Northwest in search of the tallest public viewing area west of the Mississippi, set your sights on the Sky View Observatory in downtown Seattle, Washington, in the Columbia Center. Constructed in 1985 with many technical innovations, including viscoelastic dampers, the tall building is one of the strongest and safest in the region. At seventy-six stories, the Observatory offers panoramic views of the city, Elliot Bay, and the Cascade and Olympic Mountains.

In Misty Falls, our tallest building was also built in 1985. It's called the Mesa Office Tower, though it hardly qualifies as a tower at a mere five stories. The building was originally named the Mesa Office Block, but people thought Block sounded too institutional, and businesses were reluctant to move in, so it was changed to Tower.

I turned into Mesa's parking entrance and spiraled down toward the visitor spots.

The building had one of the few underground parking lots in town, extending down into the earth at least six stories. The Tower was like a sturdy weed with more roots than leaves.

I parked and took the elevator up to the fifth floor, the offices of Tyger & Behr.

Logan had been with the law firm since his arrival in Misty Falls nine months earlier, and plans were underway for him to become a named partner. As I pulled open the door, I imagined the etched title on the brass plate being changed to Tyger, Behr & Sanderson. The change would probably happen sooner than later, given the fact Logan had brought in Dieter Koenig's business.

The receptionist, Corine, greeted me warmly. She eyed the brown paper bag in my hand.

"Delicious carbohydrates," she moaned. "Those bagels smell like my downfall."

"They're fresh from the wood-burning oven," I said. "So doughy and soft, you can eat them plain, like donuts."

Corine crossed her arms and whimpered dramatically. She looked radiant in her tropical-print dress. Corine was trying to lose a few pounds before she met her internet boyfriend in real life.

I pulled out the mini-bagel I'd gotten for her and handed it over. Her new diet didn't allow full-size bagels, but she could indulge in a miniature version, which had the same number of carbohydrates as the pita bread she usually had for lunch.

She opened the paper wrapper and inhaled deeply. "Stormy, you're such a darling." She folded the wrapper shut and set the mini-bagel aside.

"Unfortunately, I can't let you back to see Logan. He's in a private meeting with a client."

"Can you let him know I'm here?"

Corine shook her head. "He's got his phone turned off. It's a really important meeting, and he didn't want to be disturbed."

"Is it something to do with the Koenig Estate?"

"Nope." She glanced around furtively. We were the only two people in the reception area. She leaned forward and whispered, "I'm not supposed to tell anyone, but he's meeting with that singer girl. Della."

I nodded as the information sunk in. Corine didn't know of Della's connection to the Koenig Estate. How on earth was that even possible? And how had I not heard of it before Logan told me? Della wasn't the discreet type. The only explanation was that the idea of the dramatic karaoke singer being involved with the wealthy millionaire was so preposterous, nobody believed it even when the story did leak out.

"Then I'll wait around," I said, sitting on a visitor's chair. "You don't mind if I hang out here at reception and eat my lunch, do you?"

Corine made a strangled noise and disappeared behind the reception desk with a thud.

"I'm okay," she said, jumping up. "It's this crazy ball of mine. Sometimes I forget I'm not sitting on a chair." To illustrate, she held up the inflatable ball that served as her chair. About half of the people at the law firm had taken to sitting on exercise balls or converting their desks to standing desks, ever since an ergonomic expert gave everyone a demonstration earlier in the summer. Logan hadn't gotten rid of his comfortable leather executive chair, because he already spent a good portion of his day pacing around his office, dictating into a recorder.

Corine came around the reception desk and motioned for me to follow her. "You're welcome to wait for Logan to be done with his top-secret meeting. Let's get you set up in the staff break room. This way."

"The staff break room," I commented with reverence. "I feel like I'm being promoted."

Corine laughed. "Don't get your hopes up."

She showed me into a room I'd never seen before. My hopes were neither exceeded nor dashed. The staff break room at Tyger & Behr was a typical staff lunchroom, except for the five-foot-wide corkboard displaying photos of dogs, cats, weddings, and children of various sizes. Above the corkboard was a banner reading OUR LOVED ONES.

I nearly choked when I saw a large photo of myself and my Russian blue cat, Jeffrey. As if there were any doubt in my mind the picture was me, it was labeled *Stormy and Jeffrey, loved ones of Logan Sanderson.*

Corine looked at the photo over my shoulder. "He talks about you two all the time."

"And here we are." I stepped back to admire the whole board. "Corine, which ones are yours?"

She pointed out some of her nieces and nephews, I offered the usual compliments about their cuteness, and then she excused herself to answer the phone.

I made myself comfortable in the small kitchen, preparing a fresh pot of coffee and sitting at the sleek glass table to eat my bagel sandwich.

Over the next hour, staff members came in and out, grabbing food from the refrigerator, using the microwave, refilling their coffee mugs, and then returning to their desks to eat at their computers while they worked.

The few people who noticed me sitting there offered a polite *hello* and *good-bye* as they went about their business.

Two women came in together and exchanged gossip while they waited for their diet entrées to finish being microwaved.

The curly-haired woman said to her friend, "I hear Della might be getting her own reality TV show. I guess she would sing or something. I can't imagine what the show would be about, but I'm not ashamed to admit I would *totally* watch it."

Her short-haired girlfriend replied, "Don't you dare"—she paused dramatically—"watch that show without me!"

"What if we got to be in the show somehow? There could be an episode where we have to meet with her to get some important legal paperwork signed."

The women both laughed, and the short-haired one said, "I know you're joking, but Della really could make anything interesting. She's got that star quality." She gasped excitedly and jumped up and down. "I could say something mean about her short skirt, and she could slap me or throw a drink in my face."

The other one joked, "I'm so glad we went to law school, so we could get these amazing career opportunities."

Giggling hysterically, the two women left the kitchen with their Parmesan-scented entrées.

By then, I'd had enough of waiting around for Logan. I cleaned up my dishes, put Logan's sandwich in the fridge with a note on it, and left the staff break room. The ladies' washroom was directly across the hall, so I freshened up before my drive home.

As I was washing my hands, the door opened, and in walked trouble.

"Della," I said, pretending to be surprised to see her.

"Hello, Stormy," she breathed dramatically.

Logan's coworkers were right about Della's star quality. For a moment, I suffered Della-proximity amnesia and couldn't figure out how to use the fancy hand dryer. I tapped the silver thing that seemed to be a button and waved my hands frantically. When the blower finally came on, my hands were already dry from my flailing.

"You look well," I said.

Her dark-brown eyes flashed with apparent delight. "Thank you," she cooed. "That means so much coming from you. I think you and Logie are becoming my favorite people."

I tipped my head to the side. "Logie?"

She turned to the mirror and squared herself with her reflection. With laser focus, she smoothed her glossy black waves with one hand, adjusted the loftiness of her bosom, and scratched a speck of lipstick off her tooth with one thick-lacquered fingernail.

Without taking her eyes off herself, she said, "You don't have to pretend you don't know."

"That you were dating Dieter Koenig?" I asked. "I heard about it, but not through Mr. Sanderson."

"Yeah, right." She reapplied more lipstick and blew herself a kiss. "I'm sure Logie already told you *everything*."

"He didn't tell me his nickname was Logie."

Della shot me a self-satisfied look. "I just came up with that today. You can use it. You have my permission."

"Thanks," I said. "Did your meeting with *Logie* go well today?" It was hard for me to keep a straight face calling my respectable lawyer boyfriend a nickname that sounded like something a baby would say... or spit up.

Della shook her shining mane of hair and sighed, still facing her reflection. "Whatever happens, I'm just so happy you're going to be on my side."

"On your side? Me? Or are you talking to your reflection?"

Ignoring my question, she said, "It's going to be a battle. An actual war. Literally! On a battlefield."

I smiled broadly. "I don't know if I'm battle-ready, but I have been jogging regularly."

She turned to give me a pitying look, her cute nose wrinkled. "Stormy Day, you are *so* weird."

"Coming from you, I'll take that as a compliment."

Without warning, Della threw her arms in the air and launched herself at me. I became the recipient of an enthusiastic, very chesty hug. When she pulled away I checked my shoulder blades for knives. With no signs of any sharp objects lodged in my back, I had to assume the unthinkable.

Della thought we were friends.

She adjusted her cleavage again. "I'm so glad I got to see you today," she said.

"Me, too," I lied.

Her expression grew serious. "Now go," she commanded, pointing one long fingernail at the door. "I can't go you-know-what if anyone else is in the bathroom."

"Fair enough. I was just leaving."

"See you around. Give Logie a kiss for me!"

I left Della to her privacy in the washroom and stood in the hallway for a minute.

The only thing more unsettling than having Della as an enemy was having her as a friend.

But my father had urged me to have an open mind. Was she really so bad?

We'd met under stressful circumstances, and she'd suffered huge losses within the last six months. I could give her a second chance, setting aside the whole mud-wrestling incident and everything else that happened at the Flying Squirrel Lodge in February. I might forgive and pretend to forget, the way Officer Kyle Dempsey had declined to report the exact manner in which Della had taken possession of his firearm.

Sometimes letting things go as water under the bridge was the peaceful way to live. At the very least, I could stay neutral and simply do my job.

I walked down the hall to Logan's office. His leather chair was empty, as was his office. I made my way back out to the reception desk.

Corine was holding the mini-bagel with both hands and inhaling deeply. She explained, "If you really smell your food, you get satisfied faster. Most of our sense of taste comes through the nose."

"And here I've just been using my mouth this whole time."

She smiled. "Did you have a nice lunch with Logan?"

"I haven't seen him. I thought you'd know where he was."

She picked up her phone and called the boardroom and a few other places before reporting back, "He must have slipped out of the office when I was downstairs getting the mail." She gestured to a stack of envelopes and flyers secured by a blue elastic band. "I was only gone for a few minutes."

"Our Logie—I mean Logan—can be sneaky," I said.

"I'm sorry you missed him," she said. "If you run, you might be able to catch him in the parkade." She sounded and looked extremely apologetic.

"Thanks, but I can always catch up with him later." I gave her a sly look. "I happen to know where he lives."

On the elevator ride down to the parkade, my mind was very open. I had new information that could be shifted to form new pictures.

Della was preparing for a battle, and meeting with a lawyer. Had I detected any sign of a baby bump on her slim midsection? I'd placed my hands on her waist during our hug and felt her as much as I dared, just short of groping. If she was pregnant, she wasn't showing yet.

The math was easy. One third of thirty million dollars was a sweet ten million.

But carrying an heir to the fortune made her *less* likely to kill Dieter. If there was a pregnancy, it was still in its early stages and nowhere near a sure thing.

By the time I reached my car, I'd run dozens of scenarios. He could have been pressuring her to terminate the pregnancy. That gave her motivation. Then again, she could have simply left town and had the kid then sued him for support.

What if she wasn't pregnant? Would she still be entitled to anything? I'd have to talk to Logan and get the real scoop. If she was trying to get her own reality TV show, as the women in the office had mentioned, she could be launching a frivolous lawsuit solely for publicity.

One thing was clear. Della was very much mixed up in whatever had happened.

CHAPTER 11

THERE'S NOTHING QUITE like a smudge of lipstick on your collar, courtesy of a dame in distress, to make you feel like a cheap detective in a classic movie.

When Della hugged me at Logan's office, I was so busy trying to frisk her for a baby bump that I didn't notice she'd left a souvenir of her lips on my shirt. I toyed with the idea that if the makeup stain didn't come out, I'd bill it to Logan.

After leaving the Mesa Office Tower, I drove to Broad Avenue and my store, Glorious Gifts.

My employee, Brianna Chang, filled me in on what the whole town already knew—Dieter Koenig had hit his head on the diving board and expired just as his two heirs were flying in for a landing.

"Talk about the perfect alibi," Brianna said. "Those rich boys had it all figured out."

As we talked, Brianna grabbed the cleaning supplies and wiped up a coffee ring from what we called our butler shelf. The shelf was her idea. Rather than getting annoyed at people for setting their takeout coffee cups within product displays and dribbling on everything, or forgetting their beverages entirely, we decided to accommodate our customers' needs. We installed an extra shelf on our central island and left it empty, so shoppers could set down their drinks when they wanted to use both hands to consider a purchase. In the first month, the custom-built shelf had paid for itself.

Brianna was a great hire, and older than she looked, which was about fourteen if she didn't wear makeup. Her disposition was an entertaining mix of sweetness and sarcasm, which was probably why we got along so well. Plus she did an excellent job of running the store so I could traipse around town playing private eye.

I asked her, "Is that what people in town are saying? That Drake or Brandon planned this?"

She shuffled a display of teddy bears to dust their shelf. "Nobody else is saying that," she said. "Just me. And you know I wouldn't talk about my crazy conspiracy theories with anyone but you."

"I am the resident expert on crazy." I stepped behind the counter and checked our supply of coins for the till. "What makes you suspicious?"

"I was sleeping Sunday morning," she said. "Like a regular person, sprawled out in bed, sleeping off the weekend's fun. Nobody ever has an alibi for Sunday morning. But those two were on an airplane. A bullet-proof alibi."

The till drawer closed with a satisfying click. "Brianna, have you been watching true-crime shows?"

"Just for research." She waggled her eyebrows. "I'm thinking of doing a spinoff of my webcomic. It would be a murder mystery."

"I thought your webcomic was supposed to be funny." I gave her a teasing eyebrow waggle of my own. Her webcomic actually was funny, but one of our running gags was that I pretended to not get her humor.

She replied, "And what's more zany than people trying to get away with the perfect crime?" She rubbed her hands together. "I could totally pull it off. The trick is to make it look like an accident."

I shook my head. "You would frighten me if you weren't so adorable."

She picked up the big-eyed doll we agreed was her doppelgänger and blinked innocently, her face next to the doll version.

"Is this the face of a killer?" she asked sweetly.

"You're about as terrifying as Jeffrey when he decides my shoelaces are snakes that must be murdered."

* * *

After closing up the shop for the day and taking a deposit to the bank, I went home. Logan's truck wasn't in the driveway. We didn't exactly live together, but he did rent the tenant side of the duplex I owned. He lived there alone, and I lived with my cat and a roommate.

My roommate and best friend, Jessica Kelly, wouldn't be home until eight o'clock. She'd left me a note with detailed instructions for heating up the casserole she'd made that morning, and when I say detailed, I mean *detailed*. I had to tent the tinfoil a certain way so it didn't stick to the cheese topping, and also put a cookie sheet on the lower tray so the bubbling sauce wouldn't drip onto the stove interior and set off the smoke detector, which would give Jeffrey a scaredy-cat tail all night.

Logan still hadn't returned when Jessica got home at quarter past eight. He did send me one text message at seven, telling me he was working late and not to wait up.

I pulled the casserole from the oven while Jessica got changed out of her Olive Grove uniform, a cream blouse and green slacks. She emerged in her usual all-pink wardrobe, with hot-pink jean shorts and a pale-pink sleeveless top, her red hair back in a loose braid.

We started eating dinner while I caught her up on the day's activities.

"Your father loves playing detective with you," she said. "And you make such an adorable father-daughter team."

"You should have seen him in his suit, with the hat and the sunglasses and everything. I don't know if I'm cool enough to be his partner."

"Oh, please," she said with a laugh. "What did Erica say about the general mood at the house?"

"It's more what she didn't say." I gave her a look as I dug the serving spoon into the hot pan of food.

"Do tell," she urged, so I did.

Since she'd moved in with me in February, I'd been sharing details of my casework with her. We made our arrangement official in March, when Logan drew up some basic paperwork, and she signed a non-disclosure agreement. She became a consultant for my detective business, and I paid her a nominal monthly fee. It wasn't much, because she was too proud to take more, but I had other ways of helping her. Jessica wasn't a shopaholic or willfully irresponsible with money, but cash seemed to slip through her fingers like water.

Our consulting arrangement had several benefits. Detective work could sometimes be dangerous, so if something were to happen to me, at least Jessica would know what I was currently working on, or who I'd gone to meet.

More importantly, when I hit a wall in an investigation, complaining to her about how impossible something was could open up my mind to the answers. We called this the Rubber Duck Effect, a term I'd learned years ago from a software engineer friend. My friend's boss would have frustrated programmers explain to a yellow rubber duck how something worked and where they were stuck. Because of the wonderful layers of the human mind, when they reframed the problem in terms easy enough for a yellow tub toy to understand, the programmers would lead themselves to the solution.

We ate the delicious casserole and talked about how Della might figure into the Koenig case. All I knew for sure was that she'd been dating Dieter Koenig, she was taking meetings with Logan, and she thought a battle was coming.

"Della would have gorgeous babies," Jessica said. "But I think her career comes before having a family. If I had to guess, I'd say she's not pregnant."

"If she is and she's hiding it, she can't hide it forever," I said.

"Not in those tiny dresses of hers," she agreed. "Fashion might actually come first before career, then family."

I rolled my eyes. I'd seen her hike up a mountain in heels. They were chunky heels, not stilettos, but *still*.

"Della is a talented singer," Jessica said. "I've always been a fan, right from the first time I heard her hosting karaoke. Her meetings with Logan could be about music contracts."

I had to agree it was a possibility. It was just like Jessica to point out Della's talent. Whereas my employee, Brianna, always came up with dark and twisted backstories, Jessica had a wonderful way of pointing out innocent intentions and seeing the good in people. She reminded me of a sheltered princess in a children's storybook, with her bright-blue eyes and her thick, red hair that she was always braiding and twisting into elaborate hairstyles. Jessica had never left Misty Falls, and it showed in her trusting nature.

"She *might* have a music contract in the works," I said. "But there has to be something else. Come on, Jessica. Just try to think like a devious person for a minute."

She snorted and added some spinach salad to her plate.

"Was Della wearing any new jewelry?" Jessica asked. "Maybe Mr. Koenig bought her something expensive or gave her a family heirloom, and she's worried the sons are going to try to get it back. That could be the battle."

I didn't remember any jewelry standing out, but we'd only seen each other briefly, and the way Della dressed, there was always a lot to look at.

"I could check with Ruby," I said. "If Dieter bought something locally or had an heirloom ring resized, it would have gone through the Treasure Trove."

Jessica let Jeffrey jump up onto her lap and pretended not to notice him licking the cheese sauce from the edge of her plate. If she and I were in a contest to see who could spoil him the most, she was winning. The little brat looked me right in the eyes, daring me to say something.

"You should call Samantha Sweet," she said, referring to my real estate agent. "Rich old guys like to buy penthouse apartments for their girlfriends. Since we don't have any penthouses in town, maybe he bought her a house."

"A love shack," I said. "Must be nice to be Dieter Koenig. Except for the whole dying part." I shook my head. "Poor guy. He ducked out right when his life was about to get extremely interesting. I overheard some women talking at Tyger & Behr, about Della getting her own TV show."

"I'd watch that," Jessica said.

We sat in contemplation for a few minutes before Jessica said, "That's it! She was talking about her story, her life rights, when she told you she was preparing for battle." Jessica straightened up in her chair, looking pleased with her deviousness. "She's planning to leverage herself with the Koenig name, like that curvy model who married the old billionaire."

"Maybe," I said. "But the Koenigs aren't that famous outside of Oregon, or billionaires. A billion dollars is a thousand million, and they're not even worth a hundred million."

"Everything adds up, though," she said. "She has the singing, the rich old boyfriend, plus everything that happened up at... you know."

At the mention of the Flying Squirrel Lodge, Jessica's posture crumbled, as though she were becoming smaller. She hunched over Jeffrey, kissing his ears and hand-feeding him morsels of leftovers.

Ever since our trip in February, my best friend hadn't been the same. She'd fainted during the worst of it, but she had to live with the memory that she'd been in the arms of a killer. In some ways, she seemed stronger and braver, more willing to take risks. But other times, like now, she seemed to be less of herself. Broken. Or at least fractured. Like a beautiful dish with a chip and a fault line, holding together day to day, withstanding continuous use, but ready to fall apart with one good bump.

* * *

I was brushing my teeth and getting ready for bed when my father phoned.

Cryptically, he said, "You should come join me at the casino."

"Very funny. I'm in my pajamas."

"I don't see anyone else here in pajamas, so you'd better get changed if you want to blend in. I'll watch the door for you. If you leave now, you can be here in forty-five minutes."

I said I planned to be in dreamland in forty-five minutes, but he'd ended the call.

With a sigh, I put on more of the makeup I'd just washed off.

My father liked to joke around, but he wouldn't send me driving out past town limits purely for amusement. If he requested my presence at the Canuso Lake Casino on the reservation lands, he had good reason.

I removed my comfy pajamas and searched my closet for appropriate detective wear. A good detective aims to be a Gray Person, like a background actor filling out a crowd scene in a movie—not too flashy, unless there's a good reason, but not too conspicuously clandestine, either. It does no good to dress like a ninja in all black when everyone else is wearing jeans and polar fleece.

The Monday-night crowd at the casino would be wearing jeans, so that's what I chose, along with a gray shirt and a zip-up summer jacket.

Jessica was curled up on the couch, eating air-popped popcorn and watching a late-night talk show. I told her where I was going and invited her along, but she declined.

"I'm afraid to set foot in a casino," she said. "Gambling is the last bad money habit a girl like me needs to pick up."

I laced up my shoes and hesitated at the front door.

She turned off the TV and gave me a concerned look. "Stormy, you look like you need me. Give me a sec to get changed."

"No, don't worry. My dad's there. It should be safe enough."

She snuggled Jeffrey, who was also giving me a concerned look. "Are you sure?"

I twisted the door handle and said bravely, "If I don't return, avenge my death."

"As always," she promised.

I left for the casino and whatever or whomever my father had found.

CHAPTER 12

PEOPLE SAY THE ONLY WAY to leave the casino with a small fortune is to arrive with a much larger one.

I drove to the Canuso Lake Casino with fifty dollars in my pocket.

I hadn't spoken to Logan all day, and he seemed to have his phone switched off, but that wasn't unusual for when he was focused on a case.

When I walked into the casino, I nearly bumped into the owner of Wild Buck's, Mr. Owen Johnson. The small, bald man grinned and gave me a warm handshake.

"Sheesh, look at you," Owen said in his squeaky voice. "Coming to haul your father out of here before he goes bust?"

"How much is he up by?" I asked.

"I'm not sure about the cash situation, but he's got two different women blowing on his dice for good luck, and they've got a couple of husbands who don't seem none too impressed."

I shook my head. "Typical."

He yawned and patted my shoulder. "I'm glad you're here to keep an eye on him, because it's past my bedtime."

"Mine, too," I said with a nod.

He laughed and carried on toward the cashier's cage to cash out his chips.

If my father had women blowing on his dice, that meant he was at the craps table. I proceeded there and found the scene Owen Johnson had described.

"Dad!" I exclaimed loudly. I gave him a hug and squeezed in between him and a lady in a tight sweater. I said to the woman, "You don't mind if I stand here next to my father, do you?"

"Not at all," she said with a shrug. The man on the other side of her gave me a grateful look then selected two dice and prepared to roll. The table hushed.

I turned to my father and whispered, "How goes? I bumped into Owen Johnson on the way in, and he says you're hot tonight."

"Owen's got a funny definition of hot. I just rolled a big red, but at least I'm having fun." He handed me a roll of quarters. "Here. Go check out Canuso's new one-armed bandits."

"Really?" I accepted the roll of coins.

He looked me steadily in the eyes. "The machine on the far end is bound to pay out soon." He blinked slowly. "Trust me."

I took the quarters and made my way over to the slot machines. The Canuso Lake Casino had a cornucopia of brand-new machines, with high-definition screens and comfy bucket seats, but they'd recently added a dozen classic slots, vintage one-armed bandits. Over the cacophony of computerized sound effects, I heard the clinking and pinging of coins on metal.

The old machine at the end was unoccupied, so I took a seat on a wooden chair, plugged in a quarter, and pulled the lever. My father must have sent me to that particular spot for a reason, so I scanned the casino while the symbols whirled in front of me. The whirling stopped, and I felt a twinge of something. *Hopes dashed.* I wasn't a winner. I plunked in another quarter and promptly lost it. I put in more quarters, quickly forgetting my original purpose.

The machine ate my final quarter, hadn't paid out once, and showed absolutely no remorse. I called it some choice words and left in search of more quarters. I changed forty of my fifty dollars, which seemed reasonable, and got back to my machine, whom I had nicknamed Jerkface.

I was running low on funds when noise at one of the blackjack tables drew me out of my hypnotic daze.

Finally, I saw what my father had called me out to the casino to see. Tim Barber, the sixty-something employee from the Koenig Estate, was making a fuss at a blackjack table. I couldn't tell if he was celebrating or complaining, but his stacks of colored chips exceeded the amount I'd expect to see in front of someone on a handyman's salary.

Was he spending the cash he'd earned on the side as a hit man? Jackpot! I started taking pictures with my phone.

A man in a suit with a bolo tie blocked my view.

"Has someone at the blackjack table caught your eye?" he asked.

I plugged another quarter into my vintage machine. "Ginger ale, please," I said without looking up.

"Stormy, I thought you were a root beer gal." The man leaned against the money muncher I'd named Jerkface. "Root beer floats in particular," he said. "I cherish the memories of the few times you let me buy you one, anyway."

I looked up into the face of Colt Canuso. I hadn't talked to him since high school, but his name came to me instantly, along with a flood of memories that gave me a teenage flutter.

"Colt Canuso, you never bought me one single root beer float," I said.

He flicked his lanky black hair off his forehead and turned on his megawatt grin. "Are you calling me a liar?"

"You bought yourself one, with two straws, and you went around trying to get girls to share with you."

He chuckled and turned his brown eyes down to his pointed, western-style boots. "I regret my youthful ways," he said. "My intentions were good, but I didn't understand generosity the way I do now."

He flicked his eyes up to mine and said huskily, "Let me buy you a root beer float, and you'll see."

"Another time," I said as I turned toward the slot machine. "Now, if you'll excuse me, I need to feed the rest of my pocket change to Jerkface here."

He remained leaning against the machine, moving only to adjust his bolo string tie. "You want me to leave so you can keep taking pictures inside my casino. I know all about your new career as a detective, and I'm sure you're not here just to get grime on your fingers from a bucket of coins. You're watching someone. But why bother with your little phone when you can get footage from my eyes in the sky?"

I looked him in the eyes. "You'd give me footage?"

He shrugged. "Would it hurt to ask? You might find me very generous."

I scanned down to his hand, stopping on his wedding band. "Your wife might not like you being so generous," I said.

He pulled away from the slot machine and fidgeted with the ring. "She's the one who taught me what it means," he said. "We had a good six years followed by two bad ones. She's gone now, free of her pain."

"Colt, I'm so sorry. I didn't know. Was that Susan?" I shook my head. "Of course it was, and I knew about her passing. She was friends with my friend Jessica."

"How is Jessica? She never comes around. You should bring her with you. Are you coming Friday? You won't believe who we have playing in the lounge." He continued to tell me about the upcoming weekend's entertainment, but I wasn't listening. I'd pushed my chair back enough to afford me a view of the blackjack table.

Tim Barber had been joined by another Koenig employee. The butler, Randy, was tugging on Tim's arm, trying to get him away from the table. After a flurry of arm waving, Tim gathered his chips and allowed himself to be led away by Randy.

I stood and shocked Colt into silence by giving him a hug. He was no longer the scrawny kid I'd grown up with, but a broad-shouldered man whose athletic physique was barely disguised by his suit.

"Good to see you, Colt. I'll tell Jessica you said hello."

He stepped back and glanced over his shoulder. "Your mark is leaving," he said.

I plugged my last quarter into Jerkface and pulled the handle. "Not at all," I said. "But I'm out of dough. You know what they say. Eat your gambling money, but don't gamble your eating money."

He gave me a slow smile. "Don't worry so much about eating money. I'll buy you dinner any time."

I thanked him and walked away, slowing to let Tim and Randy stay ahead of me. They stopped at the cashier's cage, cashed Tim's chips quickly, and went toward the exit. They seemed unaware I was following, but spoke in hushed voices I couldn't hear.

Once they got outside, away from the clatter of the casino, I could hear snippets of their conversation. They stood near the entrance, not far from the taxi stand.

Tim was saying, "But fun money's for spending. It was just a bit of cash I got as a bonus."

Randy growled something in a tone too low for me to catch.

Tim cried, "But I'm supposed to spend it. Fun money's for spending!"

Randy told him to be quiet and looked around. I pretended to be checking something on my phone.

Tim continued to complain, but his words were drowned out by the engine of a dark vehicle pulling up.

The two men climbed into the vehicle, joining at least one other person, possibly more. The SUV's windows were tinted, so I couldn't identify its occupants.

I made certain the flash was turned off before I snapped some images of the truck's license plate as it drove away.

CHAPTER 13

Tuesday morning, I awoke to knocking.

That was unusual, because I was used to being woken by either my digital alarm clock or my cat alarm clock, the latter being the more persistent one, with his raspy tongue licking on my forehead.

Because I assumed the knock belonged to Logan, I ran to answer the door clad only in a thin sleeping camisole. I unlatched the door and threw it open.

On my step, in his dark police uniform, stood Captain Tony Milano.

"Good morning, Miss Day," Tony said stiffly.

As his eyes roved down my camisole and bare legs, his expression went from surprised to agitated, which was a look I knew well. Ever since my return to Misty Falls nearly a year earlier, he and I had been butting heads and trading threats. He'd always been arrogant, but his promotion to captain had actually made him less agreeable.

It hadn't always been that way between us. Back when Tony was a twenty-three-year-old rookie with big brown eyes and a dark buzzcut, he'd trained with my father and spent a lot of time at our house. I was just a teen and as impressionable as any girl. Though I pretended my biggest crushes were on singers and actors, if there'd been a magazine poster of Tony Milano, I would have put it on my wall.

My fixation on my father's partner was why I rebuffed the advances of guys my age, like Colt Canuso, who would have been a great high school sweetheart. My life might have been very different if only I could have viewed the scrawny teen version of Colt in the same fawning light as I saw Tony.

Once I was much older, I did have a secret fling with Tony. It was brief, and while it got him out of my system, it only got me more into his. But then I left town, and he didn't waste time getting a wife and the first of three kids. Since then, the unsaid things between us had remained mostly unsaid.

Tony said, "Do you always answer the door like this?"

"Just when I'm really excited about early-morning guests waking me from good dreams."

His eye twitched. "Put some clothes on. I'm here for official police business."

I put my hand on my hip. "Are you saying clothes would be optional if you were here for *unofficial* business?"

He made a flustered, irritated noise as he came inside and closed the door behind him.

I excused myself, quickly pulled on some clothes, and poked my head into Jessica's room to warn her about our guest. She grunted and rolled over. Jeffrey, sprawled on her spare pillow, showed more concern. He walked over Jessica and trotted out, accompanying me back to the kitchen, his sleek gray tail flashing curious question marks.

He paused when he saw Tony seated at the table, gray ears twitching as he sniffed the air. He padded over and jumped onto Tony's lap without an invitation.

Tony's expression lightened. "Aren't you friendly?" He looked up at me. "How long have you had this cat?"

"If you didn't meet Jeffrey the last time you were over, it's because he's afraid of boots. If he hears heavy footsteps, he hides."

Tony tentatively patted Jeffrey's head. "Who's a scaredy cat? Is it you? Are you the scaredy cat?"

"Don't tease him," I said defensively. "He's very brave. Avoiding people wearing boots is good sense for someone with four paws and a tail."

"The kids are bugging me for a dog," Tony said with a tired sigh. "They wanted to prove they could take care of one, so we looked after the neighbor's German shepherd for a few days while they were out of town. Everything was going fine until Harry went missing."

I measured out some coffee grounds and put on the coffee. "Harry? Don't tell me your kids lost the dog."

"Harry Potter is the name of our guinea pig. He's got a little white streak on his head, like this." Tony used his fingertip to trace a lightning bolt on his forehead. "You don't think you're going to get attached to a furry rodent, but the darn things steal your heart." He scratched under Jeffrey's chin and leaned forward to kiss the top of his head.

I was so taken aback by this kinder, gentler, pet-loving version of Tony that I forgot where we kept the coffee mugs and had to search all the cupboards.

Tony continued, "The kids were devastated, and the owners of the German shepherd were horrified. We all thought the dog ate the guinea pig."

"Did he?" I joined him at the table.

"Tony Junior said his heart was broken, and the only way it could be healed was if we got a dog. He already had one picked out. A Jack Russell terrier." Tony paused, and much to Jeffrey's apparent delight, began petting him with both hands. "I suspected things were moving along a little too conveniently," he said. "So, I went looking for Harry Potter, and I found him." His expression turned grim.

I gasped and raised my hand to my mouth. "Your kids killed him and buried him in the backyard."

"God, no," Tony said. "Harry was in his older, smaller cage, at the back of my daughter's closet. The two of them were in on it together."

"The little brats," I said. "How did you know?"

"You can hide a guinea pig, but you can't hide the smell."

I breathed a sigh of relief. "I've never met Harry, but I'm so glad he's okay."

"Sometimes everything works out how it ought to," he said.

"Are you still getting a dog?"

"And reward those two future con artists for what they did? I don't think so. Would you?"

"Probably," I said with a laugh. "Jeffrey's just a cat, but I spoil him rotten. I'd be a lot worse with kids."

Tony fixed me with his dark-brown eyes, suddenly serious. "You'd be great with kids."

I swallowed hard and jumped up to fill our mugs. The coffeemaker wasn't quite finished and spat onto the hotplate with a hiss while I poured.

"What brings you here?" I asked. "You said there was official police business. Don't tell me I changed out of my pajamas for nothing."

"What were you doing at the casino last night? Colt told me you were trying to film someone."

"You're friends with Colt? Since when?"

"Since his band opened the casino, more or less. We share information and keep tabs on certain people."

I set the mugs and creamer on the table and took a seat, pulling my zip-up sweatshirt closed self-consciously. In my rush to get dressed, I hadn't pulled on a bra, and Tony's eyes had been trained on my chest. He was still petting Jeffrey on his lap and, despite his police uniform, looked almost gentle and vulnerable.

"You and Colt keep tabs on *certain people*," I mused. "Like me?"

Jeffrey reached his limit for cuddles and abruptly jumped off Tony and ran to his food dish. "Now I'm covered in fur," Tony said. "Do all cats shed so much?" He swiped clumsily at the fur on his dark-blue uniform.

"You're just spreading it around," I said. "I've got a sticky roller in the bathroom you can use before you go."

He didn't say anything, apparently distracted by Jeffrey's generous gray souvenirs.

I asked, "What else did you and Colt talk about?"

"Mainly about Tim Barber. I saw the footage, courtesy of Colt. The old handyman was throwing around a lot of money at the casino last night."

"And you think someone paid him off to do something to Dieter Koenig."

"It does appear that way." He gave up on the fur and started drinking his coffee. "But I think someone gave him the money as a distraction. We're supposed to *think* Tim did something. It's so obvious that even Tim figured out something was up. He knows he's in danger. He came into the station early this morning, looking like he hadn't slept all night, asking to give a statement on the lie detector."

"Really?"

Tony gave me a playful look. We'd had some fun playing around with the department's equipment— fun that my father, not to mention the chief, wouldn't have been pleased about.

I prompted, "And? How'd that go? I thought you guys didn't use the polygraph anymore."

"We don't," he said. "We had to send Tim home to get some sleep. Once we locate a machine and someone trained to use it, we'll have Tim come back in. I tried to figure out what else he had on his mind this morning, but he wouldn't talk. He said he wanted it all recorded while he was on the machine, and nothing less would do. Strange guy."

I raised my eyebrows and sipped my coffee while everything sunk in. "Dad says Tim Barber has some memory loss from shock therapy a long time ago."

Tony agreed, "He never was quite right in the head, and he's got some wild stories about cops and abductions." He pursed his lips and broke into a grin. "Alien abductions."

I smirked. "Two questions. When are you interviewing him on the polygraph? And how much are you charging for admission?"

Tony chortled. "I'll let you know how it goes. In exchange, why don't you tell me how long your boyfriend, Mr. Beardy Man, has been working for our favorite future pop star?"

"Working for Della? I don't know how long. Who told you?"

"You did. Just now."

I held my hands up. "I don't know anything, and I haven't told you anything."

"But you know she's guilty," he said.

"Guilty of being tacky," I said. "What is it you think she did?"

He shrugged. "Not much. Just bashing Dieter Koenig in the back of the head and staging his murder to look like an accident. She was there at the mansion that morning. She claims she slept right through the whole thing. We were doing a sweep of the mansion when Kyle found her, sprawled out on the bed in a guest room, naked except for one of those satin sleep masks."

"That's quite the visual," I commented.

"Kyle may never be the same again."

"Poor Dimples."

"He needs to toughen up anyway," Tony said. "Do you have anything you'd like to share with me?"

I shrugged. "I didn't know anything you don't, Tony. What we told Kyle at the scene was the whole truth. Logan brought me out there to have breakfast with Dieter Koenig. I swear I had no idea Della was there, or even that the two were dating."

But now I understood why Logan had held back some details. If I'd known the erratic, prone-to-violence woman was there, I might have brought pepper spray or other weapons to breakfast.

"What about the obvious?" I asked. "Isn't it possible Dieter Koenig slipped on the diving board and died by a simple accident?"

"People worth a billion don't die by accidents."

"He wasn't worth a billion," I said. "More like thirty million. But you didn't hear that from me."

"Either way, things are going to get ugly," Tony said. "We may be going into a battle. You need to think very carefully about which side you'll be on."

"A battle," I said. "Funny. Della said the same thing."

"When was that?"

I shook my head. I'd already said far too much.

CHAPTER 14

FOR THE SECOND TIME that morning, someone was banging on my front door.

I opened the door.

"Mr. Sanderson," I said with mock surprise. "I haven't seen you around. I thought I was going to have to find a new tenant."

"Oh, Stormy," he said tenderly, reaching up to stroke the side of my face. "Nobody else would rent this dump."

"Especially not with the colorblind previous tenant's hideous furniture all over the place."

"You don't find my couch so hideous when you're flopped out on it, eating potato chips and getting crumbs between the cushions."

"Me? I think you're mixing up me and you." I stepped back and ushered him inside. In a more serious tone I asked, "How are you?" We hadn't talked at all for the last twenty-four hours.

I started putting on a fresh pot of coffee while he took off his shoes and light summer coat.

"I've been pushing paper around and doing research. What was this big news you alluded to in your voicemail?"

"Just that I found our Running Man." While I prepared the coffee, I filled him in on the previous morning's interviews as well as what I'd seen at the casino.

"Interesting," he said once I was done. "I guess time will tell how all of this shakes out."

"Are you going to tell me about this battle Della is planning for?" I turned on the sink water to wash my hands. "Do you have anything to share with me?"

He stepped in close behind me and wrapped his arms around my chest. "Just that I missed you," he said, nuzzling my neck.

I curled against him, closing my eyes. "We've already talked about business, so today's not a personal day."

His lips brushed my ear. "We could throw those silly rules out the window."

I pulled away and turned to face him. "We have the rules for a reason." I crossed my arms. When we'd started dating, we agreed on the simple rule that we didn't mix business and pleasure. If we used our mouths to talk about a case during the day, we wouldn't use them for kissing until the next day. We hoped these boundaries would protect the romance in our relationship from the strain of working together. I'd had issues in the past, mainly with my ex-fiancé, and I didn't want to repeat the same mistakes.

"Today's a work day," he said solemnly, as though breaking the worst of news.

I nodded and offered my hand to shake. "A work day." We shook hands. "Very well then, Mr. Sanderson. What's happening with the Koenig case?"

"I've got a new assignment for you," he said.

"Tell me it's not babysitting your diva client. I ran into her at your office yesterday, and she got lipstick all over my shirt collar. She's a messy person, in more ways than one."

He chuckled. "Corine gave me heck for missing you. Thanks for the sandwich."

"And thanks for..." *Thanks for putting a photo of me and Jeffrey on your Wall of Loved Ones? Thanks for making me tear up in front of your receptionist?* "I mean, you're welcome. What's the assignment?"

He rubbed his beard. "Having you babysit Della is not such a bad idea. She's highly excitable at the best of times, but she's really on edge now. Did you hear the cops have been tailing her around town, watching her?"

Guiltily, I said, "I haven't heard that, specifically."

He tilted his head to the side. "What have you heard? Have you been talking to Tony Baloney?"

Right then, Tony emerged from the hallway and cleared his throat. He'd finally finished removing Jeffrey's fur gifts using the sticky roll in the bathroom. "That's pronounced *Milano*," he said tersely.

Logan wheeled around. "What are you doing here?"

"I can't discuss an ongoing investigation." Tony inhaled, his chest flaring. "Especially not with the legal representation for a person of interest."

Logan shot me a glance. "You told him?"

I held my hands up. "Nothing he didn't already know."

Logan squared off with Tony. "You order your boys to back off my client, or we'll have you for harassment."

Tony didn't flinch. "Which client? The one who applies makeup while speeding around town in her green Volkswagen Beetle? That girl is a menace to polite society."

"You're a menace," Logan said.

Tony retorted, "Your beard is a menace."

"What have you got against my beard?"

"It's attached to your face." Tony smirked at his joke. "Though I suppose I should thank your beard for covering part of your mug."

Logan didn't smile. "I think you're done here, Officer Milano. Thanks for stopping by."

Tony walked over to the door and pulled on his boots. The boots looked similar to a pair of Logan's, so he hadn't noticed them by the entrance mat.

Once the boots were laced, Tony said to Logan, "If your diva client is allergic to the attention of a few hard-working police officers, she might want to consider a new line of work." He waved a hand dismissively. "Never mind. A singing career may be the least of her concerns where she's going."

Logan said grimly, "We'll see about that."

Tony left, and Logan paced the open space between the table and my living room furniture. He slowed down only when Jeffrey jumped onto the coffee table and meowed for attention. He picked up the cat and nuzzled his gray fur before looking up at me with an expression of disgust on his face.

Logan growled, "Was your friend Tony touching Jeffrey?"

"What if he was?"

Logan smelled the cat again, his expression darkening. "The cat stinks of Tony's bad cologne."

I walked over and took the cat. Holding Jeffrey's front paws like puppet arms, I moved them as I spoke in a kitty voice, "Logan, I'm sorry I was unfaithful to you. I only sat on Tony Baloney's lap for a few minutes. It meant nothing to me. It was *just pets*."

Logan didn't crack. "Maybe I'll give him a bath," he said.

We'd never given Jeffrey a bath, but he seemed to recognize the word and squirmed in my arms.

I rolled my eyes. "You're so jealous. You know how friendly Jeffrey is. He loves to make new friends."

Dryly, Logan said, "Sure. Jeffrey's the friendly one." He continued to pace, looking toward the hallway entrance. "What was Tony doing back there?"

"Using the washroom. He had three cups of coffee, so I figured it was only fair."

He crossed over to the front door and grabbed his jacket from the hook. "You have to be more careful. Don't let your guard down around Tony. Try to remember you're supposed to be on my side."

I hugged Jeffrey tighter. "I am on your side, Logan. Do you want to talk about whatever's got you upset, or about this assignment?"

He looked as if he was trying to make a difficult decision. "I'll let you know," he said, and he left.

After the door closed, I hugged Jeffrey tighter and nuzzled him.

To my surprise, I realized Logan had been right.

The cat did smell like Tony.

CHAPTER 15

"I THOUGHT FOR SURE I was going to hear thumping," Jessica said. "The thumping of two big apes beating their chests."

We were folding laundry in the living room, working together to tackle the near-impossible fitted sheets. Jessica had a special way of turning them into tidy triangles and then neat squares. She also had a knack for making me laugh at what could have been an upsetting experience.

"You should have seen them," I said, acting out their body language. "Tony was all, 'Your client is a menace,' then Logan was all, 'You're the menace,' then Tony said, 'Your beard is a menace.' And the whole time, they were shooting dagger eyes at each other, like two apex predators at a watering hole."

Jessica smoothed the neatly folded sheet. "It must be nice to have two men fighting over you."

"Over me?" I groaned. "More like over territory. They both want to be the big men in a small town. I don't take their fighting personally. Tony's married with kids, so it's not like he's trying to get me in any romantic sense."

"He's still in love with you," she said.

"Gross." I started folding the towels. We didn't usually do laundry on Tuesdays, but we'd started the process on the weekend, before everything got turned upside down at the Koenig Estate on Sunday, and hadn't finished our chores.

"Your mouth says *gross*, but your eyes say something else," Jessica teased. "Admit you still carry a torch for Tony Baloney."

"Don't make me throw up all over our clean laundry."

She rolled her eyes.

Once we finished with that dryer-load of laundry, we started dealing with the other household tasks that had been left since the weekend, including the unopened mail and stacks of flyers.

Jessica handed me a real estate flyer. "Samantha Sweet is running an open house in the neighborhood. Looks cute."

I looked over the listing details, since I was still on the lookout for investments. She'd run this house past me a few weeks earlier, and I hadn't been interested, but the house had cleaned up nicely, according to the photo.

"I love the gingerbread detail," I said.

"Now you're making me hungry for gingerbread."

"Nice stained-glass windows," I said. "I'm not sure about the overall color scheme."

"You could paint the front door a festive color. The front door is like the bowtie of the house. It shouldn't be tan."

"Our doors are tan."

"But our doors are on the sides of the house, and there are two of them. This house isn't about looks, anyway. It's more about maximizing livable square footage." She quickly added, "And I love this house, of course."

"It's not my dream home," I admitted. "I bought it because of the rental income from the other side. It's just a practical investment that I can live in."

"And it's a *great* house," she said. "I love having Logan on the other side, too. It's perfect. He opened a pickle jar for me the other day."

"But this house doesn't look like an adorably kooky old manor that witches in storybooks live in."

"Is that what you want?" she asked. "I don't know the first thing about witchcraft. Is there something you want to tell me?"

I laughed. "I'm being silly. I'm romanticizing what should be a purely economic decision. That's how people get in trouble." I tried to sort through the rest of the flyers and junk mail, but my eyes kept going back to the house listing.

"That porch is to die for," Jessica said.

"You could sleep on that porch. Just screen it in and you've got a whole 'nother room."

"Can't you picture yourself there, rocking in your chair, knitting baby booties while your grandkids play on the front lawn?"

"Easy now. We need kids before we worry about grandkids."

She smiled as she sorted through the rest of the flyers. "My grandma always says she would have skipped right to the grandkids if she'd known. Of course my mother didn't find that nearly as amusing."

I flipped over the flyer. "Samantha's running the open house right now," I said. "If we blow off housecleaning, we could go check it out. Samantha always puts out yummy olives and crackers."

Jessica was already putting on her shoes.

CHAPTER 16

"Photos lie," Jessica said. "Real estate listings are just like internet dating profiles, only instead of shaving off twenty pounds, they get the photographer to hang outside the window on ropes and take room pictures from ten yards back."

The house was gorgeous, and would have been perfect, if I were one of those people whose only possessions were three changes of clothes and a tiny laptop. None of the rooms had closets, and the beds were suspiciously small.

While the real estate agent talked to interested buyers downstairs in the standing-room-only kitchen, Jessica and I did some detective work in the master bedroom. She pulled a tiny measuring tape from her purse and sized up the bed.

"Non-standard," she hissed. "I knew it. The homeowners have staged the home with three-quarters-sized furniture, to make the rooms look bigger." She lay on the bed to show me her feet hanging off the end.

"So sneaky," I agreed. "I wonder if Samantha thought this up herself, or if she's got a clever home stager."

Jessica climbed off the bed, giving me a dirty look. "I don't think it's very clever to rip people off. It's hard enough for people to save a few dollars after all the taxes come off their paychecks, without having to worry about someone tricking them out of what's left."

I held my hands up. "Hey, don't get mad at me. I'm on your side." I shook my head. "What's with everyone getting mad at me today, anyway?"

Jessica apologized for misdirecting her anger at me, and we continued touring the house. The upstairs bathroom was so ridiculously compact, it gave us the giggles. The arrangement was such that a person using the toilet would need to tuck their legs under the sink or else ride sidesaddle, which we both agreed brought little dignity to the act.

We went downstairs and found the real estate agent, our friend Samantha Sweet, alone and stuffing her face with cheese and crackers. She waved us over and poured some sparkling water into champagne flutes.

"I heard you two girls laughing up there," Samantha said. "You got a kick out of the sidesaddle powder room, didn't you?"

We were the only ones in the house, since the interested parties had come to their senses and fled.

Jessica asked, "Who designed that washroom? Why would someone do that?"

Samantha answered, "The upstairs didn't have a washroom, so the owners converted the linen closet."

"That explains why there's no linen closet," I said.

Samantha sighed as she unfastened her bun and let her blond hair fall around her shoulders. "This house may be the death of me," she said. "I know it's only been on the market a short time, but I've got a bad feeling about this one." She gave me a knowing look. "I should have listened to your advice about the fundamentals, Stormy. I should have let your lack of interest be my guide."

I helped myself to the offered snacks and sparkling water. "Don't be so tough on yourself, Sam. The house really is adorable, and people who are looking for a home to live in don't look with the same eyes an investor does. It only takes one person to walk in that front door and fall in love."

The three of us looked expectantly at the door. Nobody came in. We turned our attention back to the food, with Samantha begging us to help her finish the crackers so that her efforts weren't a complete waste.

I'd spent a lot of time with Samantha during the first months I'd moved back to Misty Falls. She'd sold me the duplex and the gift shop business. Ever since then, she'd been keeping an eye open for more investments for me. I'd done well in my venture capital career, earning a number of bonuses and saving everything because I was too busy working to spend it. I was happy to have the cash in the bank, and I could have played it safe with stocks or bonds, but I loved the idea of investing in my town and owning things I could touch and feel... as long as they were good investments that didn't come with sidesaddle powder rooms.

Samantha Sweet had been a great ally in my quest. I'd accidentally made her cry a time or two, but she was very diligent and hardworking. It wasn't easy for her to raise small children while pursuing a career, but she did everything with her whole heart, which was a trait I admired.

The three of us caught up on current events, and Samantha confessed that she'd gone way over her time budget in preparing the tiny house for sale. The owners were out of town, so she'd spent the entire weekend digging up the front garden and transplanting some mature, late-blooming perennials from her own yard.

"Michael wasn't too happy with me," she said, referring to her husband.

"Do I need to talk to him?" I asked, playfully rolling up my sleeves and looking tough. Samantha was relatively new in town, but I'd gone to school with her husband, Michael Sweet, and I'd played an important role in teaching him manners.

Samantha chuckled. "That won't be necessary, but thanks. He wasn't impressed about spending his weekend painting the front porch here, but he had to agree it looks great."

Jessica agreed, "The house does look beautiful. Hang in there."

Samantha turned her pretty emerald-green eyes my way. "Speaking of exciting weekends, I heard you and your handsome lawyer boyfriend were up at the Koenig Estate the exact same time as the old guy drowned."

I winced. "It sounds bad when you phrase it that way, but we were there."

"That's not all," Jessica said. "She also met Brandon and Drake. Oh, and Drake was exactly like how people around town say he is. Very flirty."

"Really?" Samantha's green eyes widened, and she bounced excitedly, making me feel as if I were back in the ninth grade, sharing gossip.

"Nothing happened," I said. "But since we're on the topic, do you know if any of the Koenigs have bought or sold real estate in town recently?"

"Are you investigating something?" she asked. "You're still doing the detective thing, right?"

"I'm just curious," I said.

Samantha gave me a knowing look. "How many months of recent transactions are you"—she made air quotes—"*just curious* about?"

"The past three to six months."

Samantha told me to wait a moment, and she pulled out her laptop.

Jessica caught my eye and gave me a sly smile. She knew what I was up to because she'd been the one who suggested the line of investigation in the first place. We wanted to know if Dieter Koenig had bought any houses for his girlfriend, Della.

"That's odd," Samantha said, clicking away.

We both leaned over her shoulder, expecting to see something interesting. Listings and images scrolled across the screen in a blur as Samantha did search after search.

"What's so odd?" I asked.

"The internet access is really fast here," she said.

We left her to her database and helped out with the remaining open-house snacks.

After ten minutes, she said, "Sorry, but I've looked at everything local for the past six months, and none of it's tied to the Koenigs. They actually don't own much real estate, other than the mansion and the surrounding land with the airstrip. If you're looking for a real estate family, that would be the Canusos."

"Thanks for looking," I said. "I owe you one."

Samantha closed the laptop and gave me a mischievous grin. "Buy this little dollhouse, and we'll call it even."

I patted my pockets. "I would, but I think I left my darn wallet at home."

"Maybe next month," she said. "I'm having another open house in September. You two should come. There'll be cupcakes." She started packing up her display materials and tidying the dishes. "Just come and say nice things to get other people excited."

"Like shills?" Jessica asked. "You shouldn't have to be dishonest to sell something." By the arch of her eyebrows, she seemed to be on the verge of saying something about the undersized beds.

I gently grabbed my best friend by the arm and pulled her toward the front door.

"We'll drop by," I promised Samantha. "For the cupcakes."

I managed to get Jessica safely outside and down the street before she started ranting about the undersized beds. I interrupted only to make sympathetic sounds. The staged beds were only a few inches shorter than regular ones, and the rooms would accommodate regular-sized beds, albeit with less walking space around the furniture, but I understood that for Jessica, it was about the principle of the thing. She was perfectly fine with telling white lies to protect someone's feelings, and she was fine with me fudging the truth to get information for a case, but she hated the notion of a business or person scamming people out of their hard-earned money.

I stayed agreeable as we walked back to the duplex. I understood where she was coming from. Her father had been known as a con man, and even though he disappeared when she was quite young, his reputation lingered, and she rebelled against it.

We reached our boring tan door, and she paused. "But at least the porch was really sweet," she said.

"The porch was the best," I agreed.

My phone started buzzing with an incoming call. As I pulled it out to answer, I said to Jessica, "Go ahead and get started on the dusting and mopping while I take this call." I winked. "I shouldn't be too long."

She looked skyward and shook her head as she went inside.

"Day Investigations," I answered. The number had come up with no caller identification, so I assumed it was business.

A woman replied, "Is this Logan Sanderson's assistant?"

"Sure," I said, gritting my teeth. I was becoming one of those people who gets her knickers in a twist when someone gets her job title slightly wrong. I liked to think of myself as easygoing, but it bothered me when people called me an assistant or a paralegal or a secretary. Those were all respectable jobs, and I didn't think being a consultant was any more dignified, but I still wanted people to call me what I was.

"Hello? Are you still there?" She had a European-sounding accent that, combined with her impatience, made her sound cartoonish, as though she were about to order someone beheaded. "Speak up!"

"Yes, I'm here. I'm Stormy Day, Logan Sanderson's *assistant*. How may I be of assistance to you?"

She breathed, "I need to meet with you. Can you come right now?"

"Let me check my calendar." I stared up at the blue sky. "Yes."

She rattled off an address. It was just outside of town, in a pocket of luxury rentals not far from the Koenig Estate.

She added, even more breathily and urgently, "It's very important. And very private. You mustn't tell anyone."

CHAPTER 17

THE FIRST THING I did after my phone conversation with the mysterious woman was call Logan's office.

The receptionist at Tyger & Behr, Corine, couldn't put me through to Logan, but she did give me some reassurance about our breathy new client.

"She's the Countess of Krengerborg," Corine said. "I thought she was just a kook, but I've done some digging, and she's actually some sort of Danish royalty. She's divorced from an earl but still has the title. You should refer to her as Lady Octavia."

"I assume that means Lady Octavia can pay for my visit," I said as I walked into the house. Jessica gave me a curious look. "A member of the Danish royal family should be able to afford my services," I said into the phone, more for Jessica's benefit than Corine's.

"Of course," Corine answered. "Just track your time. And since it's a new client, and you're meeting at her location, bring someone with you for security."

"Like my father?" I laughed. "Finnegan Day would just *love* to meet a breathy-voiced, divorced countess."

"Anyone will do," Corine said. "How is Finnegan, by the way?"

I frowned up at the living room ceiling as I kicked off my shoes. The way Corine said my father's name, it sounded as though cartoon hearts were floating around in the air.

I thanked her for the information on the countess and told her I'd try to rope my roommate into coming along as security.

When I ended the call, Jessica let out a whoop of excitement and demanded details.

I told her what little I knew, and we hit our wardrobes, jewelry, and makeup stashes like two teens getting ready for prom. Then we spent another twenty minutes removing half our makeup and scaling back on the jewels.

Looking as if we were attending high tea at a fancy hotel, we blew ladylike air kisses at Jeffrey as we left the house. I drove while Jessica did background research on her phone.

We learned that the Countess of Krengerborg was forty-one and had been divorced for three years. Following the royal breakup, she'd dated a number of European aristocrats, playboys, and even a few actors, including a man who was best known for his role as one of the world's favorite spies.

"That poor woman," Jessica said. "Going from one broken heart to another, all of it blasted over the internet for the world to laugh at."

"But she got to have martinis with the man who made martinis *sexy*."

Jessica made the neutral *hmm* noise I'd come to think of as her way of disagreeing without being disagreeable.

My car hummed as we left town limits, driving past the hill with the town's infamous scary-faced house. The house had been renovated years ago for the filming of a horror movie and had recently been the site of a murder. The victim had been a similar age as the countess and even unluckier in love. A shiver crept up my spine as I got a premonition of finding the countess in a pool of blood. She'd sounded frightened on the phone.

"Jackpot," Jessica said, still focused on the screen of her phone. "This story was buried, but I cross-referenced the countess and the name Koenig and found something. Last summer, Lady Octavia was seen leaving the master bedroom of Dieter Koenig."

"The plot thickens," I said.

"Wasn't he about a hundred?"

"Seventy-five." I checked the map on my car's navigation system and watched for the turn-off road. "Was the countess here in Misty Falls last summer? I don't remember that. There's usually tons of gossip if someone from a royal family is in town. They would have mentioned it in the *Mirror*."

"Last summer you hadn't moved back here yet," she said.

"Right." Sometimes I forgot about the entire decade I hadn't been part of the town. "What else does it say about Lady Octavia and Dieter Koenig? Were they officially an item? If she got divorced three years ago, that's around the same time his wife passed away. Maybe it's just a coincidence, but it makes you wonder."

"These stories aren't much more than rumors," Jessica said. "There are no photos of the two together, but things have been quiet for the countess lately. It seems she's been traveling around America for the last year and keeping a low profile. There's some speculation about health problems and visiting wellness spas for alternative treatments. Her official statement is that she's suffering from *exhaustion*."

"Exhaustion," I mused. "That's code for either rehab or facelift."

"Facelift," Jessica said. "She strikes me as the vain type. I say facelift, and maybe new boobs, too."

"You have to make the boobs match the face."

We shared an uncomfortable laugh. Making jokes about plastic surgery was preferable to imagining we were on our way to meet a heartbroken woman with a life-threatening illness. Was she really Dieter Koenig's lover?

"Where does the countess live?" I asked Jessica.

"Not in Misty Falls," she said, laughing. "But I read something about her splitting her time between Denmark and a penthouse in New York."

"Aha!" I said. "I bet she's the family friend that Drake and Brandon Koenig were visiting before they flew home on Sunday."

"So, she wasn't at the mansion pushing him off the diving board."

"Not unless she has a teleportation device."

CHAPTER 18

WE ARRIVED AT the luxury rental house, which shared a quiet cul-de-sac with two other homes of equal majesty. The homes were newly constructed but made to resemble turn-of-the-century Victorians, three stories high and with grand porches.

Jessica stepped out of the car and gazed admiringly at the home as she smoothed the car wrinkles from her pale-pink skirt.

"Nice," she said. "I bet this house doesn't have a sidesaddle toilet in a former linen closet."

"The linen closet probably has its own *en suite* bathroom."

She arched her red eyebrows in agreement as we approached the door. "With one of those fancy foot-washin' thingamajiggies."

I snorted. Jessica enjoyed pretending to be less sophisticated than she was, misunderstanding the proper use of a bidet.

The front door had both a brass knocker and a doorbell. We were on time, not a minute early or late for our two o'clock appointment. I rang the doorbell.

A woman in a summer-weight houndstooth suit opened the door. I'd never been one to pore over Vogue magazines or worry about high-end couture, but even I could tell it was a Chanel suit. The jacket and skirt fit perfectly, and the woman looked anything but ill or in recovery from surgery. Platinum hair framed an elegant face with what seemed to be its original layout, with just a few wrinkles that were as stylish as her Chanel. Her body was more voluptuous than I expected, with healthy curves drawing my eyes up and down. It was possible she had gotten something inflated in the chest area.

"I'm Stormy Day. We spoke on the phone. And this is my associate, Jessica Kelly."

Jessica curtsied.

"Aren't you two adorable," the woman said, her Danish accent peppering her words.

"It's so nice to meet you, your excellency," I said.

"Call me Tavi," she said. "All my friends call me Tavi, not that I have many of those these days."

"We'll be your friends," Jessica said warmly. If someone else had made a similar offer within a minute of meeting someone, I would have rolled my eyes, but Jessica was one of those people who genuinely led with friendship and treated everyone as worthy until they proved otherwise.

Lady Octavia looked back and forth between the two of us. "If we're friends, I don't need to wear these tight shoes." With a girlish laugh, she pried off the shiny pumps that matched her outfit perfectly.

"Much better," she said, beckoning us to follow her deeper into the house.

She led us to the kitchen, where we found evidence of a battle with coffee supplies. The luxury rental was equipped, as most are, with the latest and greatest in specialty coffee dispensers. From the look of the sprayed coffee grounds and coffee-spattered knives strewn about, Lady Octavia had fought the coffeemaker, and the coffeemaker had won.

"My English," she explained, pointing to a sheet of paper taped to the inside of an upper cupboard. "I can speak English fine, but reading this small print is impossible."

"You poor thing," Jessica said sympathetically. "I'll take care of this while you and Stormy get started on your business." At our house, Jessica and I preferred the low-tech, brew-a-pot method, but thanks to her experience in foodservice, there wasn't a food-related machine Jessica couldn't master.

Lady Octavia said, "*Tak.* That's thank-you in Danish," and the two of us left the kitchen for a bright sitting room at the back of the house.

The room overlooked an attractive flower garden, a meadow-sized green lawn, and mountains in the distance. Butterflies winged gracefully from flower to flower.

I pulled a new hard-covered notebook from my purse and wrote the date and time across the first page.

"Ready when you are," I said. Below the date, I wrote *Countess Octavia of Krengerborg.*

The air in the sunny room seemed to thicken at the mention of business. She turned to look at the mountains and twisted the glinting buttons on her houndstooth jacket.

"I don't know how to say this," she said. "How can I get a copy of Dieter Koenig's will?"

"Everyone who's named in the will is going to be contacted by Mr. Koenig's lawyer."

"Has that already happened?" she asked.

"I'll have to get back to you on that," I said, writing a note in my book. "Mr. Sanderson is a very busy man, but I'm sure he has everything under control."

She whipped her head to face me, her gray-blue eyes suddenly regal and cold. "Busy men are always thinking about control." Her eyes narrowed. "That's why they're so busy all the time. Control and power. It takes all their resources, and they have little left to give."

I wrote down every word she said before asking softly, "Do you have concerns about the will? There's a legal process for contesting wills in Oregon. Even the most thorough and legal will can be overturned legally, if there's an appropriate reason."

"I do have concerns," she said.

"Which are?"

She turned to the view again. "Private," she said.

Jessica came in with a tray and coffee for everyone.

"Sweetheart," the countess cooed, her chest heaving, straining against the shiny Chanel buttons. "You are a jewel. I really need this, too. I've been in too many time zones lately, and I made a mistake and thought you two were coming an hour before you did." She fluffed her platinum hair with one hand. She had no manicure or polish on her nails, and they were trimmed shorter than my own.

Jessica took a seat next to me on the tightly upholstered settee and complimented the view.

"Let's get to know each other," the countess said. "You girls must tell me about your life here in this adorable town. Dieter always spoke so fondly of his home."

"Are you sure?" I asked. "Did you really have me come out to meet with you just so you could ask for a copy of the will? You could have done that over the phone." I smiled to soften my tone but didn't take my eyes off her.

She sipped her coffee, staring down into the dark-brown brew as though it might have answers. In my experience, coffee usually did have answers, but not until the last sip. Patience, however, was never my strong suit. I preferred to cut through the icing and get to the cake.

I gave Jessica an eye-flash of warning then turned to the countess. It was time to cut into the cake, so to speak.

"Your child is entitled to be taken care of," I said.

The room was silent; even the chirping birds outside went quiet.

I continued, "Even a child who is born out of wedlock and off the record. Lady Octavia, we don't live in medieval times. Genetic testing is commonplace these days."

On one side of me, Jessica made a tiny surprised noise, and on the other side, the Countess of Krengerborg made a louder surprised noise.

"The labs will run a simple test," I said. "It can be done by swabbing the baby's cheek, and you'll have the basis of a very good case for contesting the will. At the very least, you're entitled to child support."

"How did you know?" she gasped. "Have you been following me? What have you seen?"

I nodded to her chest. "That's a beautiful suit you're wearing. I've been admiring it since we arrived. I'm not the queen of fashion, so I don't know if it's this season's design, but I do know it was fitting you perfectly when we arrived. Now, however, it's too snug at the top. The button that's been impeccably placed at the apex of your bosom is threatening to pop off."

She self-consciously pulled at the jacket, trying to find more room where there was none.

"You got your time mixed up," I said. "Your milk might not have come down this much an hour earlier, but now you're overdue for a feeding, aren't you?"

She got to her feet and covered her chest with crossed arms. "That's none of your business," she hissed.

Jessica's clothes rustled as she fidgeted next to me. I remained seated and touched Jessica's knee to keep her calm.

"I understand," I said. "You didn't want to tell me right away because you want to keep this out of the press, or maybe you don't want to appear greedy."

She quickly answered, "The reporters. It's them."

"They're vultures," I said. "But you aren't. You're not greedy. You just care about your child and seeing that he or she gets taken care of."

"Yes." She nodded vehemently. "That's all. I'm a good mother."

"And a good mother protects her offspring," I said.

She remained standing, still nodding. Her posture was slowly softening.

I glanced over to Jessica, hoping she'd take my hint and say something reassuring.

"Congratulations," Jessica said. "I'd love to meet your baby. I'm sure he or she is the sweetest thing."

Something outside the window moved, drawing our attention. There was a flicker of darkness and motion, then nothing but the peaceful meadow.

The countess stepped closer to the window and pressed her palms against the glass. "What was that?" she breathed.

"Just a deer," Jessica said. "I'm surprised you have any flowers at all, considering how many deer graze around this area."

The countess turned toward us again, her face and movements stiff with fear. "I didn't see any deer," she said.

I leaned over and patted the arm of the chair she'd been sitting in. "Do you want to get your baby and nurse while you talk to us some more?"

"I don't know," she said. "What happens next?"

I explained, "I'm not a lawyer, but I have helped Mr. Sanderson with a similar paternity case. We finished one just last month."

Jessica elbowed me and shot me a quizzical look. The case I was referring to had been a bitter dispute between two dog breeders, over the parentage of a litter of chihuahua-daschund puppies. I bounced my eyebrows at Jessica. Sure, the case hadn't been over millions of dollars, or even about humans, but I'd still learned plenty about paternity suits.

"This is happening too fast," Lady Octavia said. "I can't think." She didn't return to her seat but moved toward the door. "You'd better go now. Thank you for driving out of the way to come see me."

She led us all the way to the front door, where she grabbed a pocketbook and pulled out a handful of bills that she shoved at me. "Take this," she said. "I always pay my debts."

Jessica's eyes bulged at the sight of the wad of cash.

I had to refuse the money, explaining that any billing would be done through the law firm, and that Corine would be in touch as needed.

"Just one more question," I said.

"No." Lady Octavia shook her head. "I shouldn't have called you."

"Where were you on Sunday? Were you in New York?"

She narrowed her eyes. "Why? Who is asking?"

"Were you entertaining the Koenig brothers in New York?"

She blinked repeatedly. "They are dear family friends, and we share a love for the opera."

"Were you at the opera together on Saturday?"

"Friday," she said. "Now, please go. Thank you. *Tak.*"

CHAPTER 19

"THAT WAS BANANAS," Jessica said. "Like feeding-time-at-the-gorilla-pen bananas."

We were driving back into town, and it had taken her five minutes of contemplation to craft an adequate response to our meeting with the countess.

"Bananas," I agreed. "Get it all out of your system now, because you can't tell anyone at work tonight."

"I know, I know," she said. "I'm going to get changed now so nobody at the Olive Grove gets suspicious about why I was dressed up so fancy. I hate lying, so it's better if nobody asks any questions."

She lowered the back of the passenger seat to maximum reclining position and climbed over the headrest, into the backseat.

"Speaking of gorillas," I commented as her feet whipped by my head.

"We're in the boonies," she said, unzipping the bag she'd brought along with her change of clothes for work. "Nobody's going to see my boobage if I'm quick." She whipped her pink blouse off with an exotic flourish, revealing her colorful daisy-print bra and pale, lightly freckled skin.

"Are you sure it was a deer back there in the backyard?" I asked. "Because if Dieter Koenig was murdered for his fortune, it stands to reason that anyone threatening to split the honeypot to pay for an additional heir might also be in danger."

Jessica continued her quick change in the backseat, wriggling out of the skirt and into dark-green slacks. At least she was right about nobody being around on the deserted roads outside town limits.

"It was a young buck," she said. "He was giving me a flirty look with his big deer eyes before he bounced off into the trees."

"Wild animals love you," I said.

"That's because I always bring peanuts on my walks and throw them to the crows. They have a language, you know. The crows tell everyone to be nice to the cute redhead." She pulled on her cream waitress blouse and climbed up into the passenger seat.

"What did you think of the countess?" I asked.

Jessica fastened her seat belt. "She was magical. So regal, and she had that glow of specialness around her."

"Glow of specialness?"

"You know. Like a princess," Jessica said airily, as though she'd met other princesses and could pick them out, the way she could spot the best, nearly ripe avocados and cantaloups.

"I'll put that in my notes," I said.

After a moment, Jessica asked, "Do you really think she might be in danger?"

"She was definitely nervous, and where was the baby? I didn't hear a peep, and you'd expect him or her to be crying out for that milk."

"Maybe she pumps," Jessica said. "She probably has a nanny, because all rich people do. Maybe they were on the top floor where we wouldn't hear them." She was quiet for a moment then asked, "Is it a boy or a girl?"

"How should I know?"

She leaned over and playfully socked me on the shoulder. "You're the brilliant detective who's always two steps ahead of everyone. Boy or girl?"

"You're putting me on the spot," I said.

"And?"

"Girl," I said. "She made some strangely barbed comments about men and control, right before you came into the room. If she had a baby boy, something tells me she wouldn't have been so harsh."

"Or maybe it is a boy, and she's worried her son will grow up to be a jerk."

"You could be right, Detective Kelly. Is boy your official guess?"

She cracked the window for some fresh air. "Yes. I'll take boy, and you take girl. Care to make things more interesting?"

"Sure," I said. "The loser has to wear the furry costume in the Forest Folk Fun Run next month." I shot her an evil look.

"Ew," she said.

"Don't worry. My father had it professionally dry-cleaned after last year's incident. You won't smell a thing."

She gave me a squinty look. "The baby's definitely a boy, and you'll be wearing that furry monster costume."

"Assuming we find out by then, or even if we find out at all."

"I have faith in you," she said. "You'll figure it out. Nobody can keep their secrets from you for very long."

I didn't respond. I wish I had the same unshakable faith in myself that Jessica had.

* * *

Our meeting with the countess hadn't taken as long as we'd planned, so we browsed the bookstore for a while before I dropped Jessica off at the Olive Grove for her shift.

From the parking lot, I called Logan's office. This time Corine put me straight through to him.

"How are things?" I asked breezily.

"I don't know," he said, which didn't put me at ease. Was he still sore at me for whatever it was that had happened earlier that day at my house? When I'd been blamed for letting the cat smell like Tony?

"I met with the countess," I said.

"How did that go?"

"She let me wear her tiara."

"What?" He sounded more horrified than amused.

Adopting a more serious attitude, I relayed all the details of my afternoon meeting with Countess Octavia of Krengerborg while he said almost nothing.

"What does this mean?" I asked when I was out of details.

"It means that Deets is a baby daddy," he said.

I groaned. "Don't tell me Della has infected you this badly. *Baby daddy?* And you're calling him *Deets*? And what's the deal with her calling you Logie? It sounds like something baseball players spit up."

Ignoring my question, he asked, "What are you doing right now?"

"Nothing. Do you want me to come over there and kidnap you away from that place? It's almost four o'clock. You should get off early to make up for all the overtime you've been putting in."

"Stormy," he said with irritation. "I have to work. It doesn't get done when I'm not there. The law isn't like your gift shop, where you have Brianna taking care of everything."

"Oh," I said, hurt by his tone, not to mention his complete disregard of how hard I'd been working at my private investigation business. "Well, I'd better let you get back to your very important job of lawyering. Get those billable hours."

He started saying something, but it didn't sound anything like an apology, so I ended the call abruptly. Holding the phone in my hand, I sensed an incoming text message, followed by an inevitable fight. I shut off the power for the phone before it could get started, and put the thing in the glove box.

I thought about going home but then remembered the unfinished laundry that awaited on the sofa.

I tapped my steering wheel as a father and young daughter walked by on the sidewalk. The little girl danced ahead of him, excitedly showing him what I guessed was a brand new bracelet.

Ruby's Treasure Trove was within walking distance, and the August weather was pleasantly inviting. I gathered my purse and casebook, left the car, and set off toward the jewelry shop.

The owner of the store, Ruby Sparkes, knew everyone and everything. She should have been the first person I talked to after the accident at the Koenig Estate, but talking to her right now was better than never.

CHAPTER 20

WALKING INTO RUBY'S Treasure Trove, located at the corner of Broad Avenue and Bergamot Street, immediately improved my mood. The jewelry and collectibles store was still every bit as magical as it had been when I was a child, back when I'd come in with my father to pick out my birthday present.

The beach-hued interior was brightly lit by a multitude of spotlights. A royal fortune in jewelry lay attractively in sand-colored cases, as though a pirate's chest of treasure had busted open and washed up on lush, velvet shores. A dark-blue carpet completed the seaside feeling.

The shop's owner wasn't in sight. Her young employee, Hayley, was helping a tall, thin man. Hayley, the little sister of my friend Harper, who worked at the Olive Grove with Jessica, was working full-time for the summer, but would have her hours scaled back to part-time when she returned to school in the fall.

Hayley gave me about as cheerful of a greeting as the teen could muster. "What's up, Stormy?"

I replied, "I hear your sister isn't keen to have you driving her car."

Hayley rolled her eyes hard enough to do damage. "She's in complete denial that I'm a better driver than she is."

I leaned over the display case to look at some earrings that caught my attention. "I'm sure that's the reason," I said with a smile.

The man she'd been helping turned to me. "Stormy Day! How are things at the gift shop?" Before I could answer, he said, "You should know, your presence is sorely missed at our monthly storeowner meetings. Everyone who cares about Broad Avenue's future should be there."

"Mr. Jenkins, I swear I'll make it one of these days," I said.

The man was Leo Jenkins, the owner of Masquerade. He'd gained a few pounds since his health scare the previous year but still dressed in black and looked like a grim reaper. At least he was sweeter than he appeared, assuming you didn't get him talking about experimental health treatments and his biological functions. I'd heard phrases from his thin lips that should never be uttered in a retail establishment.

"Call me Leo," he said.

"I'll try," I replied politely, but I didn't mean it. Call him Leo? I had a hard enough time not calling him Creepy Jeepers.

He held up his left hand. "The old wedding band fits again. Thanks again for tracking it down for me."

"My pleasure. How's Mrs. Jeepers? I mean, Mrs. Jenkins?"

His deep-set eyes crinkled behind his rectangular-framed glasses. "As lovely as the day we met. I'm picking up a little something for our anniversary. Another decade's gone by, and I'm hoping she'll agree to a renewal of our vows."

"What?" asked Hayley. "What do you mean, *renew*? Like a rental agreement? Is that normal for married people?"

Leo Jenkins and I shared a knowing look and a special grown-ups' moment over the teenager's naivety.

Somewhere in the showroom, a speaker crackled to life, and out came Ruby's voice. "Hayley, you can send Stormy back here. Unless she wants to buy those earrings. Then you can send her back after she buys them."

I waved at the newest camera and walked around the display counter to the door leading to the back of the shop. Behind me, I could hear Leo Jenkins spinning a wild tale about standard marriage contracts and little-known legal clauses. I had to chuckle to myself. Some older men loved nothing more than telling harmless lies to wide-eyed younger girls. I saw no malice in it; if anything, the jokes taught girls to have skepticism. Being raised the way I was, by my father the perpetual prankster, I probably had five times the usual amount of skepticism.

Ruby was pouring hot water into a teapot when I made my way into the tiny kitchenette.

"Earl Grey?" she asked.

"We can't break tradition," I answered. "How's the new intercom and camera working out?"

She gave me a big grin. "I feel omniscient. I know all, see all." She let out a witchy cackle. "I'll be unstoppable."

"I'm glad all this power hasn't gone to your head."

She made a fist with one jeweled hand. "Now if only the breeder would hurry up with my winged monkeys."

"Ruby Sparkes, you'd scare me if you weren't so adorable."

She grabbed the tray and nodded for me to follow her into the secret tearoom. "It's the purple clothes," she said. "Nobody fears a little old lady dressed in purple. We can do anything. We could get away with murder."

I took a seat at the round bistro table next to the secret window that, as far as the rest of town was concerned, was just a round mirror embedded in a decorative mosaic wall.

Ruby sat across from me and poured the fragrant tea into dainty cups. Ruby was an energetic single lady of sixty-something, with curly hair colored a purple-red shade between auburn and grape soda. She'd never had children but treated every child she met with love and affection. With her friendly voice, warm smile, and matronly bosom, it was no wonder she was a friend and confidante to almost everyone in town, and that her jewelry store had been a fixture of the community for over thirty years.

"Speaking of murder," she said, raising her eyebrows.

I sipped my tea and raised my eyebrows to match.

"Was it murder?" she asked. "I understand you were there when they discovered Dieter Koenig searching the bottom of his swimming pool for another billion dollars."

"He wasn't a billionaire. A billion dollars is a thousand million."

She sipped her tea, eyebrows still raised. Now it was her turn to stare until I cracked.

"Off the record, I don't know if it was murder," I said. "The whole thing smells fishy to me, but maybe it's just the money that puts things into a different light. He was found dead in a swimming pool, which isn't that crazy. You know the statistics as well as I do. A swimming pool is more likely to kill someone than a gun, sadly."

She swished her mouth from side to side, pondering. "That's what makes a pool the perfect murder weapon."

"Technically, I think it was the diving board."

"Someone hit him with a diving board? Brilliant! Bravo." Affecting an upper-crust English accent, she said, "Jolly good sport."

I gave her a suspicious look. "Ruby, is there something you want to tell me? You don't usually speak ill of the dead."

She twirled one of her bouncy purple-red curls and batted her eyelashes. "Last Sunday, I was in Las Vegas at a trade show, picking out treasures for the store and making sure the gentlemen dancers got a few tips tucked into their underpants."

"Thanks for the visual, but why are you telling me this?"

"My alibi," she said. "I certainly didn't hit the old cheapskate with a diving board."

"Cheapskate? I've never heard anyone say that about Dieter Koenig. Everyone says he loved this town and tried to support it as much as he could."

"He never spent one crusty penny here! And I've had some lean years where I could have used his pennies, crusty or otherwise!"

"I'm sorry to hear that," I said. "He must have had terrible taste. Your selection was too good for him."

At my compliment, Ruby calmed down, to my relief. She wasn't usually so excitable, but something had gotten into her.

"That's kind of you," she said softly. "You're so good with words. You obviously inherited your father's charm."

"And my mother's temper, unfortunately." I sipped my tea and gazed out the round window at Broad Avenue. A woman walked by, frowning and talking on her phone. By the look of it, whoever was on the other end of the line was in trouble. I thought of my recent blow-up at Logan and felt ashamed. Why couldn't I just take a deep breath and count to ten? Since when did hanging up on people ever solve anyone's problems?

"It was his wife," Ruby said with finality, as though making a declaration.

"Dieter Koenig's wife has been dead for years," I said. "She didn't kill him, unless it was her ghost."

"No. I mean she was the one who blackballed my store. She and I used to be friends. She actually babysat me when I was a little girl. Later, when I was a teenager, I idolized her. Followed her everywhere, like one of those dogs you pack in your purse. Did you know that? Then she started dating Dieter, and she couldn't get away from her old friends and her old life fast enough."

"That sucks," I said sympathetically. For Ruby to carry a grudge, she must have been hurt. "Why would Mrs. Koenig blackball your store, though? That sounds like some serious hate."

Ruby drew herself up taller. "She didn't like me dating Tim Barber. He was quite the catch, back in the day."

"Tim Barber? That guy?" I was shocked to hear Dieter's late wife had been involved with the handyman, but within seconds, I formulated a scenario in which Tim Barber had killed old Dieter Koenig over some forty-year-old rivalry. The handyman had means and opportunity, and now, if Ruby's memory was to be trusted, he also had motive.

Ruby waved one jeweled hand. "Oh, please. Tim. Dave. Harry. The old ho-bag was involved with anyone and everyone. I could make a list."

I scrunched my lips together to keep from laughing. *Ho-bag?* That wasn't a term I'd ever heard applied to the deceased Mrs. Koenig.

Ruby gave me a dead-serious look and whispered, "There are even a few women's names on that list. Not that you heard it from me." Ruby looked very pleased with herself, as though outliving the woman had been her sweet revenge.

"Sounds like the first Mrs. Koenig was a wild woman."

Ruby nodded. "That was long ago, though. She settled down, and then she had the two boys and dedicated herself to raising them. Oh, she loved those boys. You could tell how proud she was. I remember one time I saw them at the bank, and the manager made a joke about her having two sons. He called the boys *an heir and a spare*. Well, she just reached out and slapped him across the face. The poor gentleman tried to explain to her that it was just a colorful expression, and he hadn't meant anything by it, but she left in a huff. I'm sure she would have blackballed the bank, too, if the town had another one she could have used."

"Who else did she have an issue with?" I asked. "Are there other businesses you know of that were blackballed by the Koenigs?"

Ruby stared down the street for a breath before sighing, "Just me."

"And you have an airtight Las Vegas alibi," I said.

She pretended to wipe sweat from her brow. "Phew!"

I followed her gaze to the window and watched as customers from the bagel store next door stopped at the two-way mirror to check their teeth for poppyseeds.

"There's something going on that I can't quite figure out," I said. "Maybe his death was an accident, but I feel like if I keep digging, I'll find out something important about Dieter Koenig. Something that will illuminate everything." And if it was something Logan had been keeping from me, all the better.

"Now that I think about it, I did hear something," Ruby said. "Someone was complaining about the Koenigs costing him money. Now... who was it?" She tapped her fingers on the table in a rhythm that reminded me of Tony Milano and his tapping, which always annoyed my father. I didn't mind.

I waited quietly while she thought. My visit to the jewelry store had been productive. I'd come by mainly to hear if Dieter had been making large purchases for his new girlfriend, and without even having to ask, I'd found out the answer was no. As a bonus, I'd learned Della wasn't the first high-strung, slaphappy woman the old man had fallen for. He had a type, and that type was Trouble with a capital T.

Ruby snapped her fingers. "Accio Bistro. It was the manager. He was drinking at the Fox & Hound last night when I stopped in for a nightcap with a friend. I heard him calling Dieter Koenig some names I won't repeat."

If she wouldn't repeat the names, they had to be a lot worse than *ho-bag*.

I asked, "Did he say why?"

"No, but have you eaten? It's not too early for dinner. My treat."

I flashed her a nervous, embarrassed smile. I hadn't been to the Accio Bistro very many times since February, when my ex-fiancé had terrorized all the diners in a drug-induced lapse of sanity. When I did dine there, it felt like I was getting away with something. Based on some rumblings I'd heard, I believed I was on the bistro's do-not-serve list, or worse, on the drop-her-food-on-the-floor list.

"Sounds fun," I lied, and off we went to Accio Bistro.

CHAPTER 21

"I'M ASHAMED TO admit I don't remember much of last night," said the manager of Accio Bistro.

Ruby and I were seated at a cozy table for two not far from where the bread bandit had struck back in February. A few of the waiters were looking at me with suspicion, but nobody had tried to ban me. Truth be told, I was innocent. But on the night of the Rainforest Delight scandal, my name had been unfairly linked with the events. It wasn't the first time I'd gotten caught up in trouble and likely wouldn't be the last.

Tonight, though, I was just a regular citizen having an early dinner with a dear friend, who had a few questions for the manager of the restaurant.

The manager, a rubber-faced man named Howard Blight, stared at our pitcher of water. His eyes bulged as he licked his thick lips. Ruby had called him over to our table and asked him to expand on whatever had been bothering him the night before, over at the Fox & Hound.

"Howard, sit with us a moment," Ruby said, pouring ice water into an unused glass. "You'll remember if you try."

He swayed from side to side but didn't sit. "I shouldn't drink at all," he said. "When I drink that devil's brew, my brain shuts off and my mouth keeps talking."

"Sit down and keep us company a moment," she said sweetly. "It's the least you can do to make up for what I heard last night. Do you kiss your mother with that mouth?"

He bowed his head and took a seat. "I was blowing off steam. I didn't mean anything by it. Mr. Koenig was a great and wonderful man, and he will be sorely missed."

She asked, "Then what were you so worked up about?"

Howard Blight glanced around nervously and shuffled his chair closer. I caught a whiff of him, which did little to inspire my appetite for dinner. He'd showered, I guessed, but something seemed to be wafting from his pores.

"Tequila," I said. "You were worked up over tequila, weren't you?"

His bulging eyes got even more wide and bulging. "How'd you know? Have you been spying on me? I know you're a detective, Stormy Day. Sometimes I see you in that black car of yours, always behind me. Never in front of me. What's that all about?"

I held my hands up and nodded for Ruby to continue with the questioning, since apparently I made Howard Blight nervous and paranoid.

She patted his hand. "You were saying? Why were you so angry at Mr. Koenig?"

"Because of the champagne," he spluttered. "We ordered a hundred bottles of the type he asked for, and I'm the idiot who didn't take a deposit, because I figured the Koenigs wouldn't stiff me. But the party got cancelled, well, for obvious reasons."

Ruby gave him an inquisitive look.

"Because he died," Howard said. "And you don't exactly serve champagne at a funeral. I called Brandon Koenig, trying to see if we could come to some sort of agreement. He says he's going to think about it." Howard gesticulated wildly with the free hand that wasn't being patted by Ruby. "Can you believe it? He's going to *think about it*. The guy's a billionaire, but he has to *think about* paying for the champagne his father ordered."

Ruby kept patting his hand. "There, there. Sometimes the powerful are like seagulls. They eat and fly and think nothing of what they"—she made a rude brapping sound with her mouth—"crap all over."

"I'll say," Howard agreed.

"What was the party for?" I asked.

Howard shot me a bug-eyed look and slurped back his glass of water. "Beats me," he said, setting the glass on the white tablecloth. "What would you need a hundred bottles of champagne for? Something special, I bet." He pushed his chair back and stood with a groan.

Ruby said, "A tablespoon of honey, every hour, on the hour." She tapped the side of her forehead. "My grandfather's secret hangover cure."

Howard got down on one knee next to where Ruby sat and kissed the top of her hand. "Lady Ruby, you are a treasure," he said, and then he was gone, heading in the direction of the kitchen.

"You really are a treasure," I said. "And that's a tasty-sounding hangover cure."

She winked. "The only true cure for a hangover is the bottlecap." She winked again. "The trick is you leave the bottlecap on the bottle the night before."

* * *

We ordered the day's special, which was chicken with a cream-and-champagne sauce, paired with a champagne-and-wild mushroom risotto. The food was so delicious, we couldn't feel bad about enjoying a dead man's champagne.

Ruby fished for information from me, but I couldn't tell her confidential details about the case, such as the fact that Dieter Koenig had been dating Della, or that he might have an illegitimate child by way of Danish royalty. If I'd been looking into the mysterious death out of my own curiosity, I might have laid it all out, along with charts and timelines, but the investigation was being paid for by Tyger & Behr, so the information belonged to them.

Without me spilling any beans, however, Ruby's guesses were remarkably similar to the ones in my head.

She surmised that a hundred bottles of champagne would go equally well with a baby shower, a wedding engagement, or even an actual wedding.

We finished our dinner and talked each other into sharing a slice of Accio Bistro's infamous mouth-watering lemon chiffon. The dessert went perfectly with more Earl Grey tea.

We'd been some of the first customers to arrive for dinner, but by the time we were quibbling over who ought to help herself to the last lemony bite, the dining room had filled up. It was busy for a Tuesday. Ruby and I agreed that word must have gotten out about the champagne-themed dinner specials.

Once we were done with eating, I visited the powder room to freshen up before going home. Ruby had already powdered her nose before dessert, so I went alone.

I stepped out of the washroom, searching through my purse for my phone and not looking where I was going. Just as I realized my cell phone was actually switched off and in the glovebox of my car, I noticed I'd taken a wrong turn and wasn't back in the dining room. Thinking I'd eventually pop out somewhere familiar, I kept walking.

At the end of the hallway was a door marked Office, and around the corner was a dead end and a mop bucket. I turned around to head back but paused when I heard a voice coming from the office.

Ordinarily, I wouldn't be such an eavesdropper, but the voice belonged to the manager, Howard Blight, and I heard him say *Koenig*.

I stood still, listening to what I assumed was Howard on the phone, trying to sell ninety-some bottles of champagne to the Koenig family.

"My chef is threatening to quit," Howard said. "He says I'm making him commit culinary crimes, putting bubbly wine in dishes where it doesn't belong. He says he's going to report me to the Institute, whatever that is. I don't know if he's kidding. I do know I have ninety-four bottles that I can't afford to store and can't afford to pour over the specials. We'll be out of business by the end of summer. Do you really want that to be your father's legacy?"

A man with a refined, deep voice replied calmly, "You need not concern yourself with my father's legacy."

I clapped my hand to my mouth. Howard wasn't on the phone after all. Which son was he talking to?

Another voice, similarly refined, said, "Dad wouldn't leave a bill unpaid, and neither would we."

I almost couldn't believe my ears. Both sons were in the office with the manager. How much could the bottles of champagne cost? What could have made the catering bill important enough for both Drake and Brandon to personally visit the Accio Bistro?

I heard the sound of a check being ripped along its perforated edge.

"This should cover the damage," said the first brother.

"Not so fast," said the other. "We need to know what we're paying for."

"Bu-bu-but I told you already," spluttered Howard. "And here's the itemized bill, all printed out for you. We're not charging for the service or most of the food, but we are asking for the cost of the champagne and the caviar, plus a small cancellation fee."

"Don't play stupid with us. I know you're not as dumb as you look, Mr. Blight. We're asking you what the party was in celebration of."

Howard's voice pitched up high and squeaky. "How should I know?"

There was the sound of a scuffle, and of the items atop a desk being rearranged violently.

Howard squeaked, "Honestly, I don't know." He gasped, coughed, and continued raspily, "Your father never told me why. He just said it was a surprise, and he was planning it himself, without getting his staff involved."

I'd been edging my way closer to the door. I leaned over to peer through the open crack. Just as it sounded, the Koenig brothers were working as a team to put physical pressure on the manager. Drake had him in a headlock, and Brandon was gripping the man's tie, threatening to choke him.

I was just about to kick the door and demand they release him when they did. Within seconds, Drake was laughing and ruffling Howard's hair.

"Good ol' Howie," Drake said. "You always were a snitch. It's a good thing I've known you since we were all kids. I can tell when you really don't know anything."

Howard coughed again and smoothed down his sparse hair. "I know plenty of things," he retorted.

"Like what?" asked the glasses-wearing brother, Brandon. "Things about our father?"

"He said you two were going to be livid," Howard said. "He said he'd already done it, so you couldn't stop him. And he sounded so excited about it, too."

The brothers exchanged a look.

Howard looked down at the small slip of paper on his freshly cleared desk. "Hey, this check isn't signed."

"Dummy," Drake said, giving his brother a shove.

"You're the dummy." Brandon shoved him right back.

Howard whined, "Please, would one of you sign the check?"

The brothers ignored him and continued to fight like a couple of twelve-year-olds in the backseat on a long road trip.

From behind me came Ruby's voice. "There you are," she said.

I jumped from the cracked-open door and hustled down the hall toward her as quickly as I could without making noise.

"I got lost on my way back from the bathroom," I said softly.

She shook her head. "How did you ever survive in the big city?"

I shrugged and glanced over my shoulder to make sure I wasn't being followed. If Howard or the brothers had noticed me spying, they hadn't been worried enough to come after me.

I tried to return to our table to settle the bill, but Ruby grabbed my arm and tugged me toward the door.

"Already paid," she said. When I reached for my wallet, she swatted my hand. "You don't owe me anything. It was a two-for-one special, so yours was free."

I gave her a skeptical look. The old yours-was-free trick was one I used on my too-proud-for-charity roommate.

Ruby was a sly one.

And so was Dieter Koenig. If the squealing of Howard Blight was to be believed, the old multi-millionaire had done something shortly before his death that he knew would upset his sons, and he was going to break the news with a hundred bottles of champagne. I had a few ideas what that news might be.

I'd been planning to go home straight after dinner and finish my chores like a good roommate, but I was so close to figuring out Dieter's secret, I couldn't stop now.

CHAPTER 22

IF A MAN ORDERS a hundred bottles of champagne, chances are his girlfriend knows why.

Dieter Koenig's sons didn't know what event Accio Bistro had been hired to cater, but his girlfriend might. And since Della had been spending so much time with *Logie*, I had a hunch he knew as well.

After retrieving my car from the Olive Grove parking lot, I drove to Logan's office. Corine, who often worked until six or seven, was just leaving for the day. She let me in the front door and waved me down the hall with her blessing.

I found Logan in his office, eating noodles from a square takeout box and staring at his computer screen.

I announced my presence by saying, "Either your hair's turning bright orange or you've got carrot shreds in your beard."

He paused his fork and smiled with his eyes. "I'm saving those for later."

"So that's what the beard is for! You use it to squirrel away food."

"Winter is coming."

He didn't invite me to sit down, but I did anyway, dropping with a sigh onto the button-tufted leather sofa in the lounging part of his office. The room was L-shaped, and thanks to Logan's exquisite taste, resembled a posh bachelor's apartment.

I lay back on the sofa, pretending to begin psychoanalysis. I'd started doing this a month ago as a joke, calling Logan by the made-up title of Dr. Feelgreat, but I'd discovered it to be surprisingly effective. It was easier to be open and calm while staring at the ceiling. We humans are so attuned to each other's microreactions that it's little wonder the best conversations happen on long road trips, when we're rocked gently by the motion of the vehicle and not overreacting to the smallest of facial expressions.

"Well?" he said.

"I'm sorry I hung up on you," I said.

"I'm over it," he said.

"And Jeffrey is sorry he let Tony get his stinky cologne all over his fur."

"He said that?" His voice was neutral. I wished we were in my car, driving somewhere fun.

I fluffed a pillow to get more comfortable on my back. "Dr. Feelgreat, sometimes my temper makes me do things. I try to get ahead of it, but everything happens so fast and spirals out of control."

"That's where you and I are different," he said. "When I get angry, I feel even more in control."

I reached up and air-traced the square lines of the ceiling with my fingertip. "What does that feel like?"

"Like standing in the middle of a terrible storm, in the only place that's calm. Time can slow down, if you want it to." His chair squeaked as he stood. "Not the years. The years will never slow down, but if you hold very still, a minute can stretch out to eternity."

"That's how I feel waiting in line at the grocery store. Like every minute is an eternity. Is it like that? Does it make you hungry? I always get hungry in line."

He came over and lifted my legs so he could sit with me on the leather sofa. He settled my legs back down on his lap and rested his hands on my shins. The heat from his palms made me realize how chilly I was, despite the warm late-summer weather. The air conditioning was always set to meat-locker levels in Logan's office.

His voice low and gruff, he asked, "Have you eaten dinner?"

"I'm not interested in whatever you've got hiding in your beard."

He chuckled, the vibrations of his voice warming my body. "We've got some more Golden Wok in the staff fridge."

"Ruby already treated me to dinner at Accio Bistro."

"They let you eat there?" He gently massaged the sides of my calves. "That's the first bit of good news I've heard today."

I asked him, "Did you find out anything else about the countess and her baby?"

"Not much," he said. "She should have her own lawyer, though. She shouldn't have been contacting me directly."

"Does attorney-client privilege still apply?"

"Yes," he said. "Even though I won't be taking her case, I can't share anything from the initial meeting with anyone, especially not Della."

I snorted. "That's probably for the best. Della doesn't strike me as the type to welcome her boyfriend's other girlfriend with open arms. Especially not one who made ol' Deets a baby daddy."

"We wouldn't want to have another murder on our hands."

I sat upright. "Another one? Logan, did Della kill him? What do you know?"

He stared straight ahead, avoiding my eyes. "Our client hasn't done anything illegal. Just between us, I think she genuinely loved the man."

"But if she had murdered him, we couldn't exactly tell the police, could we?"

"Speaking hypothetically, if we had a client who committed a crime, we couldn't report it. Not unless our client was actively planning to commit future crimes, or fraud, or commit perjury."

"Ouch." I pulled my legs off his lap, as his gentle calf massage had turned into unwanted deep-tissue prodding. "So, is she? Is she planning something?" I pulled my knees up under me and shuffled closer to him, the tightly tufted leather sofa squeaking with my movements. "What else is going on?" I twirled my finger around a short lock of dark hair behind his ear.

He pulled his head away. "Stormy, don't. Today's a working day for us."

I moved in closer. "You can bruise my calves, but I can't fix your hair?"

He slid away, putting a foot of space between us. "My hair's fine. Cool it, will you? We're in my office."

"But I have information. New information. To trade for a kiss."

He shot me a look, his blue eyes showing both annoyance and curiosity. "That's not how we do this."

"Fine," I sighed. "I did some research on my own. After my meeting with the countess, I popped in to see Ruby. As usual, she had plenty of interesting gossip."

His eyes burned with cold fire. "Are you going to make me beg?"

I pretended to consider my options just long enough to get him a little riled. He'd been holding out on me lately, and I wanted him to see how it felt.

Flatly, he asked, "And what was Ruby's gossip?"

"Before Mrs. Koenig married Dieter, she and Ruby were involved in a love triangle with the groundskeeper, Tim Barber."

"Della? No way."

I jumped to my feet and began dancing around.

Logan tilted his head and stared at me. "What's wrong with you?"

"This is my figured-it-out dance." I wiggled my hips.

The corner of his mouth twitched up. "You look ridiculous. This is exactly why I don't dance." He waved one hand at me. "But I don't mind watching you dance, so keep going."

I danced some more, until finally he said, "What is it you've figured out?"

"They're married," I said. "That's the thing you haven't told me. This explains all the secrecy. Della and Dieter got married, so she really is legally entitled to some of that fortune, and that's why she's getting ready for battle!"

He crossed his arms. "I don't know what you're talking about." He scratched his head. "How did you know?"

"You slipped up. I said *Mrs. Koenig*, and you assumed I was talking about Della. I was talking about the man's late wife, but you thought I meant the new one." I continued my dance, aware that I was gloating but unable to quelch my excitement.

Logan asked, "Who else knows?"

"I hope nobody else figured it out before I did, but you should know the sons are hot on the trail. When I was at Accio Bistro, I happened to overhear Brandon and Drake talking to the manager. They were paying for some champagne Dieter ordered for a catering job, and they were trying to find out what the surprise party had been for."

"Sounds like it would have been quite the surprise." Logan got up and walked toward his desk, giving me and my dance moves a wide berth. "And it sounds like something a man in love would do. He was going to share the news with everyone at once."

"You make it sound sweet, but I'm not so sure that was his plan."

"How would you know? You never even met the man."

"I heard the catering manager say Mr. Koenig sounded gleeful about how much it would upset his sons."

Logan flicked on his computer monitor and settled into his desk. A minute later, he was typing like mad.

He abruptly looked up. "How did you come by this information?"

"I got lost on my way back from the bathroom and accidentally overheard the three talking in the manager's office."

"Accidentally." Logan raised his eyebrows and returned to typing. "A likely story," he muttered.

"What's with the judgment? I'm helping you out. And you love my outside-the-box methods."

"Were you ever inside the box to begin with?" He kept typing.

"When did the lovebirds tie the knot, anyway?"

"Recently." He gave me a serious look. "And that's all I'm telling you. Go ahead and torture me with more dancing. I'm not going to crack."

I was just about to begin my second performance when the phone on his desk started ringing. The receptionist was gone for the day, so it had to be someone who suspected he was there and used his direct line.

He answered, "Sanderson." His eyes flicked to me. "Yes, she's right here. Who? Where? No, she's fine. Her dance moves haven't proven fatal... yet." He nodded. "I'll let her know. How are you doing?" He nodded again, listening for a while, then said, "Okay, Slugger. Have a good shift, and I'll see you at home."

"What did Jessica want?" I asked.

"Switch your phone back on. You've probably got a dozen messages."

"All the more reason to leave it off," I said.

He shook his head. We both hated voicemail.

"You should check anyway," he said. "The cops are looking for you. Specifically, Officer Kyle Dempsey is looking for you. He stopped by the Olive Grove to talk to Jessica when you weren't home or picking up your phone."

"Should I talk to him? I mean, without you?"

"If he just wanted to follow up on our report from the day at the mansion, you should be fine. If he asks about anything else and you're not sure, call me. I'll be here for a few hours."

"Talking to him may not be safe," I said. "You've seen his dimples. When he turns those on full-blast, a girl's resolve gets rather weak."

"Stormy, you've never had a weak moment in your life." He held up his hand to shush me. "Except for when you agreed to date me. There, I said it so you don't have to. Now go. Get out of here so I can get some work done."

I danced my way out of Logan's office, much to his amusement.

CHAPTER 23

"WHERE'S TONY BALONEY?" I asked.

"Captain Milano's out on business," Kyle answered.

Officer Kyle Dempsey had come to the police station's reception area to meet me and bring me back with him. I'd stopped by the station rather than call him because I was hoping he'd spill more juicy details in person. I'd already uncovered two of Dieter Koenig's secrets that day and was hoping for a third.

"Did he track down a functioning polygraph machine?"

Kyle stopped walking and turned to face me. We were halfway to the first interview room, within smelling distance of coffee and what I guessed was donuts.

"You're full of questions," Kyle said. "How do you know about the polygraph?"

"Tony came by my house this morning. He told me Tim Barber wanted to report something, on the record and hooked up to a lie detector. He strikes me as a bit cuckoo, so I bet whatever he says is good stuff. Maybe aliens."

Kyle nodded for me to follow him. He turned down a hallway that led to the parking lot rather than to the interview room.

"Let's go for a drive," he said. "We can talk while we drive. That's always nice. Maybe we'll catch the sunset."

"I'm not sure if my lawyer-boyfriend would approve of that."

Kyle flashed his dimples. "I don't see him here."

I followed him out the door, blinded by his dimples and trying to keep up with his long strides so I wouldn't be forced to see his butt, which, if memory served, was equally blinding.

Kyle led me to an unmarked police car and held open the passenger-side door for me. He put his hand on top of my head and told me to be careful as I slid in.

"Thanks, Officer," I said in a girlie voice. "I'm always bumping my head when I get into cars unassisted."

"Force of habit," he said.

He got in and started driving. It was now half past seven, and the summer sun was low enough that we flipped down the visors to save our eyes.

I took a wild guess we were driving to the Koenig Estate, and after a few turns in that direction, decided my hunch was right.

He was the first to break the silence. "We got the report from the medical examiner's office," he said.

"Oh?" I couldn't tell him privileged information, but I had no problem listening to his. "Was there water in his lungs?"

"No. He'd stopped breathing before he hit the water."

"I knew it! He was murdered and tossed into the pool."

"Not necessarily," he said, looking both ways as we stopped for a stop sign. "The ME report hasn't ruled out an accident."

"It's not their job to prove things. That's for the jury."

"But there was tanning oil on the diving board," he said.

"Suntan lotion?"

"No, the tanning oil stuff that you use to get more sun, not less."

I rubbed my chin, thinking. "That's a bit strange, but rich people have all the money for facelifts and laser treatments, so maybe they don't care about sun damage."

"Erica Garcia, the housekeeper, said that Dieter Koenig didn't use tanning oil, but that his girlfriend did. She was trying to darken her skin to look more exotic for him. What do you think of that?"

"A deep tan looks amazing with crisp, white clothing."

He let out an exasperated huff. "Like father, like daughter. Just like a member of the Day family to never give a straight answer."

"You could try asking a straight question."

"Did you know Della was dating the old man?"

I answered, "If I didn't before, I do now."

"You knew," he said. "I went over your statement from that day, and you lied to me. That's why you were so concerned about those drink tumblers. You think she did something."

I squirmed in my seat. Kyle had always been friendly to me, a sweet kid with a puppy-dog crush. He'd been getting mentored by my father for several months, and I'd come to think of him as a member of the family. I didn't need his respect, but it hurt more than I'd expected to be at risk of losing it.

"Kyle, I didn't lie to you," I said. "As of the morning of Mr. Koenig's accident, I had no more than a whiff of a clue that he was dating anyone, let alone her."

He stared straight ahead, focused on the road.

"I swear," I said. "If you guys round up a lie detector, I'll go a round on it."

"Don't tempt me," he said.

"Is that all you wanted to talk to me about?"

He flicked his eyes off the road to look at me briefly. "Why did Della murder Dieter Koenig?"

"If you think she did something like that, you should arrest her. But bring reinforcements, and keep an eye on your sidearm, Dimples."

He didn't say anything. The case had to be taking a toll on him if he wasn't even going to smile at my comment. We turned again, and he pressed the accelerator, exceeding the speed limit on our way out of town.

We weren't just going for a drive past the mansion to jog my memory. Where was he taking me? What else did he know about Della? A few wild theories came to mind.

"No way," I said. "Nope. Turn around. I can't be part of this."

"Part of what?" he asked innocently.

"Kyle, if you value your friendship with my father at all, you won't drag me into whatever you have planned."

"We're just checking on a nuisance call," he said.

"Who's the nuisance?" I had a feeling it was Della, and he was planning to use me as a bluffing tool.

To my surprise, he turned off the main road before we reached the road for the Koenig Estate.

After a mile, I realized we were heading back to the place I'd visited earlier that afternoon, the luxury rental where Lady Octavia was staying.

"This won't take long," Kyle said. "This lady has called to say someone's hiding in her bushes. I'll get out my stick and beat the bushes, like a good cop. You can help with my spare baton."

"I'll stay in the car."

"Less fun but safer," he said. "Thanks for being honest with me about the other stuff."

I said nothing, because saying nothing was the safest. I ached to tell him everything I'd learned that day, but breaking privilege would be the end of my investigation career. Knowing that didn't make keeping secrets from the police any easier. It was possibly why I still hadn't taken my test and gotten my license. I had enough hours to apply but kept coming up with excuses.

Did I even want to be a private investigator? Sitting quietly in the passenger seat, I was experiencing the exact opposite emotion of the jubilation that had made me dance an hour earlier. What a roller coaster ride the day had been.

We pulled up in front of the luxury rental house and parked.

Kyle used the radio to call in his location to dispatch and then stepped out.

I didn't want the countess to see me and think I blabbed. I slouched down in my seat and willed myself to be invisible. It had never worked before, but I figured it was worth a shot.

CHAPTER 24

I WATCHED FROM the car as Countess Octavia of Krengerborg answered the door with a baby in one arm. She'd changed out of her Chanel suit into jeans and a blouse that still looked too expensive to be near a baby's food-return system. As for the wee royal one, it was dressed in mint green, so I couldn't tell if it was a boy or a girl, or whether Jessica or I would be the one wearing the furry monster suit in the upcoming quarter marathon.

The countess didn't invite Officer Kyle Dempsey inside. She stepped out to join him on the porch. She used her free arm to make sweeping gestures. He spoke for a bit, puffing out his chest. She took on a coquettish stance, probably admiring his dimples. After a moment, she reached out and squeezed his bicep. Kyle responded by flexing for her.

What was he up to? Had he brought me along with him to use my presence to bluff his way into information? He hadn't tried hard to get me to come with him, and now he wasn't pointing me out. The countess didn't even glance in the direction of the car. Had he just brought me along to talk on the drive, or was young Kyle far more devious than he looked?

Perhaps my father had answers. I reached for my phone, but it was still in the glovebox of my car, which was parked at the police station. I looked at the radio. I knew how to use it, but doing so wouldn't do anything but get me in trouble.

I looked up just as Kyle disappeared into the house with the countess and her green-clad baby.

I opened my new casebook and added more notes to the page I'd started on my first visit of the day to that location.

Fifteen minutes passed before Kyle emerged from the front door, alone. He waved to me and walked around to the side of the house, where he disappeared from view.

The sparsely populated country cul-de-sac was quiet. The sun dropped lower, and the glints on the Victorian-style windows took on a golden hue.

Kyle returned and knocked on the front door again. I couldn't lower my window without the keys, which Kyle had wisely taken with him, so I cracked open my door, hoping to overhear their conversation. The countess returned with her green-clad baby in one arm.

"Nobody was hiding in the back bushes," I heard Kyle tell her. "It might have been some local wildlife moving around back there. We have plenty of deer in this area."

"But I saw flashes," she said. "Like a camera lens, or the sight on an assassin's rifle."

"An assassin?" He looked over his shoulder at me, then back to the countess. "Ma'am, do you have any reason to believe you might be in danger?"

"Oh, no," she said. "No, no, no. Of course not."

"Are you sure? It's my job to protect people in this town, and that includes visitors."

"Thank you," she said. "It must have been my imagination. I felt like I was being watched."

"Ma'am, some people find the quiet of the country to be disturbing. It's so different from life in a big European city. In the absence of cars honking and strangers yelling, you start to imagine things."

She said something too quiet for me to catch.

He reached for the baby. "Let me hold the little one while you get a glass of water. I have a way with kids."

She handed him the child and disappeared into the house, leaving the door wide open.

Kyle bounced the baby and walked toward the car. My mind's eye snapped a still picture of him, the young police officer in full uniform, his weapon holster visible just inches below the baby's small booties. Somewhere in the Day family's photo collection was a similar image of my father, holding me.

For an instant, I was somewhere else in time, a witness to a moment I couldn't comprehend, only feel.

Kyle used his toe to open the car door all the way.

"Look what I've got," he said.

"What are you up to?"

He grinned as the baby plumbed his dimples with pudgy baby fingers. "I'm serving and protecting," he said.

"Did you really bring me out here to watch you babysit?"

He waved the baby in front of me. "Look, it's a baby king. Get it?"

I kept my expression neutral, though I *did* get it. Koenig was German for king. Somehow, he'd figured out the child was an heir to Dieter Koenig's fortune, and he was fishing to find out what I knew. Had he only just figured it out, or was this why he'd brought me with him on the call? I didn't dare ask, lest I give away information with my curiosity.

He prompted, "Stormy, don't you know who this little cutie-pie is?"

I answered evenly and honestly, "I've never seen that baby in my life."

He smelled the baby's downy crown. "Smells good."

"Are you even qualified to hold that baby? It's not like a sidearm, Dimples. You have to know where a baby is at all times."

"Want to see me toss it in the air? My nieces love being tossed up." He made a practice motion with the wide-eyed baby.

I couldn't take it anymore. I pushed open the car door and grabbed the baby from him. He was right about it smelling delicious. I cuddled the tiny heir and murmured some of the sweet syrupy nothings I usually reserved for Jeffrey. To settle the matter of the bet with my roommate, I did a quick visual inspection down the front of the green pants and diaper. The baby king was indeed a king and not a queen.

The boy responded by gazing up at me, smiling, and letting the pacifier fall from his rosebud mouth.

"Hello," called out Lady Octavia, back at the front door. "Thank you, Officer. I'm feeling much better now. It was just, what's the word? Panic. It was just a panic attack."

Kyle took the baby from me and returned him to his mother. Lady Octavia was so focused on her child and Kyle, she didn't seem to notice me there. I slid back into the car and closed the door carefully. If she had noticed me, we could sort it out later, and not in front of the police. In the meantime, I had to do something sneaky, in private.

A few minutes later, Kyle returned to the car.

He got in, turned to me, and held out his hand, palm up. "Hand it over."

"I don't like this new sneaky side of yours, Kyle. And I don't have anything to hand over to you."

"You have the baby's pacifier," he said. "I was going to swipe it myself, but you beat me to it, because you're the sneaky one." He wiggled his fingers. "Hand it over."

I reached into my purse and pulled out the small plastic baggie with the pacifier.

"You carry evidence bags in your purse," he said, taking the pacifier. "So sneaky."

"They're just sandwich bags," I said. "I'm environmentally friendly. I use them in restaurants when I don't finish my dinner and want to take a doggy bag home." I sighed. "And for evidence, when needed." I sighed again. "How did you know about the heir?"

"I googled the countess and found a story about her hooking up with Dieter Koenig."

"You googled her," I said with a chuckle. "That's some top-shelf detective work."

He asked, "Did you notice anything about the baby?"

"It smelled yummier than fresh bread."

"I meant, did you notice something unusual?"

"No," I said. "Did you?"

"The booties were for two left feet," he said.

"Mismatched?"

"Exact same style."

I shrugged. "That poor baby, having two left feet. You know what they say about the genes of royal families, though."

Kyle grinned, turning his dimples up to maximum. "Having two left feet isn't a bad tradeoff for millions of dollars." He started the car's engine.

I said, "The other possibility is that the baby king has a twin."

"Exactly."

"Which would be scandalous for different reasons," I said. The math was easy, and the ramifications were obvious.

"Exactly," he said. "Instead of splitting the inheritance two or three ways, we're now up to four. As their legal guardian, that puts the Duchess of Kankersores in control of half the Koenig fortune."

I snickered. "She's not a duchess. She's a countess, and it's Krengerborg."

"That's what I said."

"Sure it is."

He waved the baggie with the pacifier. "Let's not get ahead of ourselves until we get the lab results."

"Will there be enough DNA for an accurate test?" I asked innocently.

I knew darn well there would be but figured it didn't hurt to play dumb with Kyle. If he could use his dimples, I could bat my eyelashes and ask simple questions.

He turned his head and watched as a large, dark vehicle passed behind us on the road. I turned as well. The quiet lane had only three homes and culminated in a dead end.

Kyle backed the cruiser out of the driveway and turned to follow the vehicle, which was a black truck.

"What do we have here?"

"You don't need to call in the license plate," I said. "That truck's from the Koenig Estate. I saw the butler driving it last night, when he picked up Tim Barber from the casino."

"The butler did it," Kyle said wryly.

"Did what? Drive innocently along a road?"

"That truck's up to something," Kyle said. "I can feel it."

We turned onto the road and followed the vehicle, which wasn't even speeding.

Kyle continued, "If whoever's in this truck isn't up to anything, they shouldn't mind stopping to answer a few questions."

The truck reached the end of the road and used the final home's driveway to turn around.

Kyle tapped a switch to flash the lights and sirens once in a polite request.

The vehicle slowed as it neared us, as though considering stopping. The dark tint on the windows, combined with the glare of the setting sun, made seeing the driver impossible. Once it was alongside us, the truck's engine roared. Dirt and gravel from the unpaved country lane sprayed up from the tires as it raced away from us.

Kyle flicked on the lights and siren and said, "Stormy, buckle up!"

CHAPTER 25

Scenery whipped past the windows as we pursued the black truck.

"If someone bolts, I'm a bloodhound," Kyle said. "I'm going to chase them like a rabbit."

I clung to a handhold above the door as we careened through a curve in the country road.

"You mean like a *fox*," I said. "Bloodhounds chase foxes. It's greyhounds who chase rabbits at the racetrack."

"What?" His dimples were gone, smoothed out as he concentrated on the black truck kicking up dust in front of us.

"You're a greyhound, because you're fast."

"Bloodhounds are still fast. Dogs are faster than people."

"Not chiweenies."

"Huh?" He hazarded me a quick glance as he cranked the wheel for a bigger turn.

I added a second hand to my hold on the strap above my head.

I explained, "Chiweenies are a cross between dachshunds and Chihuahuas. They're both burrowing dogs, so they like to dig their way into piles of blankets."

"This is what you do during a car chase?" he asked with disbelief. "You spout facts about dogs?"

"Would you rather hear about the life cycle of fleas?"

He shot me a look that said *no*.

I would have told him about fleas anyway, but something was happening with the truck in front of us. It drifted erratically from one side of the road to the other and slowed down. We caught up quickly. Kyle had to brake hard to avoid running into the back of the truck.

Kyle switched off our siren but not the lights. The road dust hung in the air. All was still, except for the blue and white lights bouncing off the truck. Thanks to the glare from the setting sun, I still couldn't see through the tinted windows.

Kyle unbuckled his seat belt.

"They're going to bolt," I said.

"What makes you say that?"

"The body language of the truck."

His dimples made a brief appearance. His light-blue eyes twinkled as he opened his door and stepped out, shaking his head at my warning. I heard him mutter about the body language of trucks as he closed the door.

What I *should have said* was that the truck's tires were pointed toward the center of the road instead of straight ahead, telegraphing the driver's intention to bolt.

Sure enough, as soon as Kyle passed the rear bumper of the truck, the red brake lights flashed off. The tires kicked up dirt as it sped away, pelting the windshield. One particularly loud bang made me shriek. A spiderweb crack blossomed on my side of the glass. The impact of a flung rock, so close to my face, caused a cascade of emotions, from fear to anger. Whoever it was in the truck, they'd scared me. Now it was personal.

I pushed open my door, jumped out, and yelled at Kyle, "Shoot the tires!" I used my hands to mime my instructions, in case he couldn't understand English.

Kyle, who was running back to the vehicle, yelled, "Get back in the car!"

"They're getting away! Shoot their tires! Do something!" I jumped up and down, shooting with both of my finger guns enthusiastically.

Kyle seemed to consider my request, his hand on his holster. Then he shook his head and jumped back into the car. I got in as well, quickly fastening my seat belt and reaching for the overhead strap. I pressed my foot impatiently against the ghost accelerator on the passenger side.

He flicked the siren on and grabbed the radio as we took off. He told the dispatcher he needed backup. He gave our location, and the female voice on the other end asked him to clarify the situation.

"It's a ten-twenty-five," he said.

"No, Dimples," I said. "It's a ten-thirty. And it may turn into a ten-thirty-three if you don't watch where you're going."

The dispatcher asked, "Who's that? Who's there with you?"

"Ten-fifty-nine," Kyle said.

They spoke for a few more seconds about his location, speed, and direction, and he set the radio handset back into its cradle.

Before I could ask him what a ten-fifty-nine meant, we reached the main road. The truck veered left, nearly cutting off an oncoming vehicle. Kyle braked hard to avoid being T-boned, and then we were off again, shooting like a bullet down the paved road. Here, on the smooth surface, the car had the advantage on the truck. We started catching up.

We hit a curving section of road that took us through a dip, a natural slough that was too damp to be used for growing hay. The trees were just thick enough to hide the suspect's truck from sight. As we sped along the road, the setting sun strobed between the trees.

Suddenly, a dark vehicle whipped by us, going in the opposite direction. It was the truck, which must have doubled back the instant it was behind the blind.

Kyle and I swore in unison.

The road was too narrow for a U-turn, so he had to make a three-point turn. To Kyle's credit, it was the fastest three-point turn I'd ever witnessed. The wild movement of the vehicle made me glad I'd split dessert with Ruby rather than overdo it on my own.

Kyle used the radio to report our new direction then commented to me, "Whoever's in that truck, I guarantee you it's not dumb kids on a joyride."

"If it's the butler, he may be a bodyguard, too. It sure looks like he's familiar with evasive driving techniques."

Kyle snorted. "My training's better than a butler's."

"Sure, but do you know which tiny fork is used for escargot?"

He shot me a look that said my silence might be more helpful than my commentary about fancy silverware.

We pursued the truck for another five minutes before Kyle groaned. "Great," he said flatly.

As we crested the hill, I saw what had him down. We were nearing a forested area with trails the locals used for riding dirt bikes and horses. Most of the trails were little more than a horse-width wide, but there were a few with double ruts suitable for Jeeps and off-road vehicles.

The black truck didn't even wait for the exit. It veered off the road, down a ditch, and into a field, speeding toward the trail entrance at an angle.

"We can still get them," Kyle growled.

I thought he meant someone from the backup detail could get them. The police had a few off-road vehicles that could handle the rutted goat trail of a road.

But he didn't mean we would wait for backup. He thought we could head them off, our speed on the access road superior to their speed over the bumpy hay field.

We'd barely slowed when we reached the access road exit. Kyle hit the brakes, we fishtailed, and he grunted as he cranked the steering wheel.

As the world spun, an image of playing cards came to mind.

The king of diamonds.

A royal flush.

Something was making a horrible grinding noise.

CHAPTER 26

ONE HOUR LATER.

I THOUGHT I'D SEEN every variation of Captain Tony Milano's unhappy expressions, but it turned out there was another layer to the irritation onion.

"You two are as bad as my children," Tony said.

"Ouch," Kyle said.

"Burn," I said.

We were inside a hospital treatment room, waiting for the emergency room's admitting doctor to officially release us. I was sitting on a hard-backed chair, admiring the interesting colors appearing on my bruised elbow and forearm. Kyle sat on the treatment bed, shirtless, getting splinters removed from his shoulder and pretending it didn't hurt.

"At least we're okay," I said to Tony. "Isn't that the most important thing?"

"But you're *not* okay," Tony spluttered. "Your arm is all mangled, and Dimples is broken." The nurse looked up from the bloody splinter extraction.

"Dempsey," Tony corrected. "I meant Officer Dempsey."

Smiling, she went back to the splinter extraction.

"You're overreacting," I said. "We're not mangled or broken."

"Don't try to diminish what's happened," Tony said. "You two really are as bad as my children."

I raised my hand and asked impishly, "Dad, if we had a puppy, we'd be too busy with the puppy to chase after bad guys."

His face went through three new variations of peeved. He did not appreciate the humor in me calling him Dad.

"Nobody's getting a puppy," he growled.

I put my hand down and tried to look sorry, even though, once again, I was innocent of the trouble I'd been caught up in.

When Kyle thought he could outrace the truck to the forest trail, he'd been realistic about his driving abilities. Unfortunately, one of the tires must have snagged a clump of dirt and thrown us off course.

The only thing we succeeded in apprehending was a giant billboard for the Canuso Lake Casino. When the sliding police car struck the post for the billboard, the whole sign toppled over and broke apart. The spiderweb crack on my side of the windshield was obliterated by a corner of plywood smashing through. The king of diamonds nearly lopped off my head, acting like some mad royal working creatively around the issue of not being granted a divorce.

When we stopped sliding, poor Kyle was so shocked by the proximity of splintering wood near my throat, he didn't even notice the injury to his shoulder until I pointed it out to him.

We'd climbed out of the car and were assessing the damage when backup arrived. Officer Gary Gomez was in an off-road vehicle and continued the pursuit into the forest, but we didn't have high hopes.

When the paramedics showed up, they found me dazed and trying to put the billboard sign back together, treating it like a giant jigsaw puzzle. I would have solved it, too, if Kyle hadn't been bleeding all over the edge pieces and making the picture hard to see. At least that's what the first responders reported me as saying. I was in shock, as was Kyle, and couldn't remember much more than flashes.

Of course I was happy to be alive, I'd told Tony. But I wasn't taking the blame for wrecking the police car, and I wasn't going to sit seriously through a scolding from a disappointed father who wasn't even my father.

"Are you even listening?" Tony snapped his fingers in front of my face. "What did I just say?"

"We're never, ever, ever getting a puppy," I answered.

He kneeled down in front of my chair and looked into my eyes. "How hard did you bump your noggin?"

I rubbed the right side of my head, where I had a tender spot between the top of my ear and crown of my head.

"Just enough for a nice goose egg," I said. "I'm fine, and I really am sorry about your police car. Sorry in the way that a person can be sorry even when they had *absolutely no responsibility* for the thing that happened."

"I don't care about the car," he said. "We can get another one." He glanced around then asked softly, "You haven't seen Tim Barber around lately, have you?"

"No, why? Do you think he was in the truck with the butler? You think the two of them are up to something?"

Tony raised a finger to his lips and shushed me. "Not here," he said. "And not tonight." He reached up and touched the tender spot on the side of my head. "That is quite the goose egg."

"Tony, what's a ten-fifty-nine?" I asked. I'd heard Kyle utter the code when the dispatcher asked who was in the car with him. I had a feeling it was me.

Tony frowned then stood and began asking the nurse if she thought I should stay overnight for observation, just in case.

I leaned over to look past them and make eye contact with Kyle. The nurse had finished the splinter extraction and bandages. He pulled on a gray sweatshirt the hospital had given him to wear home, since they'd cut his uniform shirt away.

Kyle looked tired as he mouthed *I want to go home.*

Me, too, I mouthed back.

Sorry, he mouthed. He looked pointedly at my arm and knitted his eyebrows.

I'm okay, I replied, waving one bruised hand. Then I started looking around for an escape route.

While Tony was distracted with the nurse, I twitched a divider curtain out of the way and made my exit.

The hospital was quiet that Tuesday night, and I didn't encounter anyone I knew on my way outside.

Night had fallen. The parking lot looked creepy in the darkness, as did the hill I would need to traverse to return to the police station to get my car and phone. I switched my purse to my left shoulder, which wasn't as sore, then back to my right, where I could use it as a makeshift sling. I was lucky my injuries hadn't been worse, but acknowledgement of fortune doesn't do much to diminish pain. At least the pills the doctor had given me were kicking in.

By the time I crossed the park and traversed several neighborhoods, I was feeling fine. Fine enough to run a quarter marathon. In a furry monster suit.

I retrieved my car and my phone and drove home, my mind pleasantly blank.

After a long day that had started with Tony banging on my door and only gotten crazier from there, all I wanted to see was my cat and my pillow, preferably at the same time.

It was nearly ten o'clock when I reached my driveway and first obstacle since the billboard that tried to kill me. I couldn't park in my usual spot due to it being occupied.

The vehicle was a lime-green Volkswagen Beetle I knew well. I'd seen the car all over town, still sporting dents in the front bumpers. The dents had been acquired back in February, when the Beetle's owner used the car as a battering ram to push my car out of her way. That had happened right after the mud wrestling. My ribs, which hadn't been injured in the evening's car crash, ached in memory of the pummeling I'd taken.

I parked on the street and walked up the driveway toward my front door, watching the Beetle warily.

The car's front doors popped open, and two women stepped out.

My day of craziness wasn't over yet.

CHAPTER 27

ALL I WANTED was a hot bath... to use for drowning anyone who stood in the way of me hitting the hay.

The driver of the green Beetle was exactly who I expected: Della. And with her was another raven-haired woman I'd never seen before.

Della ran toward me. I'd never wanted a cane sword of my own so badly.

"Stormy," she gushed. "I found her. I found our witness."

"Our witness?" I turned to the other woman and asked, "You work at the Koenig Estate?"

She blinked, frowned, and answered, "No, ma'am. I'm Saundra, and I work at the Turtledove, up in Seattle."

Della's eyes caught the light of the streetlamp and blazed at me. "Do you even know what's going on?" she demanded. "Do you know who this is?" She pointed to Saundra. "Do you know what she's worth?"

Saundra wore the gray-and-white uniform of the Turtledove, a prestigious boutique hotel in Seattle, Washington. She didn't seem to be alarmed by people discussing her value. She looked at me with a hopeful expression.

"That's Saundra," I said to Della slowly, buying time to put the puzzle pieces together. "Saundra... from the Turtledove. It's a lovely hotel, by the way. I've stayed there twice, once for business and once for pleasure. We were in the presidential suite."

Saundra looked even more hopeful. "Was it after the renovation? That suite has its own steam room now."

"Really? I'll have to make another trip up there someday."

Della made an exasperated sound as I shook hands with Saundra, the three of us still standing in my driveway.

"It's nice to meet you, Saundra," I said. "You must be the witness for the wedding. And Della brought you here to get a notarized statement."

Saundra looked at Della for guidance. For a moment, I worried I had guessed wrong.

Della answered for her, "Yes, of course. And she was the witness to the will, too."

I nodded slowly. "A witness for the wedding and the will. Saundra, you look like you left town in a hurry."

"Yes. In a hurry," she answered. The whites of Saundra's eyes were quite visible, giving her a frightened appearance and causing me some concern.

Leaning in so I could ask her a question without Della overhearing, I whispered, "Are you here of your own free will? Blink twice if you've been kidnapped."

Her eyes crinkled at the corners, but she didn't blink. Either she was there of her own volition or she was just scared of Della. I was actually glad to see Saundra was nervous. It meant she was a legitimate witness. If Della had paid off an accomplice to lie for her, they would act more confident and eager to help.

Della, meanwhile, was on my front step, standing under the motion-sensing safety light as though it were a stage spotlight. She seemed to come to life under the brightness.

"Oh how I miss my boo, my sweet, silver-haired boo!" Della's words had a melodic quality, as though she were singing. "Deets wanted to take care of me, good care of me, sweet tender care of me," she spoke-sang.

Saundra said to me, "He really did. I was there to sign their papers to witness the marriage, and he said since I was there anyway, I could put my name on his Last Will and Testament. I thought the old guy was joking around." She gave me a knowing look, eyebrows raised. "Rich people get up to all sorts of crazy stuff. I've seen things."

Della continued to speak-sing about her *boo*, some of it nonsensical, transitioning into humming.

"Della, what was the champagne for? Dieter was getting a caterer for a party at the mansion."

She sang her response, "A party? For me?"

"Probably to announce the marriage," I said. "Did you know about the party?"

Her eyes grew sad. "There won't be a party," she said. "I'm glad I didn't know, or I'd be even more brokenhearted now."

"I should warn you that Dieter's sons are trying to figure out what the party was for. They're not going to be very happy when they find out."

She shook her head, smiling. "Not very happy at all. Silly boys."

"I wonder if the party was just about the announcement or if he was planning to have another ceremony. Are you sure that first one was legal?"

Della only laughed.

I looked around my dark driveway sheepishly. She wouldn't have gone up to Seattle to kidnap Saundra if the ceremony hadn't been legal.

Either way, this wasn't a conversation for my driveway.

I asked Saundra, "Are you two here to see Della's lawyer? The lights on his side aren't on, so he's probably still at the office."

"Doesn't he live here? This Logie guy? Della told me we're staying here tonight." She looked me up and down, stopping at my bruised arm, which was resting atop my purse. "She said we'd be safe here, because you're a detective and you have special training. Like a bodyguard."

"Interesting," I said. "Well, if you're staying at Casa Day, I guess I should unlock the door and let you in." I stepped into the spotlight with Della and nudged her out of the way so I could get my key in the lock. Jessica was working a late shift, and we'd locked up when we left for our trip to see the countess.

As I pushed open the front door, Saundra pointed at my arm. "Did you get those bruises beating someone up?"

"Yes," I said, stretching the truth. "But you should have seen the other guy. I left him in pieces."

CHAPTER 28

"THIS IS WHERE you live," Della said, more statement than question.

"Thanks," I said—automatically, since people usually offered a compliment when they entered my home.

"You just moved in," she said.

"Almost a year ago."

"Maybe you should hire a decorator," she said. "Does that big wall have to be there?" She pointed to the wall separating my side from Logan's.

"Not forever," I said. "Make yourselves comfortable. Would you like some tea? The kettle's right here, and the tea's in the cupboard."

"Do you have mint tea?" Della asked. "That's what I'd love right now."

Saundra, who was in the living room petting Jeffrey, chimed in, "Mint tea sounds great."

With a sigh, I filled the kettle. I'd been hoping to escape their company to have a hot shower and rinse off the grime that had settled on me during the car chase and crash, but no such luck.

I got the two women settled in the living room with big, steaming mugs of mint tea. The mint must have been chemically similar to catnip because Jeffrey snagged a dry teabag and carried it off to be destroyed in private.

I reviewed the messages that had accumulated on my phone. There was a request from Logan that I "babysit" Della and the star witness for a few hours while he lined up a place for Saundra to spend the night.

I send him a text message: *They're here now. If it's just one night, she's welcome to my sofa. I hope she likes having a cat groom her eyebrows.*

Logan messaged back immediately: *Saundra is skittish and only agreed to come to Misty Falls if we provided a bodyguard. Don't sweat it. I've already got one lined up.*

Me: *Do I dare ask who?*

Logan: *I'll be home soon.*

Me: *Is it you? Are you the bodyguard? Or is it me?*

Logan: *It's a professional. I have to get some work done now. Call me if there's an emergency.*

I sent him one of my favorite signoff emoticons— a gray cat waving one paw—and plugged my phone into the charger.

I joined the two women in my living room, saying, "Sorry for the lack of organization and communication. I've had a very hectic day."

Saundra looked at my arm again. "Are you okay? Do you need to go to the hospital?"

"Already been. I'm not broken." I wiggled my fingers to show her the arm was still working, albeit sporting some funky shades of purple.

Della showed no signs of concern over my arm. "At least you're still alive," she said. "Unlike my old boyfriend, who died too young." She explained to Saundra, "He was *murdered*. And now my new boyfriend, my sweet boo, is gone. He was old, but he was still too young. I don't think he was murdered, but you never know, do you?"

Saundra, who'd been sitting on the front edge of the room's armchair, abruptly stood. "I shouldn't have come here," she said. "My mama told me to stay clear of this crazy business. I should have listened to my mama."

"Everything's going to be fine," I said. Then I grabbed all of my emergency junk food and started spreading it out across the coffee table like a kid's Halloween haul of trick-or-treat candy. "You just need a snack after your long road trip."

By the time the coffee table was covered in a rainbow of the finest snack foods money could buy, Saundra had settled back into the chair.

I sat next to Della and told her, softly "You might want to lay off on the M-word in front of your star witness. Besides, only one of your boyfriends has been murdered so far. What happened with Dieter might have been an accident."

She turned to me, her brown eyes glossy, and I caught a glimpse of the vulnerable girl underneath the larger-than-life stage personality.

"Do you really believe it was an accident?" she asked.

"People do have accidents," I said. "Can you think of any reason why he might have slipped on the diving board? Did you ever use the board right after applying suntan oil?"

"I don't like diving in," she said. "My hair takes forever to get straight again if I get it wet."

"How do you think your suntan oil got onto the diving board?"

"My suntan oil was on the diving board?" She frowned and looked away. "The pictures," she said. "On the day before he died, on Saturday, Dieter took some pictures of me posing on the diving board."

"Standing? I'm trying to figure out how much of your body might have been touching the diving board."

Della looked to Saundra and then to me. "A lot," she said shyly. "I'd say a lot of my body was touching the diving board."

"You were nude?"

"If you've got it, flaunt it." She sat up straighter. "But I didn't like how the pictures turned out, so I made him delete them off his phone. He was going to take more pictures, but I wouldn't let him. I felt like I was being watched. More than usual."

"Were the staff watching you? Who was it? Erica the maid? Randy the butler?"

Della crossed her arms. "I think the sons were watching me."

"But they were in New York on Saturday. They only flew home on Sunday."

She kept her arms crossed and rubbed her upper biceps. "It's just a feeling I got. You know how sometimes you walk into a room and you feel like someone you don't like was just there a minute before? It was like that. I felt like the brothers were watching me on the diving board that day."

"How about the staff? How did you get along with them?"

"Just fine," she said. "I'll probably keep them all. Except the butler. Randy gets a little too invested in organizing the drawer where I keep my underwear, if you know what I mean." She winked.

Saundra interjected, "Perv?"

"He takes a lot of *cold showers*," Della said. "If I give him any attention at all, he's got to run off on some *errand*, and when he does come back, his hair's wet."

Saundra nodded. "Perv. I know the type. At the hotel, we keep them away from the guests. Most wind up in the kitchen, where they can perv on each other to their heart's content."

"Randy's hair was wet on Sunday," I said. "And he wasn't fully dressed."

Della laughed. "Sounds like Randy. I probably gave him too much eye contact."

"But you couldn't have, because you were asleep," I said. "Weren't you sleeping during the accident? And then sleeping straight through until the police showed up?"

The smile fell off her face. "My memory is foggy," she said. "I did get up for a bit. Deets woke me up because we had that breakfast meeting with Logie. I started getting ready, and I had to go wandering around searching for whichever bathroom I used the night before, to get my hair stuff."

"Were you wandering around naked? I heard the police found you sleeping in a guest room without a stitch of clothes on."

Her nostrils flared. She spat out, "What are you saying?"

"I'm just trying to get a feel for what happened that morning."

"That's not what I'm paying you for," she said.

I leaned back and held my hands up. "My bad. Hazard of the trade. I ask too many questions."

Saundra interjected, "You are asking her a lot of questions."

I offered her a friendly grin. "I hope you're not feeling left out. I have questions for you, too."

She ripped into a bag of M&Ms. "I've got nothing to hide," she said. "Shoot."

"Did you really witness the wedding?"

She crunched on the candies. "Of course I did. That's why I'm here, isn't it? I can prove I was there."

"You have photos?" I asked.

"No," she said, crunching away on the candies as she put her phone into her purse quickly. "Della said she didn't want any pictures, because she was afraid of people selling them to the gossip sites."

I nodded. "Sure, that's what she told you. But that only made you more interested in pictures, didn't it?"

Saundra gave me a dirty look. "You really do ask a lot of nosy questions."

"Doesn't change the fact you've got photos," I said. "You took another half a dozen of Della on the sofa when she wasn't paying attention. I saw you from the kitchen."

Saundra crossed her legs. "So what?"

Della jumped up and launched herself at Saundra. Lucky for the hotel maid, I'd anticipated such a thing and caught Della with my good arm before she could get a handful of Saundra's dark locks.

Saundra grabbed her purse, clutched it to her chest, and gave me a wild-eyed look. I sensed that she was a good person, just young and in way over her head.

"Everything's going to be okay," I said as I wrangled Della back down onto the sofa and sat myself on her lap to keep her there.

Della squawked in protest, but she had no leverage.

I told Saundra, "You're not in trouble, I promise. Just email me a copy of the photos so we have them for the file."

Della squawked angrily, "Those pictures are illegal!"

Saundra retorted, "I have to look after myself! I don't have a sugar daddy!"

"You're going to delete those photos!"

"Maybe I will," Saundra said. "I'll delete them right now and tell everyone I was nowhere near your suite that night. I don't know who forged my name on the paperwork."

Della practically screamed.

"Don't be hasty," I said to Saundra. "Send me the photos. Then let Della look through them and delete the ones she doesn't like. You can sell the rest."

"I can sell them?" Saundra looked surprised.

"You'll have Della's blessing, but don't tell the press that."

"No!" cried Della. "I won't let you. Those pictures are personal and private."

I turned to put my face in hers. I was close enough to smell her lip gloss. "You can delete the bad pictures if you don't like how you look in them. Let her keep a couple good ones that she can sell. Does that work for you?"

Della gave me a confused look. "Why would I let her sell the pictures?"

"Because you can't buy publicity like leaked scandal photos. And don't you want your own TV show?"

Della's expression gradually softened, and she stopped trying to get out from underneath me.

"Okay," Della said to me. "You're kind of a genius, aren't you?"

"I must be," I said. "You're looking at me the way my cat does when I use the magical can opener."

The women both blinked at my joke. There are two kinds of people in the world: Cat people and the yet-to-be-enlightened.

Someone knocked on the front door and started pushing it open without waiting.

"Bodyguard's here," came a man's voice.

CHAPTER 29

"Did someone call for a bodyguard?" My father, Finnegan Day, walked in wearing his suit and hat, plus a pair of sunglasses, despite the fact it was dark outside.

"Hi, Dad," I said. "Give us a sec." I pointed to Saundra's purse and gestured for her to hand over the phone. "We won't delete them all," I promised.

She hesitated before handing us her phone. It was the same model as mine, so I was able to find the wedding photos easily.

Saundra seemed more concerned with the bodyguard in the kitchen.

"Wow," said Saundra. "You sure dress good for someone living in a small town like this."

"Misty Falls is full of surprises," he said. "Have you considered moving here?" He set his hat on the counter, took off his sunglasses, and refilled the kettle for tea.

Saundra, who was probably eager to put some distance between herself and Della thanks to the nearly violent altercation over the wedding photos, got up from her chair and joined him in the kitchen area.

"Not until now," Saundra said. "What's the weather like?"

"Where do you live currently?"

"Seattle," she said.

"We don't get nearly as much rain here," he said. "Don't tell me you're one of those girls who prefers gray skies."

She giggled girlishly. "I like blue skies." She held out her hand. "I'm Saundra."

He took her hand and held it. "Finnegan Day. You can call me Finn. Would you like a warm-up?"

She giggled again. "What did you have in mind?"

"Your cuppa tea," he said, laying on the Irish accent for extra charm. "Would you like a little more hot water?"

"If you think I would, then yes."

Next to me on the sofa, Della said, "Gross."

I leaned over and said, "He's always like this."

"Gross," she said again.

I looked down at her hands and realized she was referring to the wedding photos on the phone, not to my father hitting on our kidnapped witness.

Meanwhile, my father was asking Saundra if she'd seen the movie *Bodyguard*, starring Kevin Costner and Whitney Houston. She had never seen the 1992 romantic suspense film but sounded genuinely excited about watching it with my father at his house, which he kept referring to as the Safe

House, as though it were a residence kept by the FBI for housing witnesses on the run.

After another cup of tea, my father left with Saundra. Della said she was going to wait around for Logan to come home. I yawned repeatedly in front of her, hoping it would be contagious.

* * *

Wednesday morning, I woke up with my feet on the pillow and my head at the bottom of the bed. I was fully dressed, but not in the same clothes I'd worn the day before. There were only two possible explanations for my condition. Either I'd been abducted by aliens and done some time traveling, or I'd taken one of Jessica's sleeping pills the night before.

As I got up, brushed my teeth, and adjusted my bra so the front part was at the front, memories of the previous evening came back in waves.

After Saundra left with the bodyguard, Della raided my kitchen for a bit. When she discovered I didn't have her preferred brand of vodka, she left in search of a better party.

Jessica came home at eleven, saw the bruises on my arm, and dragged me away from my laptop and the photos of Della and Dieter's wedding. She fed me some deep-fried tortellini that she'd brought home from work, gave me a sleeping pill, and tucked me into bed.

With my memory restored, I could go about my day secure in the knowledge I had not been abducted by aliens and sloppily redressed.

"Good morning," I said as I entered the kitchen.

Jessica was already up and baking.

"I thought you deserved some apple turnovers," she said.

"Deserved?" I snagged a few almonds she hadn't slivered yet and munched them. "Apple turnovers are my father's favorite. Is he coming over again today? Do you know something I don't know because I slept right through it? What year is this?"

She laughed. "Finn's next door with Logan, delivering the witness." She nibbled on a thin slice of green apple and arched her red eyebrows. "She's really pretty."

I let out a sniff-laugh. "He just likes the attention. That Saundra girl is in her twenties. He does date down in age, but he'd never touch anyone younger than his daughters. That's the line."

"Did he tell you that?"

"Not in so many words."

She dusted the countertop with flour. "Remember when we were kids and we tried to set up my mother and your father?"

"We thought we were so clever," I said with a chuckle.

"It almost worked," she said.

"You have a funny definition of *almost*."

"We should keep trying," she said.

"If you go over to your mother's place and start breaking things on purpose, people might not find it so cute now that you're old enough to know better."

"There are other ways," she said.

"You're on your own with that particular project," I said, laughing.

Back when we were too young to realize how transparent we were, we'd get my father to come in and fix something at the Kelly residence whenever he picked me up from a sleepover.

At the time, we thought our plan was working well. Our two single parents would talk and laugh while he fixed things. It wasn't until the fifth or sixth time that my father asked me to ask Jessica to stop breaking things, because he couldn't handle another minute of her mother reaming him out about how terrible and useless all adult men were. That was when I realized that not all forms of grownup talking was positive. The funny thing was, Jessica wasn't breaking that many things on purpose. Her older brothers were just really hard on drawers, balustrades, and anything else they could climb on or hang from.

"Knock knock," said a voice behind me. It was my father, coming in the front door with Logan right behind him. They were alone.

"Where's Saundra?" I asked. "Don't tell me you lost your prize witness. You've got to be a better bodyguard than that, even if it was your first assignment."

Logan pointed at the wall dividing our living spaces. "She's picking out something to wear."

"You're loaning her one of your puffy pirate shirts?"

He pursed his lips, suppressing a grin. "I don't own any pirate shirts, they just look that way on tiny people." He gave me a hug and kissed my forehead. "Saundra's choosing something from the selection Corine picked out. I know Corine's taste in clothing is questionable, but it's better than the postage-stamp dresses Della would have loaned her."

"I could have loaned her something," I said.

"No, you couldn't have," said my father. "She's much bigger than you up top."

I looked to Jessica for emotional support. It was bad enough my bra didn't look too bad when it was on backwards, but now this? From my own father? Jessica gave me a sympathetic look and continued making apple turnovers.

My father and Logan thankfully moved on from Saundra's wardrobe needs to talking about other aspects of the case. They talked while I helped Jessica with the pastries by providing moral support and eating the extra fillings.

My ears perked up when my father said, "Nobody's heard from or seen Tim Barber in twenty-four hours."

"You could check the casino again," Logan said.

My father answered, "I might drive out to Canuso Lake, but I figure we'll swing by Barber's house first."

"And pay a visit to Erica Garcia?" Logan asked.

"We wouldn't want to be rude and *not* say hello, provided she's home." My father looked at me.

"What do you say? Want to go for a spin in your old man's new car?"

Jessica and I said, in unison, "New car?"

He grinned. "Now, that's exactly the reaction I was hoping for."

CHAPTER 30

THE NEW CAR wasn't new at all, and it wasn't the first time I'd seen it.

It was an older-model green Ford Torino. Unless there was a second one in town, it belonged to my friend Harper, who worked with Jessica at the Olive Grove.

"Ain't she gorgeous," my father said, patting the car on the roof. "I'm test-driving her for a few days before I make up my mind. Hopefully there aren't any major mechanical surprises. She drives like a dream, but you can't be too careful. First dates can be deceptive."

"Dad, are you ready to commit to a collectible car? It's a big commitment."

He ignored me and stroked the roof lovingly. "I don't know why anyone would sell this beauty."

"There's one good reason," I said.

He waved his hand. "I'm just puttering around town, so gas mileage isn't a huge concern."

"Dad, I know why the owner is selling."

He waved his hand again. "If it's bad, I don't want to know. When you fall in love, you want the honeymoon to last forever."

"It's not a bad reason," I said. "Did you borrow it from a girl named Harper?"

"How'd you know?"

"She's a friend, Harper, and she's probably selling her car because her younger sister wants to drive it."

"How old is the sister?"

"She's in the twelfth grade this fall."

"That settles it," he said. "The little sister's too young for a car like this. I'll have to buy it as an act of preservation. They should give tax credits for good deeds like this."

"They really should," I agreed.

He turned to Jessica and Logan for their opinions.

Logan said, "I have no opinion on the purchase or sale of used cars. Ask a mechanic." He walked away from us, toward his side of the duplex. "If you'll excuse me, I need to gather my star witness and head in to the office."

I waved good-bye. "Good luck with everything."

He paused, staring at my arm. "Stormy, why is there dirt all over your arm?"

I pulled my sleeve down to cover the bruise. "Don't worry about that."

Now both he and my father were staring at me.

Sighing, I said, "We had a little car-whoopsie when I was out with Kyle yesterday."

Jessica chimed in, "It was more than a car-whoopsie. They destroyed a billboard and a police car."

I gave her a dirty look. "You would have made a great little sister, you tattler."

She stuck her tongue out at me.

Logan came back to my side and pushed up my sleeve to look at my arm. With all the excitement of Della and Saundra showing up the previous evening, I'd only talked to Jessica so far about the accident. I assured everyone I wasn't in any pain, and I wasn't. I felt great—rested and refreshed and ready to close the case.

I finished with, "And we don't know who was in the truck, because they got away. All we know is that it belongs to the Koenig Estate."

Logan said, "It might have been the butler and the handyman." He shook his head. "That sounds funny to say out loud."

My father said, "Anything with the word *butler* in it sounds funny."

Logan hugged me—carefully, to avoid my bruised arm. "You be more careful," he said.

"Yes, Dr. Feelgreat." I pushed him away. "Go do your lawyering."

He started toward his door again, calling back, "Let me know how it goes with Tim Barber." He disappeared into his place to retrieve Saundra.

My father gave my bruises a good scowl and then returned to admire the vintage car.

Jessica walked up to the Torino and leaned over the hood as though preparing to kiss it. She fanned her hair with her fingers and let her red locks fall across the green paint.

"This car really goes nicely with redheads," she said to my father. "Hint, hint."

My father replied, "Jessica Kelly, I'm not taking your mother out unless she's wearing a muzzle."

"Dad!" I gave him a dirty look.

Jessica straightened up and also gave him a dirty look. "Mr. Day, I just meant that maybe you could bring me with you to the Show and Shine days. I could wear a vintage dress and pose with the car."

"Oh." He looked sheepish. "That would be all right," he said. "Don't tell your mother what I said about her. She's a good woman."

"It is a cool car," I said. "But it's so old. It doesn't have any modern safety features, or a navigation computer."

"Daughter dearest, are you saying old things aren't any good? That they should be left to rust somewhere, silent and forgotten?" He grinned.

I sighed. "Sometimes older things are actually the best," I said. "Let's take it for a spin and check on Tim Barber. If he was driving in that truck, I'm going to show him my bruises and make him feel awful." I turned to Jessica. "Want to come with us?"

She scooped up Jeffrey, who had come to christen the car's hood with paw prints. "I'll stay back here and get those apple turnovers in the oven. If you two don't take long, they should still be warm when you get back."

"Keep the home fires burning," my father said.

She went inside with Jeffrey, and my father tossed a set of keys at me. I caught the keys midair, but my right arm burned with pain from the sudden movement. I forced a smile onto my face. I wasn't exactly uninjured, but there was no need to worry him.

"You can drive," he said. "I've already been out with Saundra for a spin around town before we came here. The pedal heights seem fine for my new hip, but I don't want to overdo it."

I slid into the driver's seat. "Your hip is fine, Dad. You just enjoy having me as a chauffeur."

"Consider it a compliment to your driving skills."

"My driving skills in this vehicle remain to be seen." I jingled the keys in my right hand as I glanced around the interior. "And we may never find out, if I can't figure out where the key goes in."

Chuckling, he took my hand and guided it to the ignition. "New endeavors take time," he said. "Patience is your ally." He clicked his seat belt.

The engine started with a low rumble that surprised me—not the volume, but how enjoyable it was to be at the controls of the rumbling beast.

"Oh, my," I said. "It's purring like a big kitty."

"Check your blind spots," he said. "Back it down the driveway nice and easy, and once we're going, try not to hit any billboards."

CHAPTER 31

There was no answer when we knocked on Tim Barber's front door.

"Drink pineapple juice," my father said. He was looking at my bruised arm again. "There's something in pineapple that helps with bruising."

"Dad, you're turning into a real health wizard."

He patted his lower ribs. "I gotta keep up with the new hip, plus I don't want to have to replace any more parts. Pineapple juice is delicious. Add some fizzy water if you find it too sweet."

"I'll pick some up," I said, relieved that a juice recommendation was the extent of his comments on the previous night's adventures with Dimples. Although I hadn't been the one at the wheel, I did feel somewhat responsible. If I hadn't been yelling about shooting out tires, Officer Kyle Dempsey might have practiced more caution, and the casino billboard might have lived to advertise another day.

I knocked on the door again. "Maybe he's gone in to work," I said. "Or he went up the street to visit Erica Garcia. Or maybe he's at the police station right now, giving his statement on whatever lie detector Tony rustled up."

"Kyle would have let me know."

"He's at work today? His shoulder looked pretty scary last night."

"I thought you said the accident was minor?"

"It was minor! It's just that Kyle has those adorable cheeks, and when you see him hurt, it looks scary."

My father gave me a skeptical look and stepped down off Tim Barber's porch. He crossed the lawn toward the tailfins of the Fairlane that appeared to be submerged in the front lawn.

I asked, "What are you thinking about now?"

"The Torino replaced the Fairlane," he said as he leaned over the vintage tail lights.

I'd meant about Tim Barber, but I was curious about the car. I compared the back ends of the car coming out of the lawn with Harper's green Torino.

"But they're so different," I said. "They look nothing alike. Are you sure?"

"The body designers at Ford moved away from rockets as their inspiration and started looking at modern jets. Everything got sleeker and more bullet-shaped." He straightened up and looked down the street. "Now everyone drives boring gray things that look like pills or cough lozenges."

"Dad, you're doing it," I said. "You told me to warn you if you started to sound like grandpa."

He returned to Tim's door and used the end of his cane sword to ring the doorbell.

"That, I did," he said. "But maybe the old man was right all along, and things used to be better."

"You have to take it all," I said. "So what if we all drive boring, lozenge-shaped cars? We've made great strides in other fields, like forensics. Right this minute, people in a lab are analyzing microscopic skin cells taken from a baby soother, comparing it to the DNA of a dead man to determine paternity. Back in the good ol' days, you'd have to wait for the kid to grow up and see if folks could agree that he looked an awful lot like somebody, or held his caveman club the same way as the alleged father."

"Fair enough." He jabbed the doorbell again. "Did you hear that?" He cocked his head.

"I hear some warblers in the trees."

"Someone's calling for help from inside the house. You know, an old man living on his own can fall and break something. It would be a real shame if a caring citizen came all the way to the front door but didn't come inside to offer assistance."

"That *would* be a shame," I agreed.

He looked pointedly at the door handle. "Go ahead. The call for help is faint, but if you listen, you can hear it."

The warbling birds suddenly fell silent. Without sounds, the street felt flatly two-dimensional, like a postcard. I imagined Tim Barber on his floor, bleeding internally from a bad fall and break.

The handle was unlocked. I pushed the door open. "Mr. Barber?"

My father grabbed my elbow and pulled me back. "Smell that?"

I sniffed the air. An image flashed in my mind. A woman in a pool of blood. My stomach clenched. There was a smell.

As I stood in the doorway, a fat housefly buzzed past me languidly, followed by another.

"You smell it?" he asked.

"Death," I said.

His grim countenance confirmed my assessment.

He called into the house, "Mr. Barber, this is Finnegan Day. We've met before. My associate and I are about to enter the premises. We're concerned that you may be injured. We're coming inside now."

He gestured for me to stay behind him. He strode in, his head swiveling left and right as he did a professional sweep. The house was a modest-sized rancher and wouldn't take long to search.

We slowly approached the final room, a bedroom, where the foul smell of open blood was strongest. My father gestured for me to wait while he went in on his own.

A moment later, he came back, nodding grimly. "You don't need to see that unless you want to."

I had a difficult time saying I *wanted to* see a dead body, but in the end I settled on, "I'm here already, so I might as well have a glance."

"Word of warning," he said. "That's not a Jackson Pollock painting on the wall. It would appear our handyman ate a bullet."

His blunt phrasing lessened the shock of the scene, which was both terrifying and sad. Tim wore a dark suit, as though dressed for his funeral, which struck me as a not-so-prescient choice, as the shirt had blood on it and couldn't be used for burial.

On the neatly made bed, next to the body, was an ornate-handled handgun that resembled a movie prop from a Western movie. I recognized it as a collectible from the Koenig Mansion's impressive collection. Near the gun was a simple note, written on a plain white sheet of paper. The note was written in block-style neat handwriting and simply said SORRY.

"He's been gone a while," I said. "That smell is decomp." I reached for his left hand.

"Careful," my father said.

I knew he meant to be careful not to disturb the scene, not careful of Mr. Barber suddenly coming back to life. I gingerly pinched the hem of his suit jacket and lifted the arm. The body was stiff.

"My guess is he's been dead about twenty-four hours," I said.

"Sounds about right for that amount of stiffness."

"This isn't good," I said. "Not good at all."

"Let me guess. You don't think it's the simple suicide that it appears to be?"

"Dad, I might be new to homicides, but I know a thing or two about people. This scene is too tidy, too controlled of a narrative. Tim Barber didn't strike me as the type to say good-bye with a single word. He was a chatty guy."

"That he was. And what else?"

I could sense my mentor being pleased with my logic so far. Despite the gruesome scene, I found myself close to smiling.

"Plus he wanted to talk to the police about something," I said, speaking faster as I gained confidence. "He was at the station only yesterday morning, asking to give his statement while hooked up to a lie detector. Why would he change his mind so quickly?"

"Maybe he didn't."

I turned and studied the man's face, looking for insight. "He hadn't shaved in a few days," I said.

"And what does that tell you?"

"Honestly, I don't know. If his beliefs were strong enough that he'd dress up in his Sunday best to enter the afterlife, you'd think he would have taken the time to shave. You don't want the ladies in heaven to ignore you for fear of stubble burn."

My father only nodded.

I shook my head and moved toward the door in search of fresh air.

"Sorry I'm rambling about heaven and such," I said. "That's not very professional for a detective."

"Don't question your process," he said, following me down the hallway. "Killers and thieves are all humans, so exploring human thoughts, no matter how crazy they might seem when you say them out loud, is exactly how you get into their heads."

My head felt light, and my vision sparkled. "I'm barely in my own head," I muttered.

"Take it slowly," he said. "Let's get you a glass of water."

We stopped in the kitchen. The window had a screen, so we pushed it open to get some fresh air coming inside without letting flies in. We hadn't seen any more flies since the two that flew out when we arrived, which was some relief. They hadn't had time to multiply.

My father pulled out his cell phone. "I'll call this one in," he said.

I didn't like the way he said *this one*, as though he was buying this round of drinks and there'd be many more in our future.

CHAPTER 32

Officer Gary Gomez was surprisingly scary when conducting an interview.

We were at the station giving our statement about how we found Tim Barber and why we'd "just happened to be" at his house that morning.

Gomez scowled under his thick black moustache. "Am I to believe you two were on a social call?"

"Believe what you want," my father said nonchalantly. "Now that I'm retired, I have plenty of time to be social."

Gomez turned his full glare onto me. "And how about you, Miss Day? Taking a break from wrecking police cars to go trampling through more crime scenes?"

I shrugged. "It's a dirty job, but somebody's got to do it."

He leaned across the table and put his face right up to mine. "Are you telling me we're not doing our jobs?" he demanded. "You two think you can police this town better than us? Just you two?"

"We're not two people," my father said. "More like one and a half."

Gomez practically growled, "Is that supposed to be a joke?"

"Yes," my father said. "Get it? I'm not up to full speed yet with my new hip."

Gomez shook his head in slow motion. "So this is how it's going to be." He made a tsk-tsk sound. "Always gotta be the hard way."

"But we didn't do anything wrong," I said. "We stopped in to check on Mr. Barber, found that he was deceased, and called you guys."

Gomez kept his face uncomfortably close to mine. "And how long were you two chucklemonkeys snooping around inside the Barber residence?"

"Just a few minutes," I said.

"Aha!" He jerked upright and puffed out his chest. "So, you *were* snooping around. What were you doing? Planting evidence?"

"No way." I held my hands up. "And we weren't snooping."

"You didn't plant evidence?"

"No, sir," I said.

My father tented his fingers on the table. "You forgot to ask if she removed or hid evidence. If it was something large, she could have relocated it until she could come back later."

I shot my father a look. "Are you *actually* mentoring our interrogator?"

He answered, "You know how much I care about this town."

"I didn't plant evidence," I said to Officer Gomez tersely. "I didn't remove evidence or hide evidence, and I didn't snoop around, but someone else did." I pointed to my father. "He used the washroom. Maybe you should put your moustache over there, in his face."

Gomez leaned back in his seat and moved his head in slow motion again, this time nodding.

"I think we're done for now," Gomez said.

"Good," I said, pushing my chair back.

"Not so fast," Gomez said. "Where do you think you're going?"

"Aren't we done?"

A smile slowly spread across his mouth. "You've got to stay for pizza."

"Pizza?" I asked. "Since when is pizza part of the interview?"

"Captain Milano ordered it already," Gomez said. "This whole case is as good as done. *Case closed*, as they say." He mimed spinning a noisemaker. "Whee!"

"You're celebrating?" I asked. "Now?"

"Sure. We'll be busy the rest of the day processing the scene and doing all the paperwork, but Milano doesn't hold back on the celebrations. He says it's good for morale." He got up from his chair and headed toward the door, signaling us to wait. "I gotta make sure they ordered enough pizza for everyone."

As soon as he was out of the room, I turned to my father.

"They're celebrating," I said, mystified. "Another man is dead, and they're ordering pizza."

"The new body changes everything," my father said. "The evidence tells us the handyman was responsible for the death of Dieter Koenig."

"You think? Wanna run the story past me?"

"Through either negligence or malice, Tim Barber caused the death of Dieter Koenig," my father said evenly. "But then he couldn't handle the guilt. He tried to confess to the police, but it was taking too long, and he kept feeling worse and worse. The anxiety spiraled out of control. So he took his guilt and his admission to a higher court."

I finished for him, "To stand before the only judge who matters in the end."

"By killing himself, Barber saved taxpayers the cost of a trial. Everything wraps up, neat and tidy."

I looked up at the camera in the corner of the room. "A little too neat and tidy," I said to the camera. "Which is why this case can't be closed. Not yet."

The camera's red light didn't show any sign of listening.

"We'll see," he said.

"Do you actually think this case is closed? Just like that?"

"What I think doesn't matter. Now's the time for the crime scene techs to do their jobs. We have to let the police do what they do."

"But they think they're done. They won't investigate further."

He chuckled. "They're not a hive mind. They don't all share one brain. In fact, it's often the very act of one officer declaring a case closed that pushes the others into cracking it open. Sometimes pressure brings out the best in people."

"You're so calm about this." I shook my head.

"Stop thinking about the case for a few minutes," he said. "You can't always think about everything directly. Think about pizza."

"Now I'm thinking about pizza. Would it be wrong to eat pizza right after what we just saw? It seems disrespectful of the dead."

"The dead don't need to eat," he said. "They don't need much, except justice."

"Justice," I repeated.

"Pizza first, then justice."

My stomach made a noise. It was two o'clock, and not only had we missed out on getting Jessica's apple turnovers warm from the oven, but we'd missed lunch entirely. After what I'd seen at the Barber residence, I assumed I'd never have an appetite ever again, but the mention of pizza was returning me to normal.

"Sure, Dad. We can stay for pizza." I crossed my arms and tried to relax. "So, was Gomez being hard on me because he wanted to impress me? Or you?"

"I was somewhat impressed." He stared at the empty doorway. "Listen, the poor guy's been going through a divorce for the past year, and that's the sort of thing that makes a person feel useless, so we'll have to let him know he's doing okay."

"I'm not going to pay him a compliment for making me feel uncomfortable." I shuddered and rubbed my upper arms. "I'm going to take a long, hot bath as soon as I get home."

"Stormy, you're not really a bath person."

"No, but it seems like the sort of thing you do after a day like today." I leaned over the table, closed my eyes, and rubbed my temples. "How long does it take for the image to wash out of your brain?"

He patted my shoulder. "Sorry, sweetie. If you've got a good memory, that picture is yours forever. The only thing you can do is fill your mental photo album with other things, happier things."

Just then, I heard the rustling of someone coming in the door.

"Pizza's here," Gomez said. "Come on out to the lunch room. I hope you both like pepperoni."

CHAPTER 33

NOT ONLY DID my appetite come back for pizza, but I was hungry again at eight o'clock, when Jessica pulled a steaming tray of something delicious from the oven.

As the smell of sweet and spicy cornbread hit my nose, I opened my eyes and yawned. I'd been napping on the couch, where I'd temporarily taken over Jessica's nest of blankets. After my father dropped me off on his way home from the police station, I'd meant to run myself a hot bath, but what I really needed was a nap. Ever since the previous Christmas, when someone tried to drug me and drown me in a tub, I'd been leery of napping in water. My fears had only grown a few months later, when an acquaintance suffered a watery demise.

My couch, however, had never tried to murder anyone, so that was where I'd spent the afternoon following the discovery of Tim Barber's body.

"Jessica, you actually made chili and cornbread, too? Marry me!"

She snorted at my proposal, as usual. "The chili is vegetarian this time," she said. "I've been eating too much meat lately, so I got out my vegetarian cookbooks. This looked like a good recipe. There's a chunk of dark chocolate in it, plus chipotle peppers, so it's smokey and earthy."

"That does sound good."

"It'll be more filling served with the cornbread." She lifted the lid on the slow cooker and sniffed the fragrant steam. "Want yours served there on the couch?"

I moaned as I struggled with the blankets. "I'd help you set the table, but Jeffrey has me pinned down." He was sprawled on my chest, his front paws extended on either side of my neck.

Jessica let out the chirp-whistle she used in place of the traditional "here, kitty, kitty," and Jeffrey broke the sound barrier exiting our cozy couch nest.

I got up, stretched, and started setting the table for two.

"Logan's coming," she said. "He came by to check on you an hour ago. Don't worry, I rolled you over so you weren't snoring."

I snorted. "As if," I said. "I don't snore."

She handed me three squares of paper towel to fold as napkins. "The snoring I heard must have been Jeffrey," she said.

Our discussion of snoring was cut short by the arrival of Logan. He kicked off his shoes and made a beeline for me. He hugged me tightly and wouldn't let me go. Jessica knew all about my adventures that day and must have filled him in on everything.

"I'm okay," I said. "It wasn't so bad, and Dad was there with me."

"Promise me you'll be more careful from now on." He squeezed me tighter. "No more car chases or dead bodies."

"Can't breathe," I gasped, trapped by his python arms. "Let the hostage go and you get a glass of wine."

He used the top of my head as a chin rest. "What kind of wine?"

I bent my knees, dropped down, and slipped away.

"The house special," I said, "Cardbordeaux."

He gave me a skeptical look. "I don't know that vintage."

"Turn away and don't look, or you'll ruin it."

He turned to pick up Jeffrey for some whisker-on-whisker time. While he wasn't looking, I opened the cupboard and filled three glasses with Cardbordeaux, which was what we called the boxed wine in the vacuum-sealed bag.

Jessica and I finished getting everything ready for dinner while Logan showered the cat with affection.

I mentally noted that he'd forgiven Jeffrey for indiscriminately allowing himself to be snuggled by Tony. I was glad that Logan wasn't the type to hold a grudge.

"Who's the Heavyweight Champion?" he asked the cat repeatedly. "Is it you, Mr. Man? Are you the champ?"

He'd been calling Jeffrey the Heavyweight Champion for a few months. It all started with him calling the gray cat *Jefe*, pronounced *heffey*, which he mistakenly believed was Spanish for Jeff, but turned out to actually mean *chief* or *boss*. After a few weeks of calling him Jefe, it evolved into Heavy. The cat had put on about half a pound over the winter, and wasn't overweight but did appear suitably embarrassed at being called Heavy or Heavybuns or, occasionally, Hefty Bag. One day, the cat had walked across Logan's face with his full weight, and Logan reported that it felt like being punched. Thus was born the nickname of Heavyweight Champion.

"Ding, ding," Jessica said, which was her way of ringing the proverbial dinner bell, and we all took our usual seats and dug in.

The vegetarian chili was delicious, as was the cornbread, which was dotted with hot jalapeno peppers. Logan made a fuss about needing more sour cream and getting his face burned off, and we teased him about being wimpy about spicy foods. It was just the usual teasing we did over dinner, but Logan got quiet and didn't tease us back. One corner of the cornbread was blackened, and he didn't say a word to Jessica about her tendency to burn at least one portion of whatever she baked. He liked calling her Pyrocook, but, strangely enough, he didn't use the term once during dinner.

When it came time for dessert and eating the flaky apple turnovers from that morning, he excused himself, saying he had to make a few calls and get to bed early.

"No dessert?" Jessica and I asked in unison.

He patted his stomach on his way to the dishwasher. "I don't know how you girls can eat the way you do and not gain an ounce."

"We go jogging," Jessica told him.

"I know all about your jogging," he said. "You jog to the bakery to get croissants."

She gave him a perplexed look. "Why else would someone jog?"

He patted her on the head on his way back from the dishwasher. "Thanks for the amazing dinner." He walked around and gave me a similarly platonic head pat. "And you be more cautious from now on. If a house smells like a dead body, don't go inside."

"Wise words," I said.

Logan grabbed the Heavyweight Champion from his perch on the cat tree and gave him another whisker rub before leaving.

Alone, Jessica and I looked at each other.

"That was weird," she said. "You two didn't talk about case work at all during dinner. I thought that meant today was a personal day."

"Me, too. If I'd known I wasn't going to get any boyfriend time, I would have talked about the case over dinner."

"Then I would have stabbed you with a fork to make you shut up about dead bodies while I'm eating."

"Sorry about that in general," I said. "I was good tonight, but I know I drive you crazy sometimes."

She got up and grabbed the apple turnovers. We debated warming them up and having them with ice cream. The debate lasted about two seconds.

We ate our warm turnovers and ice cream on the sofa, in front of the TV. With all the excitement of the last four days, it felt good to do something so normal.

"Extra jogging tomorrow," Jessica said as she grabbed us each a second helping.

"*So much* jogging," I agreed. "And one block of lunges."

"Totally worth it."

At eleven o'clock, Jeffrey's internal alarm clock went off and he began his *parkour* routine, using every piece of living room furniture as either an obstacle to scale, jump over, or land on. It was Kitty Playtime Hour.

Jessica whipped his rainbow snake around for a bit then wandered off to get ready for bed.

"Bathroom's free," she called out on her way to her bedroom.

I clicked off the living room lights and glanced out at the lawn. I couldn't see directly into Logan's place from the front window, but I could tell by the glow on the lawn if his lights were on, and they were. He was still up.

I grabbed the two turnovers we'd saved for him, slipped on the flip-flops I used for taking out the garbage, and headed for the door. I was careful to not let Jeffrey out. He did plenty of patrolling in the daytime hours and didn't need to be out at night, making me wake up worried every time I heard something howl or bark.

The summer-night air was only slightly cooler than the inside of the house. I could feel heat radiating from the stucco exterior wall as I pulled the door shut behind me. Above, the moon glowed warmly. All was peaceful. I gazed at the night sky and tried to make the scene before me into a crisp mental picture sit in front of other images, like a new photo added to the collection on a corkboard.

I walked over to Logan's side, my flip-flops making their slap-slap sounds on the walkway.

I knocked on the door. There was no answer, so I knocked again, louder. After nearly a minute, a groggy-looking Logan opened it. He wore a pair of elastic-waisted lounging pants and no shirt.

"Pastry delivery," I said as I came inside. "You can run, but you can't hide from the apple turnovers. These ones have your name on them. Well, technically, they just have the letter L, but that's practically the same thing."

"Thank you." He gave the pastries a weak smile before putting them in his fridge.

"Sorry I woke you. I saw that the light was on, so I assumed you were awake."

"I was so tired, I forgot to switch everything off." He stretched and rubbed his stomach. The scar on his abdomen reddened under his fingers.

"Now I feel extra bad about waking you up." I turned to leave. "I'll get out of your hair."

He caught my hand and pulled me to him, almost as though we were dancing. I curled into his embrace.

I said, "You're pretty good at this for somebody who doesn't know how to dance."

He gave me a devilish look. "Who said I don't know how? Just because someone chooses not to do something doesn't mean they're inept."

I shook my head. "You are such a tease."

"What is it about girls and dancing?" His voice sounded strangely lyrical, as if he was singing or dreaming.

"If you don't already know why girls are obsessed with dancing, I'm not going to tell you." I kissed him on the side of his cheek, just above the edge of his beard. "If you need sleep, let's get you back to bed. I'll tuck you in and turn off all the lights."

He stepped back from me, which only hurt my feelings slightly less than if he'd physically pushed me away. "Thanks, but I really am tired," he said.

I snapped back, "Way to make a girl feel wanted."

"Stormy, I don't have the energy right now for this."

I bit my lip before I said something else I'd regret, and I headed for the door.

"Sleep tight," I said with forced sweetness. "Maybe I'll see you tomorrow morning for coffee."

"Maybe," he said, which wasn't the reassurance I'd been hoping for.

I kept my back to him as I let myself out.

CHAPTER 34

Since returning to Misty Falls, I had been sleeping well and forgotten what insomnia was like, but that Wednesday night, I had my first sleepless night in ages.

On Thursday morning, I made some unkind remarks toward my alarm clock—the electronic one, not the one who came in to lick my eyebrows after I'd hit the snooze button three times.

I finally got up, showered, and got dressed for the day. I told myself the rough night was due to the afternoon nap the day before, and not because of Logan's cool treatment or the Barber Residence crime scene images featured on the corkboard of my mind.

In the kitchen, I found the coffeemaker ready to go with a button press. There was a note from Jessica: *You looked tired, so I went jogging without you. I won't be back for a while. I'm going to jog twice as far to burn up some of your calories for you. You're welcome! P.S. I fed the beast his wet food, so don't believe his stories.*

I pressed the button for the coffee and checked messages on my phone. Jeffrey pranced around the kitchen meowing, pretending he hadn't been fed, despite the evidence of half a serving of his food still visible on his plate. After a few minutes of his noisemaking, I picked up the plate, hid it from sight for ten seconds, and set it back down on the floor. He dove into the food immediately.

Someone knocked on the front door. It was Logan, dressed for work in a stylish gray suit accented with a burgundy tie.

I called to the cat, "Jeffrey, your lawyer is here. Finally, you can negotiate yourself some better working conditions."

Logan caught me off-guard with a kiss that was surprisingly passionate for so early in the morning, pre-caffeine.

"Hey, gorgeous," he said huskily. "You look well-rested for someone who was running through my dreams all night."

I rolled my eyes and waved him in. "Want some scrambled eggs?" I asked, even though I knew he'd already eaten, because he never put on his tie until he'd finished his breakfast.

"I'm already taken care of," he said, smiling. "The refrigerator fairy came by last night and left me two apple turnovers. That was very sweet of you, by the way. I wish you would have woken me up so I could thank you properly."

"What?"

He glanced at the coffee pot as it gurgled to completion. "I wouldn't mind half a cup of that."

"Um, sure." I got two mugs and started pouring. Was he joking about not remembering talking to me the night before? I glanced back to check his face for signs he was pulling my leg. He was focused on his phone, scrolling through what looked like email messages. Unless I'd met Logan's evil twin from a parallel universe the night before, he must have been tired and basically sleepwalking when I stopped in.

I joined him at the table, and for the next twenty minutes, we went through our regular weekday morning routine of sipping coffee, both of us reading news, blogs, and emails, and looking up to talk about new books or movies we were interested in. We had trained ourselves to not talk about business over coffee unless it was absolutely necessary.

"About that refrigerator fairy," I said.

"Mmm?" He didn't look up from his screen.

"Never mind." I tried to let go of how I was feeling. For the next five minutes, I told myself that all he'd done was pull away from me at a time when he was so exhausted he wouldn't even remember it the next morning. But every time I looked at his face, I clenched my fists. I couldn't stop feeling hurt. My heart didn't share my brain's rational thoughts. I'd felt this way before, following a bad dream in which someone did something awful. The memory would fade, but not the hurt.

"Did something happen?" he asked. "Did you get a bad phone call this morning? You seem a bit off. Is that bruised arm bugging you?"

"I'll be fine," I said. "What's next with the case? Who do you want me to talk to next?"

"I've got everything under control." He slipped his phone into his pocket and tipped back the last sip of his coffee. "You're done with the Koenig Estate stuff. Do up an invoice for your time and send it to Corine any time."

"You're firing me? There's no way this thing is over yet."

He looked surprised by my reaction. "Stormy, the police are the ones investigating criminal matters. We aren't the police."

"Then why did you have me interview Erica Garcia in the first place?"

"To find out if anyone at the house knew about the wedding or the new will." He used his knuckles to rap on the wooden table. "So far, so good. If the sons knew something was up, they would have started removing valuables from the house by now, and it sounds as though they haven't."

"When do the boys find out about their new stepmother?"

"At the reading of the will, which is happening in three days."

"You're doing an honest-to-goodness reading? With everyone in the room when you drop the bombshell?"

He grinned, apparently looking forward to the drama. "It's not just the most fun way to do it, but also the most practical. Immediately following the reading, Della's going to lock down the property and contents. The sons will be supervised while they pack up their personal effects."

"She's kicking them out on the street? Out of the family home?"

"It's the only way to keep them from plundering the estate."

"Wait a minute. Did he will the house and contents to her?"

"No," Logan answered.

"Phew. That would be too much. No offense to your client, but they were barely married a month."

He shrugged, a playful twist to his lips.

I gave him a squinty look. "What are you not telling me?"

"She's not getting the house. She's getting everything. *Every. Last. Thing.*"

I exhaled a few choice words. "House, contents, cash, investments, everything?"

"Everything."

I was glad to be sitting, so my legs couldn't buckle under this five-ton revelation.

"She just inherited a room full of ancient weaponry," I said.

"And a mansion with a pool."

"How about the jet?" I asked.

"It's Della's plane now. She'll be flying Air Della."

I snorted. "Air Della."

"That's why we're making the announcement at the reading," he said. "Besides the big stuff, like the plane, there's a fortune in the war room collection of artifacts, and that's just the start of it. Mr. Koenig's late wife collected paintings, and some of those funny-looking squiggles are worth tens of thousands of dollars each."

"And Brandon and Drake get nothing," I said in disbelief. "They're not going to be happy."

"I wouldn't expect them to be."

"And they're getting evicted?"

"Immediately."

I sighed. "But it's their home."

"Brandon and Drake are both in their forties," he said. "It's about time the baby birds left the nest."

"I guess."

He glanced over at the living room, where Jeffrey was sunning himself on the sofa. "Since you're so sympathetic, why don't you come along to the reading of the will and offer them a couch to bunk on for a few nights?"

"Very funny," I said dryly. "But I may take you up on that offer to come to the reading. Do you have security in case things go wrong? I could bring Dad and his cane sword."

Logan sat back and winced as his hand went to his stomach.

"Sorry," I said quickly. "Sometimes I forget about what happened." And I did forget, until I saw the scar or watched him react to the memory. The last time we'd set up a dramatic conflict, Logan found himself on the pointy end of the cane sword when a dangerous killer took it from my father. I'd tried to turn my guilt into something useful, to remind myself that my actions had consequences for the people I loved.

He got up from the chair and glanced at the clock on the stove. "I should get going anyway."

"How are things going with the witness from Seattle?"

"Good and done," he said. "She's already gone home, along with the other witness from the hotel. So that's the end of Saundra, unless she gets that job offer to work at Glorious Gifts—the job your father said he might be able to hook her up with."

"That's Finnegan Day. Always trying to be helpful." I walked over to the door to say good-bye. "Hey, why didn't you have me track down the marriage witnesses?"

He got a twitchy look. "Remember, we needed to keep the whole thing quiet."

"What are you saying? I can keep things quiet."

"You're too popular," he said. "If you left here to go investigate in Seattle, it might have tipped people off. The sons knew Dieter took Della there for a trip recently. Maybe I'm paranoid." He gave me a sweet look. "Or maybe I'd just miss you too much if you left town for even a day."

"A likely story." I shooed him out the door. "Go to work, lawyer. Do all the lawyering."

"And you relax," he said. "Forget about Koenig things. It's all over."

"It's all over," I repeated, nodding, though I didn't believe it for a second.

He kissed me good-bye. "See you tonight," he said, and he was gone.

I closed the door and sat on the sofa next to Jeffrey. He had one hind paw in the air while he groomed his tummy. I couldn't pass up the opportunity to give him a tiny high five. He gave me the you're-an-idiot look, as usual.

I grabbed my laptop and caught up on some non-Koenig investigation work. After I finished typing up a report for an insurance agency, I called Glorious Gifts to check on everything. Brianna had just arrived and was getting ready to open the store for the day.

"Boss, people are lurking outside like zombies," she said.

"That settles it. If there's a zombie apocalypse happening today, I'm definitely staying home."

"They're not really zombies, but they are a bit... ghoulish, I suppose. That little goth teenager is out there licking a giant rainbow lollipop."

"She's so weird," I said. "What do the zombies want?"

"They want to see the girl who keeps turning up dead bodies. Word on the street is you found another one yesterday. Suicide, I heard. Anyway, maybe you should lie low for a while. Either that or come in and put on a big sale so we make lots of money. When life craps on you, make prune juice."

"Brianna, that's not the saying."

"I'm an original," she said. "Is it true? You found another one?"

I sighed. "You make me sound like a very dangerous collector, but yes, it's true. Apparently, it was a suicide. Very sad."

"You need to do more things that are interesting and also appropriate for my webcomic."

I told her, for the umpteenth time, to leave me out of her webcomic. She promised to do her best while keeping the retail zombies at bay, and she went to open the store.

After that phone call, I paced the room for a bit. There were a few tasks left in my inbox, but I didn't want to sit down, let alone spend the rest of the day doing paperwork.

I put in a call to Officer Kyle Dempsey.

He answered, "Stormy Day! Thank God it's you. Are you at your house?"

"Yes, I'm at home. Why? Do you want to meet somewhere to talk about... recent events?"

"Sorta. I'm at House of Bean right now. Hang on." The sound muffled, but I could hear him talking to someone. "Chad, what's that new drink on the menu all about?"

Chad, my formerly least-favorite coffee barista who had worked himself up into my good graces, replied, "Do you mean the Stormy Day? It's a latte with vanilla, cinnamon, and a hint of chili pepper."

"Give me two of those," Kyle said. "Mountain sized, and put a goat on it." To me, clearer, he said, "I'll be at your house in ten minutes."

"Do I even *want* to know what 'put a goat on it' means?"

"You'll find out," he said cheerfully.

CHAPTER 35

Apparently, "put a goat on it" means add whipped cream. The House of Bean didn't use goat's milk, just regular cow's milk. They came up with the term "put a goat on it" because the swirling pyramid of whipped cream resembled, at least to the coffee shop's manager, an upside-down billy goat's gruff.

Officer Kyle Dempsey sat across my kitchen table from me and sipped his frothy drink from the House of Bean takeout cup.

"You don't like yours?" he asked.

I frowned at the whipped cream, which was dotted with colored sprinkles. "I wouldn't know. I haven't taken a sip yet, as you can tell by my lack of milk moustache. Yours is coming in nicely, by the way."

Kyle turned on his dimples and licked the streak of whipped cream off his upper lip.

"Try your Stormy Day," he said. "And cheer up. Not everyone gets a drink named after them."

"What if I don't like myself? I'm not to everyone's taste." I pushed the cup away. "It's too much pressure. Plus it looks sweet. I had ice cream last night, and I didn't go jogging today."

"Let me help you out." He chugged the remainder of his beverage and then grabbed my cup and started on mine. "No more pressure. Better now?"

I breathed a dramatic sigh of relief and got myself a fresh cup of regular coffee.

"Do you have the day off?" I asked. He wasn't in uniform and looked ready for a day at the lake in a light-blue golf shirt that matched his bright eyes. He wore stylish jeans and a pair of leather sandals that revealed his toes. My eyes kept going to his feet, to the pale-gold hairs that dotted the knuckle of his big toe.

"Maybe I'm working undercover," he said. "This is how I dress for dog shows. I'm working on a very important dog paternity case. The fate of the whole town depends on me tracing the lineage of a litter of chiweenie puppies."

I laughed. "You heard about that?"

"I heard you solved the case. You didn't give up when it got tough. You didn't jump at the easy solution." His dimples disappeared as his expression grew serious.

"You don't think Tim Barber killed Dieter Koenig and then committed suicide out of guilt?"

"Nope, and neither do you." He tilted his head to the side and scratched his neck along the edge of the bandages that extended from his injured shoulder. "The glue on these bandages is really pulling my skin, but the cuts don't hurt at all. Funny how sometimes the cure is worse than the poison."

"What does Tony say?" I added, "About the case, not your bandages."

"He's happy to close the case. I guess he's had a few run-ins with Tim Barber over the years, and they weren't exactly pals. He says Tim was crazier than bugjuice and he probably oiled up the diving board because the voices in his head made him do it."

I ran my fingers through my hair, fluffing up the back as I considered the scenario. "Tim Barber had access to oil up the board, and he would have known Dieter's schedule," I said. "He might have hidden in the hedges surrounding the pool to watch his plot come together. Maybe Sunday morning wasn't even his first attempt. He could have been oiling up the board for weeks, just hoping for a freak accident."

"Then he ran off when you and Sanderson showed up," Kyle said. "The old guy must have been in great shape to outrun your boyfriend. Sanderson looks fit, but it's hard to tell when a guy's wearing a suit. Would you say he's... athletic?" As though competing for some imaginary muscle prize, Kyle flexed his tanned, golden-hair-dotted biceps.

"Tim Barber had a big head start," I said. "He was headed in the direction of the airstrip and just disappeared."

"Rumor is they've got a tunnel back there. It runs between the hangar and an old fallout shelter."

"A fallout shelter?" I blinked in disbelief. "Those rich people have a butler, a swimming pool, *and* a fallout shelter? Not fair."

"Do you want to come with me and check it out? Rumor is the shelter's fully stocked for any disaster."

I sipped my coffee before answering, "Just me, you, a bunker full of canned goods, and a couple of end-of-the-world cots? Kyle, you know I'm already taken. You shouldn't be taking me on romantic dates."

"How about searching for clues?"

"I'll bring my magnifying glass."

"What?"

"It just seemed like the thing to say when a person agrees to some unofficial sleuthing." I looked down. I had a cat on my lap. I hadn't noticed Jeffrey jumping up, but he looked quite comfortable.

"We'll get to the bottom of this whole thing," Kyle said.

"Did you hear back about the DNA yet? From the baby soother?"

"These things take time," he said.

"Can't you put a rush on it? The results could be really important."

He gave me a look that implied I ought to know better. "Stormy, we don't take people's DNA for kicks and giggles. Almost everything the lab receives is urgent." He glanced around the kitchen and living room, stopping when his gaze landed on my laptop. "Now, are you going to share information with me, or is it all under lock and key?"

"There are a few things I can't divulge yet," I said. "But it's minor stuff, and it'll come out in the next few days." I winced inwardly about lying. Dieter Koenig willing everything to his new bride, plus her kicking the sons out on the street, wasn't exactly minor.

"I'm guessing, by what you're saying, that there will be some revelations at the reading of the will," Kyle said knowingly.

I stared ahead blankly. "Oh?"

He nodded. "Your poker face needs work."

"We're not playing poker."

He put both elbows on the table and leaned forward, studying me intently. "Tim Barber always worked Sundays," he said. "Every Sunday for the last ten years."

"Why are you telling me this? I thought it had already been established that he was there that day, even though he'd booked it off. I saw him myself, running from the pool area."

"On the Sunday that Dieter Koenig died, Tim Barber did have the day off. It's all marked on the staff calendar. He wasn't supposed to be there on Sunday, for the first time in years. Pretty suspicious, don't you think?"

"What did he allegedly have the day off for? Are you saying he wasn't there after all? That he has an alibi?"

"These are all good questions," Kyle said. "Now grab your sleuthing kit and let's be on our way."

CHAPTER 36

"I'm really glad you called me," Kyle said.

"Funny you should say that. I'm just starting to have regrets," I said.

I strapped myself into the passenger seat of Kyle's bright-blue Jeep and looked around me for safety features. If we got ourselves into another high-speed chase, I would need something to cling to or a way to make a hasty exit. The Jeep had a black roll bar as well as a zippered, removable soft top, so I was good either way.

He started the engine, reached for the shifter, and paused. "Stormy, you can drive, if you want. I'd understand if you didn't trust my abilities after what happened Tuesday."

"No, you drive. I'm always the chauffeur when I go sleuthing, and it's nice to be the chauffee. Is that a word?"

"Sure, it is. But it's pronounced *chauffée*, and it means *heated* or *warmed up* in French."

I gave him a look of admiration. "Aren't you Mr. Smartypants?"

"Most of my family's bilingual, French Canadian. We weren't allowed to watch TV when we were growing up, but my mother let me and my brother listen to audiobooks or spoken-word albums. Our relatives in Quebec sent us French-language CDs of just about anything we showed an interest in."

We turned off my street and headed toward the Koenig Estate.

He continued, "Some of my older cousins sent us some pretty crazy stuff. My brother, Julian, got me into this sci-fi series, about the Planet Toadonx. Whoever did the French translation on the audiobooks sounded like he was trying not to laugh half the time. There was some seriously messed-up stuff, like people getting it on with space vixens and tentacle monsters."

Laughing, I said, "It's a good thing your parents didn't have a TV, then. Who knows how you might have turned out if you'd been exposed to syndicated sitcoms and *The Price Is Right*."

"I should re-read that sci-fi series," he said. "Benjamin Biggs is always talking about it. I won't go crazy like he did, though. I'd never try to recreate the toxins from the book. Mainly because I don't know the first thing about chemistry."

"You're still in contact with Benji? Did you guys become pen pals after everything that happened at the Flying Squirrel?"

"Haven't you heard? Benji's moved back to town. His aunt and uncle let him set up a games room at their gas station."

"No way," I said.

"*Yes way.* You can go in and buy Magic the Gathering cards from Benji, at his special counter. He'll buy and sell rares for a fair price, and just when you think you've got a good deck, he'll play against you and bring on a world of hurt."

"I had no idea," I said.

"Yeah, he just moved back a few weeks ago."

"No, I mean I had no idea Kyle Dempsey was a giant ultra-nerd."

He snorted. "We prefer the term *geek*. And geeks are the new chic, don't you know? All the big blockbuster movies these days are about superheroes."

"So, you geeks are the ones to blame for the lack of good romantic comedies?"

He turned his head away from the road and grinned at me. "Stormy, you don't need those movies. Your whole life is a romantic comedy."

"More like a *dramedy*. That's drama plus comedy."

He kept grinning. "You're still a superhero to me."

I pointed at the Jeep's flat windshield. "Keep your eyes on the road, geek. Let's not turn this dramedy into a tragedy."

* * *

We got to the Koenig Mansion and rang the doorbell. Kyle had spoken with Erica Garcia earlier that morning, so she was expecting us. Instead of her usual gray maid outfit, she was wearing black.

"I'm so sorry about Tim," I said.

She hugged me, trembling as she suppressed a sob. "Thank you, Miss Day," she said, her accent thick. "Tim had his troubles, but he was a very sweet man. He didn't hurt Mr. Koenig. I know what people are saying, what they are thinking, and it can't be true."

I patted her back. "I believe you," I said.

"He was confused," she said. "He only shot himself because he must have believed something that wasn't true."

I caught Kyle's eye over the maid's shoulder. He nodded to let me know he'd heard. Erica believed Tim Barber shot himself, but not that he had anything to do with Mr. Koenig's death.

"Tim was so sweet, so kind, so funny," she said. "And he loved the family. He was like an uncle to the boys. They are both very sad today. We are all so sad."

"And we're very sorry to intrude during this time of grief," I said.

Kyle added, "But we are here to help."

Erica pulled away from me, tears in her eyes. "And you will help. You will fix everything so that the spirits may rest."

I nodded. "We'll do our best."

Erica clutched the medallion at her neck. "Bless you," she said and led us through the home toward the courtyard. I didn't hear a single noise except for birds chirping.

"It feels like we're the only ones around for miles," I commented.

"Almost," she said. "Things are very quiet today. Verity is taking a day to grieve in private."

"What about the butler?" I asked. "Randy?"

"We're supposed to call him Randall," Erica said. "But we never do. We always call him Randy. He is not here right now because he's driving the boys around today. They had some errands, I think."

"The boys?" I asked. "You mean Drake and Brandon?"

"Yes. It's what we always call them, even though they are grown men." She pushed open two glass-paned doors and led us out to the pool area. "And now it is time for the boys to grow up. Things will be changing around here."

More than you know, I thought.

I asked, "Erica, does Randy always drive for Brandon and Drake?"

"Only when it's both of them going out together somewhere." Her tears had dried, and a tiny smile appeared on her lips. "Those two fight so much, one won't be in the car if the other one is driving."

I shot Kyle a look. If Randall had been driving one Koenig brother on Tuesday, chances were he had a matching set.

Kyle asked, "Was Randy driving the boys around on Tuesday afternoon?"

"Probably," she said. "They weren't around the house." Her eyes went to the bandages visible above the collar of his shirt. "Officer Dempsey, are you okay? Did you get hurt?"

"You didn't hear about my little mishap?"

Erica shook her head. "I haven't talked to people that much. Too many questions. I just want to be alone."

Kyle walked over to the pool. It had been emptied of water and looked perilously, dangerously deep.

"That looks scary," Kyle said as he approached the rim and looked down. "I hope you'll be filling this with water again soon, and not just because we're running out of good swimming weather."

"Randy is cleaning the pool," Erica said. "You know what's funny? We have all these fancy filters and machines to clean the water, and they work really good. By Monday morning, you would never know that somebody died in there the day before, with all that blood everywhere. It looked clean in the morning. Like it never happened."

I shuddered as the image of Randy, Verity, and Erica trying to resuscitate Dieter Koenig flashed in my mind.

Erica continued, "But Randy said we have to clean the pool better." She sniffed and touched the edge of her eye with her knuckle. Her tears weren't dried up after all. "Randy loved Mr. Koenig. We all did." She stood at the edge of the pool and started to sob.

Kyle reached out and pulled her back. She hurled herself into his arms and buried her face in his chest. He didn't exactly hug her so much as he held still and moved his arms so she could support herself with them.

Though her voice was muffled, I heard her saying she wasn't ready for work, yet she couldn't stay home and upset her son, either. Kyle spoke soothingly and with kindness.

After a few minutes, he got her to smile by saying, "Ms. Garcia, when I told you to get the pool filled up again, I didn't mean with your tears."

* * *

Once she'd dried her tears again, Erica asked us what we wanted to see next.

"The bunker," Kyle said.

"What bunker?" She blinked a few times. "Do you mean the hidey-hole?"

"If that's what you call it, sure."

"Why would you want to go down there?" She looked genuinely confused. "Nothing is down there, and it's so dark and spooky."

"Humor me," he said. "Please?"

She smiled slowly. "Since you asked so nicely, how can I say no?" We backtracked to go around the hedge and headed away from the house. Erica muttered to herself about spooky tunnels and the perils of being too curious.

"It's through here," she said, leading us into the groundskeeping shed that had been used by Tim Barber. The modest wood outbuilding held a workbench, tools, gardening supplies, two lawnmowers, and, hidden under an old rug, one trapdoor that led to a tunnel.

"I don't go down there," Erica said, shaking her head. "Down there are the things with too many legs." She kept shaking her head. "And the darkness that watches you, with all its eyes."

Kyle said, "You're really selling us on this bunker."

She pulled a key from her pocket and handed it to Kyle. "Here, you'll need this to get through the doors."

"You're not coming with us?" he asked.

She shook her head vigorously. "I have to go back to the house. Will you close up everything when you're done?"

We promised her we would, and she left us to the trapdoor and dark tunnel.

Kyle started to pull open the trapdoor, but I told him to wait. "Let's look around this shed a bit more," I said. "This was basically Tim Barber's office, so it should tell us more about the guy."

He agreed, and we started poking around. I was excited to tell Logan that he'd been right about Tim disappearing on him during the chase. He'd not vanished into thin air, but it must have appeared that way when he ducked into the shed and disappeared down into the tunnel.

"Look at this," Kyle said, nodding for me to come look at a note taped to a lawnmower. It was a tiny scrap of paper with a handwritten note describing the mix ratio for the machine's fuel.

"Looks like a normal fuel mix note to me," I said.

"But the note's so tiny, you can hardly see it," he said.

As we continued the search of the shed, we found a dozen other similar notes, all equally small and affixed to equipment and supplies with tape.

I commented, "It's like Tim never heard of a Post-It note."

"Waste not, want not." Kyle held up a cardboard tray that contained Tim Barber's paper supplies—a stack of old memos and junk mail flyers on every color of paper. The top sheet had a neatly torn rectangle missing. "What do we see here?" he asked.

"It's more about what we don't see," I said.

"Exactly. I don't see any of that crisp white paper that he allegedly used to write his good-bye note. If people are anything in life, it's consistent. I don't mean to make light of a man's death, but I'd believe that whole suicide scene more if he'd scrawled his final words on the back of a pizza flyer."

"Get pictures," I said. He was already taking photos for the file.

We finished searching the shed and crouched over the trapdoor leading to the tunnel.

Kyle used the key to unlock the trapdoor and pulled it open.

"Ladies first," he said graciously. "Unless you're afraid of the dark and want me to go first?"

I peered down. "No rats or snakes," I said. "I should be fine." I took my first steps on the metal rungs.

He called down, "Unless there's something bigger down there and it's what ate the rats and snakes."

"You're a real fun date, Kyle," I said flatly.

I climbed down the rungs until I reached the bottom. The tunnel had been constructed with aluminum culverts, so it was completely round inside, except for the flooring, which was a patchwork of wooden building materials. From where we stood, the tunnel was so long, I couldn't see the end of it, just darkness. It was lit—barely—by a string of small bulbs that were controlled by a switch on the wall.

Kyle flicked the switch off to test if it controlled all the lights. It did. In the darkness, all the crawly things made scratchy sounds.

"This is so cool," Kyle said.

"I wish I shared your enthusiasm for tunnels. Hey, since you don't have your duty belt, I'm guessing you don't have a flashlight, do you?"

He flicked the switch back on. "Don't need it," he said with a laugh that echoed eerily.

We set off, walking slowly. The tunnel ran in a straight line, with one branch at the halfway point. We turned right at the branch and walked in the murky near-blackness until we reached a metal door. Kyle used the key, and the door opened with a rusty squeak straight out of a horror movie.

He called out, "Hello? Anyone in here?"

No answer.

We entered the bunker, which wasn't nearly as rustic as the tunnel. The walls were square and painted a cozy tan, and the space contained simple, comfortable-looking furniture. It was practically a penthouse apartment, compared to the entry tunnel.

"Nice pad," Kyle said. "This is better than the apartment I rented when I did my training."

"I think the furniture is from IKEA," I said. "I recognize that chair from the new IKEA catalog."

"They really do make attractive, reasonably priced furniture for small spaces."

I snickered. "They should feature more bunkers in their advertising."

"What did Erica call this place? The brink?"

"The hidey-hole," I said.

"Sounds dirty."

I snickered as I looked around the space. Something odd caught my eye.

"Kyle, if we're underground, why are there curtains over there? It can't be a window." A funny thought came to me. "Do you think it's an ant farm?"

He opened the curtains. We both laughed self-consciously. It was an enormous flat-screen television on the wall.

Kyle whistled at the TV and said, "That's it. I'm moving into this hidey-hole to catch up on all the shows I missed when I was growing up."

"You'd be comfortable enough." I went over to the compact kitchen to check out the appliances. The fallout shelter had a bar-style mini fridge, a microwave, and a hotplate. The refrigerator was empty but running with a low hum that was the only sound in the place other than us.

"Someone's been living in here recently," Kyle said.

"Are you saying that because you can smell something?" I sniffed the air. "I smell food. The cupboards and fridge are empty, and the garbage can's been cleared out, but my guess is that happened recently. This place doesn't have a lot of ventilation, so the smell lingers."

"My nose doesn't work as well as yours, so I'm going by the dust pattern on the TV. It's mostly clean, but it looks like someone did a bachelor-style dusting on the screen." He lifted his elbow to demonstrate dusting the screen with his shirt. "See? There are chunks of dust in all the corners."

"Do you think Tim Barber was hanging out down here?"

Kyle nodded. "Pretending to be working but actually putting his feet up with a movie and a beer."

"Well, maybe he was down here and saw something or heard something he wasn't supposed to."

I looked over at the bed. It had been topped with round bolsters so it doubled as a lounging sofa. "Someone might have been using this place as a secret nookie den."

Kyle propped his chin with his hand in a contemplative gesture. "Tell me more about these ideas you have about secret nookie dens."

I rolled my eyes. "Don't make fun of me. It's a valid theory."

"But what does it have to do with Dieter Koenig's death? Or Tim Barber's?"

"I don't know yet, but my gut tells me this is a piece of the puzzle."

"Then we'd better be thorough. Let's do a search grid. I'll start in that corner."

I agreed and started my search at the opposite corner.

We spent close to an hour going over every square foot of the underground shelter, but we found nothing worth putting in an evidence bag. Kyle didn't have a fingerprinting kit with him, but even if he had brought it, the few surfaces that might have been handled were likely to have been touched, over the years, by many staff and family members.

As we locked up behind ourselves, I asked, "Did you ever fingerprint those glass tumblers from the sink in the hangar?"

He gave me a guilty look and scratched the back of his head. "What tumblers?"

I sighed.

"There weren't any," he said. "I did remember what you told me, but when I went back inside the hangar, the sink was empty. One of the maids must have tidied things up."

"I could kick you," I said.

"Prints on the glasses wouldn't have proved anything," he said. "So what if the boys poured themselves a post-flight drink? It didn't mean they were celebrating their murder plans."

I sighed again. "Let's have a look at the hangar again. I barely saw it last Sunday."

"Of course," he said with an enthusiastic swing of his arm. "The hangar is up next on our subterranean tour."

We proceeded along the tunnel to the end, where another ladder led up.

"Next stop, Wonderland," Kyle said, going ahead so he could shoulder the heavy trapdoor.

"I always wanted to visit a magical world," I said.

"Having your own personal jet plane and hangar is pretty magical. Even the bunker is cool, when you think about it."

"Ah, to be fabulously wealthy," I said.

"You'd get used to it fast, and then what? You'd need more money." His sandals clanged on the metal rung.

"You're right about that. I saw it happen time and time again when I was working in venture capital. Entrepreneurs are happier when they're struggling, when they're looking forward to reaching something. When they actually do hit their goals, they don't know what to do with themselves."

"That's why I'm a cop." He climbed out and reached down to help me. His hands were rougher than I expected.

I asked, "What do you mean? Because as a cop you always have clear goals?"

"Sure. And also, you might get spoiled on wealth, but you never get spoiled helping people. Money is the ruin of people, but not helping others or your community.”

“True,” I said, completely in agreement.

“Even so, I wouldn’t do it for free,” he said with a chuckle. “I have to give credit to monks and people who do.”

I finished climbing out of the tunnel and wiped my hands on my jeans.

We stood still for a moment to get our bearings in the dark hangar. It had just a few tiny windows, and with the doors closed and only safety lights on, it was darker than the tunnel we’d come from. Kyle closed the trapdoor so we didn’t have any comical leg-breaking accidents.

The jet was parked inside, and we couldn’t resist checking it out. Together, Kyle and I rolled a ramp over to the aircraft’s door and ran up the steps like a couple of kids on a field trip. The door was unlocked. Pulling it open triggered the interior lights. We walked inside, making *ooh* and *aah* sounds as we tried the comfortable leather seats and looked around. I settled in, picked up a magazine, and promptly forgot why we were there. Kyle practically had to pry me out of the comfy seat.

We closed the plane, returned the rolling ramp, and finished our search of the hangar.

“Getting any ideas?” Kyle asked. “Don’t say you aren’t, because I know you are. Suddenly, you’re awfully quiet.”

“Is it that obvious?” I started grinning and couldn’t stop.

"Your father is the same way when he's got something solved in his head and he's waiting for me to catch up."

"Yup," I said.

"You've got it all figured out, haven't you?"

I scrunched my lips and shrugged.

"Stormy, don't hold out on me. This whole investigation is a really big deal. If we don't have a good idea and soon, Milano's closing the case."

"I know, I know. Just give me a few minutes to put my thoughts in order."

Sighing, he walked toward the exterior door.

"Not that way," I said. "Instead of making the return trip above-ground, I want to go through the tunnel again."

"Really?"

"Really."

"This had better be good," he said.

"Kyle Dempsey, pull up your socks and get ready to have them blown off."

CHAPTER 37

AFTER LEAVING THE Koenig Estate, Kyle and I went for a long drive in his Jeep to talk things through. We circled the town of Misty Falls at least three times. I told him my half-baked theory, which wasn't exactly bulletproof. Then he told me his half-baked theory, and together we put together a whole new one. Both of us were convinced, but would the evidence back us up? And how would we get proof?

He put in a phone call to the crime lab, begging for the results of the DNA test on the baby soother.

"Claudette's going to call back within an hour," he reported after ending the call.

"I'm dying to know. It's not fair that she gets to find out first."

He smiled. In a radio announcer voice, he said, "Build your own multi-million-dollar lab and get specialized forensic science training, and you, too, can perform your own genetic testing."

"You've got a real corny side, Dimples."

"Um, thanks?"

"Let's head back into town. If we've got an hour to kill before we get the news, I'm going to need a root beer float."

He clicked on the turn signal to make a safe turnaround using a side road. "And nachos," he said. "I know a place that puts bacon bits on the nachos, and you're a fine lady who deserves the best."

Laughing, I said, "How are you still single?"

"It's a mystery," he replied.

* * *

The nachos were as delicious as promised, and we washed them down with root beer floats. Unfortunately, that only killed about thirty minutes, because we gobbled everything down so fast.

The phone call still hadn't come in from Claudette at the crime lab, so we went for a stroll along Broad Avenue.

We popped into the drugstore to buy some gum, where Kyle spotted *royalty* inside, and I don't mean on the cover of the gossip magazines.

He joined me at the magazine display and whispered, "Don't look now, but Countess Octavia is here."

"Does she have the twins here? I need to know if one of them is a girl, because jogging a quarter marathon is bad enough without a fur suit."

He gave me a funny look. "You have all kinds of things going on in that pretty head of yours, don't you?"

"Dad let me watch as much TV as I wanted growing up. My mind is a jungle gym of weirdness."

I turned my head so I could watch the countess in the round security mirror on the wall above the magazine stand. She didn't have any babies with her, nor did she have a shopping basket in her hands. She was here for one thing only, maybe two.

Kyle and I both watched silently as she took a box the size of a toaster off a shelf and brought it to the register. She was dressed in the same Chanel suit I'd first met her in, and she had the top unbuttoned to reveal a mile of milk-inflated cleavage.

As soon as she left, we went to the aisle where she'd been shopping and located the empty spot on the shelf. The drugstore didn't turn over high volume, and so some of the items they carried were stocked in single quantities only.

We didn't need to ask the cashier to tell us what Countess Octavia of Krengerborg had just purchased, because it was written on the price label affixed to the front of the shelf.

Kyle said, "This case just got a lot more complicated."

"I don't know about that," I said. "Sometimes what appears to be a problem is actually the solution."

He glanced around the store. There were three staff members working and two other customers shopping.

"Let's get that gum and talk elsewhere," he said.

We made our purchases and left the drugstore. We spoke in hushed tones as we made our way to Central

Park, where we selected a park bench off the busy path.

Kyle said, "I can't see how this case could possibly get any stranger."

"You're tempting fate," I said.

"I suppose I am." His phone rang. "It's the crime lab," he said.

I shook my fists in excitement. "It's time to play Who's Your Daddy!"

He was too nervous to laugh. He answered the phone while I stopped breathing for a moment.

"Claudette, I promise not to be disappointed," he said into his phone. "Just give it to me straight."

He looked right at me, the way people do when they're talking on the phone about a matter of great importance—as though he could beam the basic details straight into my head via intense eye contact.

"No way," he said. "You're kidding. No, I'm not disappointed." His pale-blue eyes grew wider and his stare even more intense. "You did that on your own? That was some smart thinking. And?" His face locked motionless, as though he'd also stopped breathing in anticipation. "NO WAY!" He jumped up from the bench. "NO WAY!"

"What?" I asked, gasping for breath. "What?"

He talked to Claudette for another minute and then ended the call.

"This might change everything," he said. "You have to promise you won't tell Logan. This is top secret. You can't tell anyone. Promise?"

Without hesitation, I said, "I promise."

And then he told me the results of the DNA testing. My mouth dropped open.

I immediately regretted making the promise.

CHAPTER 38

Logan said, "Before you say one single word, I've got something I need to tell you."

We were standing in the driveway. He'd been parking his truck when Kyle pulled up and let me out of his blue Jeep. Now Kyle was gone, and I was dying to tell Logan everything I'd learned that day, but I'd promised Kyle I wouldn't, so it was just as well he didn't want me to say one single word. I mimed zipping my lips shut and simply smiled.

"You could still say hello," he said with an apologetic grin.

I unzipped my lips. "Hello." I zipped them again.

"Can I interest you in a root beer float?" he asked.

The sugar buzz had worn off from my last one, so I nodded enthusiastically and followed him into his side of the duplex. I perched on one of the leather barstools he had set up next to the kitchen island. I didn't have barstools over on my mirror-image side, because I liked having more room for a bigger table with regular chairs, but every time I sat on his stools I questioned my decision. Just like how I questioned my hasty promise to keep Kyle's police investigation information secret.

Logan pulled two bottles of cold root beer from the fridge and made us a spectacular pair of floats with his own homemade vanilla ice cream. I wasn't saying a word, so I clapped my hands to show my appreciation.

"You're a good sport," he said.

I nodded in agreement.

"And so modest," he added.

I blew him a kiss, which he caught and tucked into his pocket.

"Listen," he said, looking into my eyes as he sat on the stool next to mine. "I came to Misty Falls in search of a different life. Not vastly different, but calmer and quieter. Being with you these last few months, however, has been anything but calm and quiet."

I blinked. He was wearing his bad-news expression and speaking with his bad-news tone.

My excited mood banked hard to the right, drifting over the edge of the road, sliding and grinding, about to crash into the billboard of bad news.

The way he was talking... was he breaking up with me? My ears began to ring so loudly I could barely hear him.

He continued, "Maybe the change I tried to make by moving here wasn't drastic enough. I don't know that I want this life. Do you know what I mean?"

I gave him a sidelong look. What was it, exactly, about his new life in Misty Falls that he didn't want? I kept blinking, my lips still zipped.

"You've been great, Stormy. As a friend, and as a landlady."

My eyebrows rose higher and higher, stretching my face.

"But I need to make more changes," he said.

I held very still, waiting for the ax to fall. Every muscle in my body tensed. I didn't dare let go and fall apart.

He winked at me and patted my shoulder. "You're a good listener," he said, and he turned to his root beer float. "Go ahead and talk now. I just wanted to get that out before you brought up something about work. Today's officially a personal day for us, and whatever work business you've got going on with Kyle, I hope it can wait until after midnight. Or, better yet, tomorrow."

I stammered, "Wha- wha- what changes?"

He turned and gave me a pensive look. "I just told you," he said.

"No, you didn't." I could barely breathe with all the tension in my body.

He frowned. "I'll start taking every second Friday off from the law office."

His words made no sense. "What?"

"Not every Friday. Every second Friday. My weekends will be two days or three days."

My heart was still pounding, and I wasn't sure if I'd heard him right.

"That's it? You're taking off two days a month?"

"You know how lawyers are. Announcing to the firm that I want a four-day work week at my age is like telling the partners I want to come in wearing pajamas and clown shoes."

"Oh. So, you want to take off every second Friday?" I felt dumb repeating the question, but it was all I could do.

"If that's okay with you. I don't want to slow you down at all. You live to work, and I don't want to drag you down. But I thought we could take some three-day mini vacations if we have longer weekends. Would you enjoy that?"

I had to think about it for a moment, since I was still reeling from the awful feeling he was going to dump me.

"Yes," I said. "I *would* enjoy some mini vacations."

"Good. I booked us a room at the Flying Squirrel Lodge."

My jaw dropped open for the second time that day.

He started to laugh. "Kidding! I really got you, didn't I?"

I started to cry. I tried not to cry. I cried harder.

He stopped laughing and slid off the barstool. He stood next to me and stooped forward to look into my eyes. I turned and hid my face. He wrapped his arms around me and hugged me to his chest.

"What's wrong?" He squeezed me and rubbed my back. "You're trembling. You're shaking like a leaf! Talk to me. Tell me what's wrong."

I didn't cry that often, and my tear ducts were making up for lost time. Blubbering, I told him what I'd thought our talk was about and how I'd been so sure he was about to break up with me. Between sad sobs and embarrassed laughter, I let it all out. What came out of my mouth was mostly vowel sounds.

Eventually, I was able to calm down enough to put in some consonant sounds between the vowels and get my message across.

"That's just bananas," he said. "To borrow an expression from Jessica, that's feeding-time-at-the-gorilla-cage bananas. Why would I ever break up with you? Stormy Day, you are smart, funny, kind, and cute as heck. I should be asking you to marry me."

I cried out some more vowel sounds.

He pulled back and got down on one knee. "Do you want to marry me?"

More crying. "Someday," I sobbed.

He grabbed my hand and held it between his. "Do you want me to ask you this question some other time?"

I nodded and pulled him back up to standing.

He hugged me again. "You really surprise me sometimes. You stumble across dead bodies and interrogate killers, but I make a few terrible word choices, and this happens."

"I'm sorry," I said into his chest. "Sorry for being such a mess."

He squeezed me and kissed the top of my head. "Don't ever apologize for caring about me. I love you so much, and knowing you feel the same way... it's such a relief. Moving here and meeting you is the best thing that's ever happened to me."

I circled his back with my arms and held him like I was never going to let go.

CHAPTER 39

AFTER OUR HEART-TO-HEART talk on Thursday night, Logan and I decided to spend a luxurious three-day weekend together. We wouldn't discuss business at all, at least not verbally. We would bend our rules by emailing each other messages about work matters, but only a couple of times.

On Friday, we started with the breakfast special at the Olive Grove and went for a long walk in the park, where we made up funny names for all the dogs playing and rolling around in the grass. We went to the Misty Falls next, where we hiked into the woods and stopped at the lake for a picnic lunch. The late-summer sun felt so good. We rolled out a blanket and napped by the lake's edge. Logan hadn't put on sunscreen, so he got a little red, but just on one side of his face.

Saturday, I took Logan to see more of the local attractions, and in the evening we caught up on some movies we'd been wanting to see.

On Sunday, we drove to Portland with Jessica for a day of shopping. She found some incredible bargains, but the real haul was the indoor climbing tree we found for Jeffrey. It was made from Oregon-coast driftwood plus other natural materials and promised to be more appealing in our living room than the carpeted monstrosity he'd ripped to shreds.

Monday morning, we were refreshed and ready for business, which was good, because it promised to be quite the day. If nobody got slapped, punched, stabbed, or pistol-whipped, we'd consider ourselves lucky.

And if the plan I'd concocted actually worked and we caught a killer, we'd be overjoyed.

Logan wished me luck over morning coffee and left to get ready.

I did some nervous cleaning around the house until it was time to leave for the reading of Dieter Koenig's will. Jessica would be going to work, where she promised to bite her nails and check her phone every thirty seconds for news.

"Not every thirty seconds," I said. "Every five minutes is fine."

"Do you have an ambulance standing by?"

"It shouldn't be that bad," I said. "My father won't be there with his cane sword."

She twirled her tiny red braids into a bigger braid. "Make sure you pat down Della for weapons."

"It won't do any good," I said. "She's a resourceful woman. I bet she could kill someone with a stapler."

"I'm glad I won't be there. It will be easy for you without me fainting at your feet like some wilting flower."

I clenched my jaw. It wouldn't be easy, no matter what.

"You'll have fun," she said. "There's nothing like a big, theatrical reading of the will. It's a shame they don't do it more often."

"There's probably a good reason lawyers don't gather family members into a room together to wage war over the estates of loved ones."

"Too many people getting clubbed with staplers," she said.

"Or chairs. Don't people throw chairs?"

"Jessica, you're not helping."

She hugged me. "You'll be fine."

I hoped so.

These days, people don't gather to hear the wills. It's usually faxed or emailed through lawyers. But Della wanted to let everyone know at once and then have bailiffs accompany the sons back to the mansion so they couldn't clear out the valuables once they got the news.

Also, Lady Octavia would be there, ostensibly as a family friend but secretly as someone who wanted in on the fortune. She would either drop the bombshell about her offspring right there, or she'd wait until later and have her new lawyer contact Logan's office. There were plenty of surprises to go around.

Whatever happened at the reading, it wasn't going to be pretty.

At 9:35 a.m., I got into my car and started driving to the Mesa Office Tower. The family had requested having the reading at the mansion, but Logan insisted they meet at the offices of Tyger & Behr.

I was still early for the meeting when I parked in the underground parkade and walked over to the elevator.

"Wait for me," called a woman's voice. It was more of a command than a request.

Della.

I stepped into the elevator car and resisted the urge to jab the Close Doors button. I held the elevator open until Della strutted in to join me.

She looked the part of a grieving widow... in a heavy-metal music video. Black lace. A dark veil over her face. Red lipstick visible through the veil. Tight dress. Bare legs. Stiletto heels. Thankfully, a tiny clutch purse, barely large enough for her car keys and a tube of red lipstick. Nowhere to hide a weapon.

Automatically, I said, "Hi, Della. How are you?"

"How do you think I am? The love of my life is dead, and now I'm rich. I'm a little mixed up, okay? Am I happy or am I sad? I don't know."

"You could write a song about your feelings," I said.

"Don't be mean. And you don't have to pretend you like me. I know you don't."

"Della..." I had no words other than, "I'm sorry for your loss."

"Thanks," she said sweetly. "Is your finger broken?"

I blinked in surprise. "No. Thanks for asking. I hurt my shoulder a little when Kyle crashed the car we were in, but I'm feeling better."

She rolled her eyes. "I mean, are you going to press the button for Logie's floor?"

Right. *Logie's floor.* I pressed the elevator button, and the doors closed.

"I saw cop cars out front," she said. "Why are they here?"

"For our protection," I answered.

She snorted. "I can protect myself just fine."

"If it comes down to a standoff, promise me you'll keep your hands off other people's guns this time."

She snorted again. "A girl's gotta do what a girl's gotta do." She stared up at the panel that displayed our floor number. "But I still don't understand why the police are here. The family's going to be surprised at the news, but they're classy people. They'll get their lawyers to fight against the will, but they won't be throwing chairs."

"I hope you're right."

She turned and narrowed her eyes at me. "You still think one of them had something to do with my darling Deets's accident?"

"Of course not," I said pleasantly. "Would I walk into a boardroom filled with people who were about to learn that they won't be getting thirty million dollars if I thought one or more of them were capable of murder?"

Della adjusted her black lace veil. "You're talking about that countess woman, aren't you? She'd better not throw me any shade, or I'll test the glue on those blond hair extensions of hers. That European skank."

The elevator dinged and opened on the lobby floor.

Countess Octavia of Krengerborg entered with a man in a suit at her side.

Della looked right at me and said, "Speak of the devil, and she appears." Her upper lip curled, and she practically meowed.

Lady Octavia looked ready to hiss right back. "Miss Day," she said to me, pointedly ignoring Della. "Have you met my attorney? You should give him your card." She turned to him and said, "Miss Day is a brilliant investigator. Very sharp."

The man, who was young and attractive in a bland sort of way, introduced himself, and we exchanged business cards. He looked terrified and sweaty.

"Everything's going to be fine," I said to him.

"If you say so." He clutched the handrail inside the elevator so tightly, his knuckles turned white.

We reached the floor for Tyger & Behr. The elevator doors opened to reveal Officer Kyle Dempsey in uniform. He squinted at Della while moving his right hand to cover the snap closure of his gun holster.

Laughing, Della said to Kyle, "Relax, cutie pie. I'm a good girl now. I've been reformed."

"By what?" he asked.

"You'll see," she teased.

We walked through the carpeted hallway. The door to the law office opened, and Corine, the receptionist, waved at us to hurry. "They're ready and waiting in the boardroom."

"Am I late?" I asked. Everything was happening so fast. I felt like I was on a conveyer belt at an amusement park.

"You're right on time," Corine said. "I guess everyone's excited about the you-know-what." She winked, not-so-subtly.

Beside me, the young lawyer's stomach made a scary rumbling sound. He asked Corine, "Is there a washroom?"

"We have our own, and there's also one behind you," she said.

The lawyer was already scrambling for the men's room off the hallway.

"Look at you three ladies," Corine said. "I know you can't see yourselves, but I can, and you're a real picture, with your nice little figures. And you each have your own exciting fashion look. You could start a girl band, like the Spice Girls, but new, and not British."

The other ladies eyed each other and didn't comment. Lady Octavia stared at Corine's floral-print romper with curiosity as we moved through the office lobby and toward the boardroom.

Corine held back, caught my arm, and whispered, "Sorry about that girl band comment. I'm so weird sometimes, and I blame it on my juice cleanse or my new diet, but the truth is I'm weird all the time. I was only trying to lighten the mood."

I gave her a smile and squeezed her arm. "I'd never be in a girl band unless you were in it with me."

"Good luck," she whispered.

"Corine, I just want you to know... I'm sorry."

"About what?"

"You'll see," I said, which was already revealing too much.

I took a deep breath and entered the boardroom, where the Koenig family was already assembled. Brandon was fastidiously cleaning his glasses with a kerchief, avoiding eye contact with anyone else. Drake was giving elaborate coffee instructions to a paralegal he'd mistaken for someone who fetched coffee. There were half a dozen other family members I didn't recognize, except for Dieter Koenig's niece, Dharma Lake. She was the daughter of his much-older sister, so she was close to his age, as well as one of the eldest family members present.

Dharma waved at me, smiling, and mouthed a *hello*. I waved back and took a seat in an empty chair near the door.

Logan caught my eye across the room and gave me a calm, supportive nod. Unlike the attorney who was using the washroom to deal with his nervous stomach, Logan was alert and eager for battle. He thrived when doing his job, and he wanted to continue loving his work, which was why he'd be taking more three-day weekends to be his non-lawyer self. I returned his nod with my own, faking calmness. I was nervous, my heart pounding and my palms moist. As of this Monday, it had been eight days since Dieter Koenig's death. It promised to be an exciting start to the week.

Logan stood, and the room hushed. He introduced himself then asked everyone present to stand briefly and do the same.

The boys spoke first but didn't stand.

Brandon said, "Brandon Koenig, eldest son."

Drake said, "Drake Koenig, youngest and best-looking son." The paralegal who'd brought him coffee tittered behind me from her station near the door.

"Alexander Vander Voss," said a white-haired man, remaining seated.

"Dierdre Koenig-Vander Voss," said his wife, also seated.

Five more Koenigs and hyphen-Koenigs introduced themselves.

Dharma stood. "Hello, everyone," she said with her usual friendly charm. "I'm Dharma Lake, Dieter's niece by his sister Corabelle. My dear mother, bless her soul, will be happy to see Dieter again in heaven—as happy as the rest of us still on earth are sad to see him go. I know the official funeral isn't until Wednesday, but after we finish up here, drinks are on the house at the Fox & Hound, courtesy of the new owner." She held up a hand and gestured to Della, who stood and bowed.

With all the action and intrigue over the past eight days, I'd forgotten Della had taken over the pub after the unfortunate events up at the Lodge. Once she acquired the Koenig Estate as well, she would have her hands full.

Logan told Della to introduce herself, since she was already standing.

With the ease of a natural performer, she announced, "I'm Della Koenig, beloved wife and devastated widow of Deets."

The boardroom froze. I could hear a photocopier running in an adjacent room.

Brandon broke the silence. "Wife?"

"That's right, honey," Della said with a wave of one hand. The other hand struck a sassy pose at her hip. "I'm your new step-mommy."

Alexander Vander Voss stood and shouted, "This is preposterous!"

His wife grabbed his arm, pulled him back to his chair, and started fishing around in her purse, all the while muttering about pills.

Logan cleared his throat to get everyone's attention. "I suppose the cat's out of the bag now. I'll get right to the reading of the will." He pulled some papers from a folder and was about to begin reading the will when he was interrupted.

"Wait!" Lady Octavia got to her feet shakily. Her Chanel suit fit perfectly that morning, and she looked downright deflated in the chest area.

"Of course," Logan said. "We didn't finish the introductions. As many of you know, this is Lady Octavia of Krengerborg, a dear friend of the family."

"More than a friend," she said. "I am *part* of the family." She made steady eye contact with Brandon Koenig, who gave her a subtle nod to continue.

The white-haired man across the table asked his wife, "Give me another one of those pills. My heart isn't made for this preposterousness." She handed him one and popped one herself.

Lady Octavia glanced around for her lawyer, who hadn't returned from the washroom yet. She remained standing and continued, "Dieter has another son you don't know about." The family members gasped. "And a daughter." Everyone gasped again.

Next to me, Della shouted, "I knew it! I knew you were up to no good, you gold-digging Eurotrash!"

Lady Octavia whirled to face her. "You should talk! You gold-digging American *Ludertæve*!"

Della growled, "I don't know what that word means, but..." Her face wrinkled in concentration. In a lighter tone, she said, "But if it's Danish for someone who takes care of their babies and provides for them, go ahead and call me that, because that's what I am."

Lady Octavia blinked. "What?"

"I just decided," Della said. "I'm a changed woman. I've been moved by love and marriage and loss."

"What are you saying?"

"You'll get your child support," Della said to the countess. She was, to my surprise, calm and steady as she continued, "Like my beloved Deets, up in heaven, my own father was a good man who looked after his own no matter how they came into his life. It didn't always work out, but he was a good man who never ran from responsibility." She patted her lacey chest. "And that's what kind of baby daddy I'm going to be. Even though I'm not technically the daddy." She shrugged. "I've got all of his money now, so I'll act on his behalf."

Across the table, Brandon yelled, "*What?*"

The other family members talked frantically amongst themselves. One woman began crying.

Logan rapped his knuckles on the boardroom table. "This is exactly why we don't do these things anymore," he said. "Would everyone please be seated again?"

The people who were standing found their seats again. The metal caster wheels of the chairs squeaked as everyone rolled in as close to Logan as they could get. A bewildered Lady Octavia turned to hug Della like a long-lost friend.

"We girls have to stick together," Della was saying. "I'll take care of you, sweet baby mamma. I need to squeeze those little cherubs if they're the last bit of my Deets left in the world."

"Hey," said Drake, who'd been relatively quiet through the drama. "What about me? And Brandon? We're *also* Dieter's little cherubs."

Della rolled her eyes. "You're both gross and old. Like, over forty. You two need to get a life. That's exactly why your father did up a new will." She reached one arm out across the table in a theatrical gesture, as though casting a spell. "Trust me, boys. This hurts me more than it hurts you. As of right now, you're evicted from the mansion." She waved her hand again. "Poof!"

Brandon reached for a coffee mug. His knuckles were white as he gripped it tightly. The mug abruptly broke in his hand, causing everyone in the room to shriek.

Drake cuffed his brother on the temple and yelled, "Walk it off!"

Brandon growled back. "Walk where?"

"It's just an expression," Drake said. "Calm down."

Brandon extracted the shards of coffee mug from his hand and glowered at Della. "You're not evicting us," he said.

"I am," she said. "I don't trust either of you."

"What did we ever do?" asked Drake.

"I don't know," she said. "But you're both shifty. That's why your father didn't invite you to the wedding. He thought you'd try to talk him out of it."

Drake laughed. "Sweetheart, there was no wedding. You're bluffing. And even if there was, we'll have it annulled."

A wicked smile crept across Brandon's face. "That's right," he said. "Dad was going senile. He didn't know what he was doing. Don't get used to using the last name of Koenig, because it's not yours. Nothing is yours."

"You can fight me all you want," she said. "Send your correspondence to the mansion, where I'll be living as of tomorrow. I'm sure you know the address."

"We're not leaving," Drake said.

"Yes, you are," Della said.

Logan chimed in, "I'm afraid it's true, sirs. After this meeting, you'll be escorted back to gather your personal items and only your personal items. You'd better not help yourselves to so much as a silver spoon."

The family side of the boardroom erupted in panic and anger. Sweet little Dharma Lake caught my attention and wheeled her chair around to be next to mine.

"Did you know about this?" she asked.

"Most of it," I said. "How are you feeling these days?"

"Great," she said. "My memory's back to normal, and I feel healthy." She glanced over at her relatives, who were wailing and gnashing their teeth.

"Sorry about all of this," I said.

"Look at those fools," she said. "Uncle Dieter was never going to give them a cent. It was all going to charity, you know. That was the most recent will, before he married Della. Nobody else knew except for me, because he trusted me. I guess he changed his mind when he fell in love."

"Charity? So, it was never supposed to go to his sons?"

"He thought the money would ruin them," she said. "He worried that it had ruined him, but then he found love, and he had hope again."

"You think he loved her? He barely knew her."

"That's the power of love. I always told him he would find love again, and I told Della the same. And then I personally invited her to the mansion for one of his parties, and I had her sing his favorite songs."

I whispered, "You sly matchmaker. Better not let the Koenigs and hyphen-Koenigs find out you were the one behind all this."

Dharma's eyes twinkled. "It's our little secret."

"Now, hold onto your hat, because things are about to get intense."

I glanced over at Kyle, who gave me the nod to go ahead and start flinging accusations.

Logan was handing out photocopies of Dieter's handwritten will to the family. "The witnesses to both the marriage and the holographic will have provided sworn statements, on video," he said. "If any of you are planning to contest the will, you may wish to use a different tactic than going after the witnesses, because I've got them, to use a not-so-legal term, *totally locked down*."

The family grumbled and roared that they would contest the will, win in court, burn down Logan's house, roast him on a spit over the coals of his burned-down house, and finally pick their teeth with his bones. Not in those exact words, but that was the gist.

The crying woman started for the door.

"Not so fast!" I yelled.

At the sound of my voice, everyone went quiet. Most of them had probably forgotten I was even there.

"You can't leave yet," I said. "We're just getting started. With all due respect to Mr. Sanderson, the reading of the will was simply the warm-up act. Grab a seat, rich folks, because we're about to unveil a murderer."

All faces turned toward me. I reached for my coffee so I could wet my dry mouth and buy a few seconds to reconfigure my strategy.

I really wished I'd planned ahead to sneak some whiskey into my coffee.

CHAPTER 40

"DIETER KOENIG'S DEATH was no accident," I said. "It was a homicide, carefully planned and executed."

Everyone in the room inhaled at once, the vacuum causing a breeze that moved my hair.

Della tugged on my elbow and hissed, "Sit down, Stormy. You're ruining everything."

I pulled my arm away and shot her a stern look. Behind her black lace veil, her eyes narrowed and her red lips scrunched.

"Don't you worry, Della," I said. "You'll get everything you deserve."

Lady Octavia muttered something in Danish under her breath. It sounded like either a prayer or a curse. By the look on her face, it had been directed at me. *Definitely a curse.*

"You, too, your highness," I said. "You'll get what you deserve."

She whipped back her blond hair, her petite nostrils flaring over lips as tightly scrunched as Della's.

Next to her at the table was Logan, who looked like he was about to give birth to kittens. During our relaxing three-day weekend together, I'd kinda-sorta forgotten to inform him of the whole plan. I tried to beam an apology from my eyes to his before turning to the others.

Brandon yanked his glasses off and began cleaning them again.

Drake scowled at me and demanded, "What is the point of this three-ring circus? We are all grieving our beloved family member."

"And your loyal staff member," I said. "Or have you forgotten about Tim Barber so quickly?"

Drake said, "Tim Barber was a disturbed individual. I can only pray that he's finally found his peace."

"What happened to Mr. Barber was a tragedy," I said. "But at least he had one great weekend in the lap of luxury, right?"

The room filled with confused murmurs. I heard one person ask another who I thought I was. Another answered, "She's the girl who found the body."

"But I'm not," I said. "I'm not the girl who found the body. The housekeeper, Erica Garcia, was the one who found Dieter dead in the pool, bleeding from a head wound."

The room got quiet again.

I continued, "Mr. Sanderson and I arrived at the scene of the crime a few minutes later. We also witnessed the killer fleeing the scene."

"You saw the handyman," Brandon said. "Everybody knows about that already. Why are you putting us through this anguish?"

"But I didn't see the handyman," I answered. "I saw his clothes. He wore loose-fitting layers and a big hat."

All eyes were on me.

I nodded at Logan. "Isn't that right? All you saw was clothes and the back of him."

Logan replied, "I chased after the guy, but he was too quick, and then suddenly he disappeared. I thought he'd slipped into a maintenance shed, so I looked in there, but the shed was empty."

I announced, "The shed was empty because the killer disappeared down a trapdoor." By the look on his face, this was news to Logan.

"Trapdoor?"

I continued, "You see, the Koenig Estate has many secrets, and one of them is an underground fallout shelter, built decades ago. The family has kept it, either as a panic room or just a curiosity. I can't really comment on the motivation for keeping a scary underground bachelor apartment. It reminds me of how kings from days gone by kept a dungeon to imprison people who caused trouble." I turned to look directly at Lady Octavia. "What do you think of that?"

Her trembling hand flew to her mouth. "He... They... A dungeon?"

"We'll come back to you," I said to the countess. I turned back to face Dieter's relatives. "I bet you're all wondering who was in Tim Barber's clothes that day, and where Tim Barber really was."

A few people nodded.

I pointed to the ceiling. "Tim Barber was in the air, flying back to Misty Falls in the Koenigs' private jet. That's why he asked for the weekend off work. He must have thought he'd died and gone to heaven when Brandon or Drake asked him to secretly travel to New York to visit Lady Octavia. He had no idea he was being set up to take the fall for a murder. And even that was just a backup plan, in case the police didn't rule Dieter's death an accident."

The white-haired man yelled, "Preposterous!"

His wife elbowed him. "Shut up, Alex. You have nothing to do with this." She turned and gave him a beady-eyed look. "Or do you?"

He crossed his arms and took his wife's advice to shut up.

I turned to Lady Octavia. "Did you enjoy entertaining the Koenig family's handyman in New York?"

Her face blanched.

"Don't say a word!" yelled her young lawyer, returning from the washroom and scrambling to sit next to her. "My client has no comment," he said.

"Not even one word?" I asked. "How about one name? How about you tell us which brother was the one flying the plane? Which one met with you in New York? We'd all like to know, because it means the other brother was back here in Oregon, wearing Tim Barber's clothes and killing Dieter Koenig."

I heard spines crackle and joints pop as everyone whipped their heads to stare at the brothers.

Drake began to smile and slowly clap. "Ladies and gentlemen, I hope you're all enjoying the show!" He kept clapping. "Around these parts, Miss Stormy Day is becoming quite the legend. I'd feel sorry for her if she weren't so adorable. The poor girl imagines murders everywhere she goes." His clapping slowed as he glanced around at his family. "Whatever you do, don't have her over for dinner. I imagine someone will be poisoned or strangled before the dessert course."

His brother laughed.

A few people tittered nervously.

Della tugged at my sleeve and asked, "Do you want me to slap a confession out of them?"

"That's not a bad idea, Della. Thank you for your generous offer." Loud enough for everyone to hear, I added, "No confession is necessary. The police lab has the work clothes that were hanging in the shed, and they're testing for DNA. It's going to match one of the brothers, and, as a bonus, we'll also find out which brother is the one who fathered those cute babies the countess gave birth to."

Lady Octavia said, "Dieter is the father! He's the father."

Her lawyer clapped his hand over her mouth to quiet her.

I gave Lady Octavia a woman-to-woman, no-bull-please stare. "You and I both know Dieter's not the father. He's been sterile for years."

Della cried out, "*What?*"

I explained to all the shocked faces, "Lady Octavia got pregnant by one of the brothers, and he saw it as the perfect opportunity to screw his brother out of a share of the inheritance by passing the child off as his father's. He's the one who started the rumor about the countess leaving Dieter's bedroom."

Across the table, Dierdre Van Voss-Koenig said, "But what about genetic testing? Wouldn't they be able to tell who the father was?"

"Not necessarily," I said. "If the alleged father's blood was degraded, say, by him already being dead, the labs would have run a test that wouldn't disprove someone who was the grandfather as being the father. I could get into the details, but it would really slow things down, and Claudette from the forensics lab explains it better than I do."

Brandon banged his fists on the table. "Enough of this travesty! We've had enough. You'll be hearing from my lawyers, and I'm suing everyone in this room."

I held up my hand. "Humor me just one more minute," I said, and I turned to Lady Octavia. "It's all up to you," I said softly. "Tell us which brother was in New York. It won't prove which one of them killed poor Tim Barber and made it look like a suicide, but at least we'll know who killed Dieter."

She leaned in toward her lawyer and whispered something in his ear.

"My client has no comment," he reported.

I sighed and bowed my head in defeat. "I guess the show's over for now. We'll wait and get the tests from the crime lab, then the police will coordinate with the NYPD and get security camera footage from one of the places where the Koenig brothers' credit cards were used, and we'll get to the bottom of this eventually." I cast one more sad look at the countess. "It's just a shame we have to wait and drag it all out."

"No comment," said the lawyer.

"Well, I hope you're cheap," I said to the lawyer. "Because your client won't be getting a dime from the estate, even if you can buy off expert witnesses to present the grandfather as the father to some gullible jury. And that's because Dieter Koenig never fathered anyone. The boys he raised and treated as sons were fathered by a man of similar height and coloring."

Ignoring her lawyer's instructions, Lady Octavia demanded, "Who? Who is their father?"

"We tested your baby's soother," I said. "I can't name the father, but I can tell you that Dieter Koenig is not the grandfather of your babies. But someone else is."

The room seemed to hold its breath.

"The handyman," I said. "Good ol' Tim Barber is the father of Drake and Brandon."

Brandon shouted, "No! Shut up! Someone, make her stop talking!"

Drake quieted his brother with a look. "Don't encourage her," he said. "Don't react."

I continued, "I hear Tim and the late Mrs. Koenig were an item back in the day. I guess they maintained their... bond, even after she got married."

Brandon's face reddened. Even Drake was showing signs of stress, with sweat running down the sides of his face.

Dierdre Van Voss-Koenig shouted, "I knew it! I knew it all along! I saw the way she looked at Tim when she thought nobody was watching! The nerve of her, passing off another man's offspring as Dieter's." She turned to her husband. "That's it. We're going to the gravestone today to spit on her grave."

The whole family erupted in outrage and accusations.

"No comment," said Lady Octavia's lawyer. "We're leaving."

"Excuse me," came a woman's voice from the door to the boardroom. "Excuse me. I'm very sorry, but it's an emergency."

We all turned to look at Corine, the receptionist. Her face was as red as the beet smoothies I'd seen her ingest during her cleanses.

"I must speak to the countess in private," Corine said.

The countess jumped to her feet and pushed her way out of the room, her lawyer right at her heels, pleading, "Please, Tavi, don't say a word!"

Corine, visibly shaking, spoke to the countess in the hallway. We couldn't hear her, but we could see all three people clearly through the glass walls.

After receiving the news from a red-faced Corine, the countess swooned as though fainting. Her lawyer caught her, righted her, and then fainted himself. He dropped like a bag of laundry, right there in the hallway. Corine shrieked and knelt over him.

The countess walked toward the glass in slow motion, her face contorted with emotion.

"MURDERER!" she screamed, loud enough for us to hear clearly. "There's blood on your hands, Brandon! All of their blood. First you killed your father, then you killed your other father, and now you've killed me! I'm as good as dead, Brandon! I will see you put in prison, and I will see you in hell!"

Brandon jumped up and tried to get out of the boardroom, but there were too many people in the way. His own family shifted into a wall to block his exit. He stepped up onto his chair and ran across the boardroom table. Lady Octavia was still screaming about him being a killer, a destroyer, and a bunch of things in Danish.

Before Brandon could get through the door, Kyle grabbed him. He was in handcuffs within seconds.

I looked around at the bewildered faces in the room. Where was Drake? He wasn't in his chair or under the glass table.

I heard a muffled plea for help near my feet. I looked down to find Drake facedown on the floor, his arm being bent at a painful-looking angle while two stiletto heels drove themselves into his back.

Breathlessly, Della said, "I got him, Stormy. I got this one for you. If he's not the killer, he's the accomplice, right?"

"That's for the law to figure out now," I said.

Drake whimpered. Della still had his arm pinned by her grip on his wrist. She had his tie in her other hand and was strangling him.

"Della, don't kill him before he goes to trial," I said.

She looked up at me, her dark, doe-like eyes gleaming beneath the lacy veil. The look on her face sent a chill up my spine. I repeated my request, and she eased up on Drake, just enough so he could breathe.

Everything whirled around me, and soon the other police officers were there, taking custody of Drake. Logan was at my side, asking, "What next?"

"Next?" I wrapped my arms around his neck. "How about lunch?"

His eyebrows raised high above his sparkling blue eyes. "Lunch? Seriously?"

"They're making a new kind of grilled cheese at the Olive Grove. Five kinds of cheese, including smoked cheddar. It's so good, it might be outlawed by the mayor."

He glanced around as his forehead wrinkled. "What do you suppose Corine told Lady Octavia? She seemed upset, and I don't know if I can do anything today if it was as bad as my imagination is telling me."

"The babies are fine," I said. "The butler, Randy, had the babies at his house. Drake and Brandon kidnapped them from the countess a few days ago to make sure she didn't turn on them. I'm guessing she got cold feet at some point, if she was in on the whole thing."

"A kidnapping? That's horrible. How did you know?"

"Kyle and I saw the countess buying a breast pump at the drugstore. He put her under surveillance to confirm the rest."

"You swear the babies are okay?"

"Yes," I said. "Officer Wiggles was watching the butler's house this morning, and they've already arrested him. Tony's been watching the babies at his house. If Tony's kids haven't traded the babies in for a puppy, they'll be back with their mother just as soon as she finishes ratting out the boys." I wrinkled my nose. "I feel awful about devastating the woman with such an awful lie, but it was actually Kyle's idea, so we can blame him."

"Sometimes the ends justify the means," Logan said.

"So, how about that grilled cheese sandwich with five kinds of cheese?"

He grinned. "You had me at grilled cheese."

"Let's invite Corine to tag along, so I can apologize for using her to deliver that fake message." I wrinkled my nose. "I'm going to be in the doghouse with her."

"She'll forgive you," he said.

I touched his stomach in the area of his scar. "The ends may justify the means, but there are always consequences."

He kissed the top of my head. "Everything's going to be okay."

CHAPTER 41

DURING THE WEEKS following the arrests of Drake and Brandon Koenig, a few facts came to light.

Countess Octavia of Krengerborg had no part in the planning or execution of the two homicides. After assisting police with the investigation, she was permitted to return to Denmark with her two children. The offspring had no claim on the Koenig fortune, since their true father, Brandon, was not legally allowed to benefit from his crime, even if he could have successfully contested Dieter's new will.

The countess would, however, be getting money from the sale of Tim Barber's home, since the babies were his grandchildren and only non-murdering heirs. My real estate agent friend, Samantha Sweet, would be listing the property on her behalf. Samantha was feeling optimistic about selling the home and predicted it would go long before the tiny dollhouse she was still trying to unload.

The Koenig family, including Dieter's niece Dharma, found that when they looked back with the knowledge that Tim Barber was the father of

Brandon and Drake, everything fit. Tim hadn't been the best employee, but Mrs. Koenig had kept him on staff no matter what. He had doted on the boys, choosing to spend his every weekend at the estate rather than starting his own family. We all hoped he was looking down from wherever he was, enjoying the adorable faces of his royal grandchildren.

The twins, a boy and a girl, would be shielded as long as possible from the history of their ancestors, but they would see the photograph of Tim Barber holding them in his arms, and they would know their grandfather delighted in their laughter and smiles for one glorious weekend in New York.

The butler, Randy, turned on his former employers after a few days of pressure. He was facing charges of kidnapping, conspiracy, and a half dozen other charges, including evading the police in a high-speed chase. It turned out he was, as I'd suspected, the person driving the vehicle that Kyle and I had been chasing near Lady Octavia's rented house. He'd been doing some surveillance work with the brothers. Once he came clean about that incident, more bombshells followed, including the fact that he'd gotten the brothers access to Tim Barber's home the day they murdered him and staged the suicide. It had been Drake who'd pulled the trigger, which put one first-degree murder charge on each brother.

As for Brandon's carefully orchestrated murder of Dieter, he'd left nothing to chance. He didn't just oil the diving board and hope for an accident. Instead, he'd gotten the butler to slip a knockout pill in

Della's morning coffee so she wouldn't be poolside that morning. Then he'd dressed in the handyman's clothes and hid in the bushes. When Dieter Koenig stepped onto the diving board for his morning swim, Brandon bludgeoned him on the back of the skull. The pipe he used had a diameter that matched the edge of the diving board. Crime scene investigators searched the entire property, including the underground tunnel and the fallout shelter where Brandon had lived during the days he was supposed to be in New York. The crime scene investigators finally found the weapon inside a toolbox in the aircraft hangar. The pipe had been thoroughly wiped clean of evidence, but it was the only clean item in the toolbox, so its use was fairly obvious.

Brandon might have gotten away with the perfect crime, if not for love.

It was because of love—Dieter Koenig's love for his new wife—that Logan and I had been invited to the mansion that day for breakfast. If we hadn't witnessed Brandon fleeing the scene in the groundskeeper's clothes, things might have played out very differently.

I tried not to think about what could have happened.

All I could do was keep looking forward, keep living my life, and try to do good in the world and in the town I loved.

* * *

As the days passed, the weather cooled, and the House of Bean rolled out their version of a pumpkin spice latte. The sweet concoction was dubbed Cinderella Got Her Fella. Their specialty drink names were getting longer and weirder, but, as I said to Chad when I first ordered the new item, I wouldn't have it any other way.

On the morning of the annual Forest Folk Run, a charity quarter-marathon that people walked or ran in costume, the sun was shining and the first leaves of autumn were turning gold and red.

My father was already dressed up and waiting at the starting location, the Olive Grove parking lot, when I arrived with Jessica.

He looked us over and let out a low whistle. "I don't know whether to scream or laugh," he said.

Jessica and I struck a pose for the event photographer, Lily Chang. Lily was laughing so hard, she nearly fell off her electric scooter.

I turned to Jessica and asked, "Why's everyone making fun of us?" Unfortunately, the fake monster teeth I was wearing made it hard to speak eloquently. What came out was, "Shy-shesherung-faffa-fa-ba-va?"

Jessica, whose monster teeth were equally magnificent, answered, "FAAAAASSSSH! GAAAAR!"

I tried to tell her she sounded like a wookie. "FOO FA FA FOOFIE!"

"GAAAAH!" She stroked her monster-fur suit, which had been custom-dyed a red shade to match her actual hair. "MAAA?"

I preened my own monster fur, which was a patchwork mashup of various colors, including purple, and grunted to her that she was beautiful to me.

Our small monster let his opinion be known.

We both turned to the vintage baby carriage we'd brought with us. Inside was Jeffrey, looking less than thrilled about his own costume. He wore a patchwork fun-fur vest over his gray fur, and a collar decorated with tiny plastic skulls. Everyone thinks their child is the cutest, but our kitty-monster was truly the most adorable of all the small monsters at the charity event.

Before the actual walk-run started, the organizers got us to assemble in our groupings of three to five for the costume contest.

Jessica and I pushed the carriage into our chalk circle, where we were joined by my father. Finnegan Day was dressed as a futuristic monster-slayer in tattered leather and punk-rock metal spikes. He'd modified his cane sword to resemble a double ax. He had a variety of tools and supplies strapped to himself, including one canteen marked "Irish." He offered us a swig.

I took out my monster teeth so I could talk and take a drink. It was iced tea.

"Dad, I thought for sure it was going to be hot coffee with whiskey."

He winked at me. "I'm a law-abiding citizen who wouldn't bring liquor to a family fun event."

"Is your Irish coffee in the canteen marked Iced Tea? This one is just a decoy, right?"

"No comment." He scanned the crowd as he twirled his battle-ax on its axis. "Where's Sanderson? Don't tell me he's stuck at work."

"He had to sign some papers, but he'll be here," I said.

A woman cried out, "Look what the cat dragged in!" It was Ruby Sparkes, wearing a judge's sash. She was one of three judges for the costume contest. Ruby was dressed as the Bride of Frankenstein, with two thick streaks of white in her purple-red curls.

My father said, "Top o' the mornin' to you, Ruby." He took a swig from the Irish canteen.

"You're looking well, Finnegan," she said, twirling one of her curls girlishly.

"I'm a monster slayer from the future," he said. "I drove here in my time machine."

"The one that looks like a green Torino?"

"That's the one," he said. "You like it?"

"I can't say for sure. You'll have to take me for a ride sometime."

"Careful what you wish for," he teased.

"Is this a teddy bear?" Ruby asked, peering into the baby buggy. Jeffrey yawned; Ruby let out a tiny shriek. "Good heavens, it's alive," she said. "You scared me so much, you little devil." She made some marks on her clipboard. "That's definitely worth a point."

Someone yelled, "Objection!" A man in a tattered-to-shreds suit ran toward us and stepped inside the chalk circle. It was Logan, or at least the zombie version of Logan. "Objection, your honor," he said to Ruby. "The parties were not all present, but now they are."

"You look hideous," she said. "Very good. The four of you are quite the sight."

"Hey," said my father, pretending to be offended. "That's my family you're talking about."

Ruby laughed and finished making her notes. "Have a good walk or run today, folks. And please take it at your own speed. Contrary to what some whippersnappers think, it's not a race. We all win if we have fun and get everyone across the finish line safely." She blew us kisses and moved on to the next grouping.

Logan hugged me tight to his side and said, "You look cute in fur."

I smiled broadly at his compliment.

He continued, "I don't know much about the legendary Forest Folk that live around these parts, but do you reckon they get along with zombies? What I mean is, do you think a cannibal sasquatch and her zombie boyfriend and her roommate and their beastly feline companion can live together in harmony, happily ever after?"

I meant to say something profound and beautiful, but I'd put my plastic monster teeth back in my mouth, so I said, "GBBBEEEEFFFULLZ!"

Soon, the event organizers were herding us toward the starting line and firing the T-shirt cannons.

We paced ourselves for the quarter-marathon, finishing in the middle of the pack. My father doubled back and brought in the stragglers.

After, we gathered with the rest of the town in Central Park, where confused dogs barked and sniffed the people in furry costumes. Jessica and I had planned to get a friend to take Jeffrey home, but he appeared to be enjoying himself from the safety of the baby buggy. We passed around refreshments, lay back on the grass, and watched the clouds float across the sky.

Everything was truly GBBBEEEEFFFFULLZ.

THE END OF

STORMY DAY BOOK #4

DEATH OF A MODERN KING

ANGELA PEPPER

TO BE CONTINUED...
IN STORMY DAY MYSTERY #5
DEATH OF A DOUBLE DIPPER

ANGELA PEPPER

www.angelapepper.com

9 781990 367182